# The Value
# of
# Nothing

*A Novel by* JOHN WEITZ

# The Value of Nothing

🕮 STEIN AND DAY/*Publishers*/New York

*For all the Kohners*

*What is a cynic? A man who knows the price of everything, and the value of nothing.*

OSCAR WILDE

# The Value of Nothing

B ᴜᴅ Grossberg and Ron Miller usually ate breakfast at Willner's, a coffee shop on Thirty-ninth Street. Their sideburns touched their jawbones, and their six-button double-breasted blazers were waist-nipped with long back vents. They mounted the leatherette counter stools, tucking their narrow asses forward like men on horseback, pants tight over Gucci shoes. It was all there. The boys grooved.

There were a dozen other sideburned, nipped-blazered salesmen among the models, buyers, production managers, and secretaries at the counter, but this was only natural. The young men of the garment center rode a new style like surfers catching the same wave.

Willner's décor had not changed since the thirties days of gilded-mosaic wall designs and cut-glass lighting fixtures. It had a certain kinship with the lobby of the Empire State Building.

Bud was tall and had a near-mahogany tan. He sold dresses at Sandy-Lou, a medium-priced house upstairs in the same building as Willner's. Ron, shorter and with a walnut tan, peddled textiles for Jaydest Mills. Recently the boys had switched from Canoe cologne to Moustache and from Sassooned brunettes to long-haired blondes. They did everything together.

Bud was pursuing their subway-born conversation: "Lissen," he said, "Ron, baby, don' gimme that! I know the broad! She pulled that schtick on the island last week an' we had a real *hassle*, you know what I mean, Ron?"

Ron-baby was stricken. All hopes for his weekend date were fading. He thought he'd had this chick all lined up, and now it turned out Bud had done her first. All broads balled, but did it have to be Bud? He hated being this *late*. Now he *had* to brush her before Friday, or he couldn't be seen with her. Everyone must know that Bud had been there, and on Fire Island cocksmanship with old material was *degrading*.

He made a quick recovery. He tweaked Bud's cheek and said, "Lissen, baby, I got other plans anyway. Sump'n groovy I borrowed at P.J.'s—"

"Ya mean Sylvia?" Bud was above it all. He'd been *there*, too.

Ron shrugged his shoulders. Enigmatic. A nose-bobbed sphinx.

Of course, there was no such girl. Ron had been to P.J.'s Sunday night, but he'd failed to score. He had tried the bar and table-hopped in the back room. Nothing. It was a shame, too! He'd looked good on Sunday: the tan, the red turtleneck, white duck pants, bare ankles, Guccis, and the Cardin blazer. It was just that every really great chick was locked in with someone, and the available ones were dogs, but dawgs. He had made the scene at four other places between Third and First Avenues—still nothing! But that was none of Bud's business, and since none of the crowd had been around, he could lie about it.

Go ahead, Bud baby. Try to guess! Eat your heart out!

Their food arrived, claiming all of Bud's attention and at least half of Ron's.

Leaning forward to sip his coffee, Ron spotted a chick halfway down the counter, in Siberia. The coffee counter had its own social structure, a good and a bad side. The girl was behind Bud, so only Ron could see her. *His* kind of face.

Square jaw with a cleft, strong neck, close-cut hair with bangs right down to the eyes, and long fur lashes. Last year's hairdo, but the rest groovy! Maybe she was a little fat? With faces like that they were sometimes fat. No. She shifted and he could see she was brick-built. He gave her the stare, but she didn't catch it. Nearsighted?

He wrinkled his brow and turned. He looked better in profile when his brows were beetled; his nose was bobbed, and the one thing the surgeon couldn't touch was the high bridge. Unless he made like Kirk Douglas, he looked weak. He had studied the whole thing. Bud's nose was fixed, too, but it looked better because he had a low bridge, lucky bastard. When Bud was a kid he'd looked like some anteater. Now he looked like Tony Curtis.

Ron glanced back at the chick, but she was busy with her goddamn prune danish. He'd get to her later. Sidney, the counter man, would give him the word at lunch time. Sidney bartended at Atlantic Beach on weekends, could tell you about every box going. He'd know if this chick was available. Maybe the weekend was saved after all.

"Ya hear about Ross?" he asked through his buttered biali. Bud could eat anything. Cream cheese and lox and bagels and danish. He never put on weight like Ron, who was always counting calories.

"What about him?"

"I heard it on WINS. He's dead."

"Dead? When?" asked Ron, who claimed to know Philip Ross well. Actually he had met him only once, when Peggy introduced them during the period she and Ron were shacking up. She had mentioned a *dozen* times that she'd worked for Ross as a sketcher at Armand-Klein when Philip Ross was their designer.

Ross had remembered her, all right. He had even hugged her and spoken to Ron before walking out to a gray Continental limousine which was waiting for him. A celebrity. Not a great big fat celebrity like Sammy Davis or Dean Martin, but at least a Suzy Knickerbocker celebrity.

Ron had made a mental note of Ross's dark blue shirt and cream tie. Beautiful! He'd worn the same outfit himself two days later. Anyway, this meeting at a party had grown in the retelling until Ron was *the* expert on Philip Ross. He knew all about every trip, showing, luncheon in Ross's life. He was also expert on Norell, Blass, Trigère, Donald Brooks, and Oscar de la Renta.

How could he have missed this piece of news? There had been nothing in *Women's Wear* that morning. Coffee and *Women's Wear Daily* were the first part of each day even if there was a chick still sacked out in the bedroom. There was a special way of reading *Women's Wear*: Who's on page one center? Who had pages four and five? Then the two gossip columns. That was the juicy stuff. The rest was straight rag trade news you could catch later at the office. But hard news was usually on page one, and this time *Women's Wear* had let him down. No word about Ross! It must have just happened.

"What'd he die of?"

"A broken head."

"Accident?"

"Like, you might call it that." Bud was arch.

"How do you mean?"

"He got cracked on the skull."

"No kiddin'. Murdered?"

"Yeah."

"They know who?"

"They didn't say. They found Ross yesterday. He'd had a helluva beating."

"Probably some guy he picked up."

"Figures . . ."

"Goddamn queens all get into trouble."

"Yeah, right!" Ron canceled his interest in Ross. He was dead, and Ron couldn't feel proprietary about him any more. There would be no more parties or luncheons to report.

"Hey," he said, "did you hear the one about the fag who . . ."

He told a stock Fire Island story. Bud cut in by waving at Sidney. Checks, please! Big deal . . .

"Like, Ron—that's an *old* goddamn story."

Time to get to work. They paid, brushed the crumbs off their blazers, and slid off the stools. When Ron passed the chick with the strong jaw, she looked up. So she wasn't near-sighted after all!

He beetled his brows on the way out to the street.

# BOOK

# 1

I N the lobby of the Stork Club there was a gold chain to the left of the checkroom. You gave the girl your coat and hat. Then you faced the forbidding maître d' behind that chain. It was he who would decide if you were fit to enter. You were not yet *inside* the Stork when you stood in the checkroom. The chain ritual came first.

From outside the chain, you were tantalized by the thump of an unseen dance band and by the sight of the glossy people at the bar. To certain initiates the Stork was home. To others it was legendary. They read about it but never expected to *be* there, in the same room with Brenda Frazier or Clark Gable.

After more than one false start, Philip Ross had finally walked through the outer doors under the front canopy and checked his cap and small zipper bag with the pretty girl at the counter. Now he turned to face the man behind the chain.

The tall, gray-haired maître d' suppressed a smile. This kid in his freshly pressed Class A uniform with the T/3 stripes was scared silly. Hundreds of Army kids had invaded the Stork since 1942, most of them trying as unsuccessfully as this one to look worldly and nonchalant. So long as they didn't get drunk or make passes at someone's wife, Mr. B. wanted these enlisted men in the club. They never spent much money, but after all there was a war on, and the service kids made the place look patriotic. Mr. B. had decided long ago that you couldn't do big business catering only to the upper crust. The Stork was very big business, and these kids spread the word about the club all over the country. Society? Exclusiveness? Let El Morocco have it. There were enough society, movie, and stage regulars who came to the Stork because they got VIP treatment. But the bulk of the clientele was, in truth, pedestrian.

"Yessir?" asked the maître d'.

"Oh," said Philip. "I just wanted a drink."

"The bar, sir?"

"Yes, please."

"Very well, sir."

The chain was lifted. Philip was *inside* the Stork Club. It was as easy as that! Each time he had gotten a pass to New York he'd wanted to come here. Twice before he had almost done it. He had actually stood on the corner of Fifth Avenue and Fifty-third Street, eyeing the Stork canopy. But the first time there had been some colonels going in, and the next time a bunch of Navy brass got out of a black limousine with admiral's stars on the front plate. He had seen newspaper photos of enlisted men at the Stork, but those could have been phony poses like the ones on recruiting posters. Philip himself had recently been photographed with a submachine gun and steel helmet, jumping over a pile of sandbags. It was strictly for publicity. Actually he did statistical work at Camp Lee, Virginia, the quartermaster center. He hadn't worn a helmet since basic training, and there wasn't a Tommy gun in the whole goddamn outfit.

There was a gap among the people at the bar, and Philip stepped into it. He ordered a beer. He knew he looked younger than twenty-two—what if they refused to serve him? Then he remembered he had been okay with the guy at the gold chain. The Stork was expensive, and he'd have to conserve his dough. It was only Friday and he had a forty-eight-hour pass. He had the ticket back to Virginia, but his twenty bucks would have to stretch over two days.

The red-jacketed bartender poured his beer with a champagne flourish. Philip nodded thanks and pushed the glass around a little, like an old barfly.

He was quite tall, nearly six feet, and just beginning to fill out the way skinny kids turn into men. His hair was still boy-blond, his face oval and soft, with a cleft chin. People found themselves concentrating on his eyes, which were gray-green and had very dark lashes. His eyebrows were sun-bleached, like a lifeguard's, although he worked in an office.

It was eleven-thirty, and the after-theater crowd was arriving. Most of the men were in uniform, nearly all officers. There were two other enlisted men at the bar, a fat-assed Marine corporal and a T/5 with thick eyeglasses and a Second Service Command patch. The Marine was bullshitting a married couple, and the T/5 was getting loaded. Philip stared at his beer, though he knew it was a stupid thing to do. He had come here to find out what it was all about and now he was staring at this goddamn beer bottle. When he finally turned to take a look at the place, his right eye caught an arm in an officer's sleeve, reaching through to grab a martini glass from the bar.

"Sorry, Sergeant, it's so darn crowded!"

The voice belonged to a very tall Air Force captain with a Gable mustache, a suntanned face, and unmilitary curly black hair. He had a chestful of fruit salad—three rows of decorations under his pilot's wings.

Philip spotted the aide's insignia and aiguillette. The captain, according to these, was an aide to a three-star general.

"Sorry, sir," said Philip. "I didn't hear you order the drink, else I would have made room."

"Oh, I didn't *have* to order. Mike there has been pouring

for me since my college days. By now he can mind-read my thirst." The captain had a very wide, white-toothed grin. He continued: "Do you get here often?"

"I've been in once or twice," Philip lied.

"Good place," nodded the captain.

"Right, sir."

"Look," said the captain, "would you mind cutting out that 'sir' crap? We're not on an airbase."

"Okay, Captain."

A tall blond girl in evening clothes tried to squeeze past. She jostled the pilot's arm and nearly spilled his drink. "Sorry!" she said without looking up.

"Liza!" said the captain.

Now she looked at him. "Hi, Johnny . . ."

"Who are you with?"

"Oh, you know, Bob Carruthers and some of the others. Want to join?"

"Thanks, no. I'll just have this drink and turn in early. Gotta work tomorrow."

"Okay, Johnny. I get it. See you . . ." She threw him a kiss, looked at Philip for a moment, and then walked toward the dancing couples in the big room behind the bar. A few minutes later a Navy jg headed in the same direction tapped the captain on the shoulder and winked at him. They were obviously friends.

The captain turned back to Philip. "Actually," he said, "I've got the day off tomorrow. But I couldn't take any of *that* tonight. I've known 'em all my life."

Philip just nodded his head. He felt uncomfortable, goddamn it to hell. Like his father was there giving him the old Army crap about officers and enlisted men and "knowing your place." His old man . . . Twenty years a Regular Army sergeant and still pissing his pants in front of junior officers.

"By the way," said the captain, "sorry I didn't introduce

you, but I don't know your name. Mine's John Evans-Greene."

"I'm Philip."

They shook hands. "Philip Ross," he added.

They were shouting now. The noise at the bar on top of the dance music made normal tones impossible.

Why the hell, thought Johnny, am I talking to this kid? And why do I bother to explain that I don't really have to fly tomorrow? And that I couldn't take Liza and Bobby any more? (When was the last time he'd bagged Liza? Two months ago? Three months? Bobby'd been in on it, and when Liza was shot, he and Bobby had had their own go-around. . . . Liza was a great watcher.)

How *about* this kid he was talking to? Blond, large hands, slim ass, about nineteen, maybe twenty. Handsome little hick. Probably first time here and very impressed by it all. What was his name again? Philip?

"Have a drink, Philip."

Philip had been nursing the beer. He shrugged and nodded at the half-full glass and bottle.

"I didn't mean another beer," said the captain. "A real drink."

Why not? thought Philip. Getting a little loaded might take the edge off the way the place made him feel, and beer was slow. "Okay, thanks."

Johnny waved at the bartender. "A martini for the sergeant, Mike." Mike had a prizefighter's face, incongruously topped by distinguished close-cropped gray hair. Within a minute he had set a generous martini with an olive in front of Philip.

Mike had served most of Johnny's pals their first drink, with Mr. Billingsley watching from afar like a permissive uncle. Mike's own little bar near Newark had been paid for with the huge tips these young society bastards handed out

23

as if cash grew on trees. They were worse than their parents, and the parents were bad enough. Anyway, Mike had no respect for people who boozed, not that it mattered. Long as they tipped him.

"Here you are, Sergeant." He smiled at Philip.

Mike knew them all. Take that girl Liza. She'd been laid by every young cocksman at the Stork. And that Navy kid, Bobby Carruthers, his father had almost been arrested for making a pass at some little boy at Exner. Some private school! Turned out drunks and queers. Maybe he was a mick from Jersey, but Mike had his standards.

Over the customers' heads he exchanged looks with the maître d'. He was a guinea from Sicily but a good guy anyway, though he couldn't even speak American and threw in a lot of French words when he talked to customers. The maître d's look said: It's only eleven-thirty and it's a long way till 2 A.M. and my feet are killing me, how about you? Mike tilted his head in agreement. Then he looked over at the boss to make sure the old man hadn't spotted him complaining.

Billingsley was tricky. He could get in a temper over the damnedest things, out of the clear blue. All these years the society people had trusted their kids to the Stork and so Billingsley was like God the Father, and everyone, the people who worked for him and even most of the customers, acted like a kid around him. By now Billingsley was probably as rich as any of them, and what with Winchell being his best pal, people—even big-time people—never wanted to cross him.

Mike mixed two more drinks for the captain and the sergeant. Those two were beginning to drink, all right. He made a mental note to check their way more often. They'd order their next round fast. Meanwhile he started cutting some more lemon peels and orange slices.

Johnny watched Philip knock off the second martini. The

24

kid's face was beginning to flush, making him look even younger. When he put his hand on Philip's shoulder he could feel the warmth all the way through the Army shirt and blouse. The shoulder was surprisingly firm. "Drink up, Philip," he said. "There's a war on."

Philip nodded and grinned. The captain was okay. He giggled. His old man should see him now!

"What's funny?" asked Johnny.

"Oh, well . . ." Philip shrugged. "Guess I'm just having a good time."

Johnny nodded and smiled, but he wasn't sure. Was the kid loaded already? Or was he making fun of him? No, he couldn't have guessed. Not yet.

"How long is your pass?" he asked.

"Forty-eight hours."

"Got some place to bunk?"

"Well," said Philip, "I haven't figured that out yet. Maybe I'll check the USO or go to the Y." He often took his chances when he got to New York; there was always someplace to sack out. It had been tougher early in the war when most soldiers were still in the country, but now there were a lot of guys overseas. Anyway, the USO and Red Cross were pretty much on the ball. A lot of the guys said they'd shack up with girls, flapped their lips on the train coming into the city, but then they'd turn up later in the same dormitories Philip usually spent his nights at. Sometimes, when they did get laid, they bought prophylactic kits at all-night drugstores. As soon as they checked into the dormitory they'd make a dive for the latrine. You had to use the stuff within one hour of getting laid. A dose of clap could cost a man his stripes or his weekend passes. Others didn't seem to give a damn—some guys had it so bad they could hardly pee.

"The Y?" said Johnny. "That doesn't sound very appealing."

"It's okay, I guess," said Philip. Of course, he hated the Y. Maybe he'd ask the captain if he knew of a better place, a cheap hotel or something. Anything but those long rows of beds in some gym. They were like the squad rooms back on the post. Maybe this guy would *buy* him a room. Christ, he really must be getting crocked! What's more, it was time for him to buy a round of drinks and he had gestured at the bartender before remembering that he had to watch his cash. What the hell, this was the Stork. No place to worry about being broke.

Behind Philip's back Johnny signaled Mike that the drinks were on him. From the way he'd nursed the beer, the kid had to be broke. There were thousands like Philip on each airbase, all nice as hell, and still wet behind the ears. Not just because they were young—he was only five or six years older than this sergeant.

The kid was probably a pushover, loaded and all razzle-dazzled with this glamour crap. Maybe he'd just take him home and let him sleep in a real bed and feed him a decent breakfast.

He said: "Look, I've got a place not far from here. Why don't you stay with me?"

"Well, Captain—"

"Let's drop the 'Captain' stuff. My name is Johnny."

"Well, *Johnny*, I appreciate it . . . Are you sure? I mean, it won't be a bother?"

"Nothing to it. Besides, I've got a barful of booze and I hate drinking alone."

Johnny signed the check and added a tip for Mike. He turned to Philip: "Where's your gear?"

"I just have a zipper bag. I checked it up front."

At the entrance, Billingsley smiled at Johnny, who waved and said, "Hi, Mr. B!" He noticed a fag press agent at Billingsley's table giving him the beady eye. That queen knew all about everyone. Fuck him. For that matter, he'd rather not.

Johnny handed tips to the maître d', to the hat-check girl, and to the doorman. Philip trailed after him, carrying the bag and trying to get his garrison cap on with his free hand. Johnny stuffed a wad of bills back into his trouser pocket as if it were Kleenex. He had huge shoulders, and his belt was pulled tight around his middle. His uniform was custom made, but despite the insignia and decorations it didn't look military. He wore it like a sport jacket and slacks.

As Johnny gave the taxi driver the address, Philip thought, This is the way it is once you get *into* the Stork. Money and beautiful girls like Liza What's-Her-Name. The officers back at Lee were peacetime teachers and storekeepers; this one was something else. A society guy who knew everyone and who handed out tips like he printed the stuff.

The taxi crawled east on two-way Fifty-third Street, turned uptown on Park Avenue, and stopped at a canopy-fronted apartment house. A doorman in gold-braided uniform opened the door, greeted Johnny, and carried Philip's bag to the elevator, where a man in similar livery took them up to the top floor. The elevator door opened into a private entrance hall. A sleepy manservant lurched into view and was quickly dismissed by the captain.

"Get some sleep, Roberts, we won't need you. Oh, and before you go, get Sergeant Ross settled in the guest room."

"Yessir," said Roberts without looking at Philip. He took the bag and disappeared.

Johnny led the way into a vast square room, dimly lit and draped on three sides. There were clusters of furniture in three corners as if they were separate rooms—in one a dining table with eight chairs, in another armchairs around a coffee table and in the third a bar under rows of bookshelves. The floor was carpeted from wall to wall in gray, with zebra hides and bearskins scattered about haphazardly.

There were dozens of photographs of John Evans-Greene: on yachts, on skis, playing polo, and in several with a tall older woman who was obviously his mother. On the "library" wall were signed photos of generals, politicians, movie stars. Johnny waved a hand at a row and said: "Those are the people I've been flying around lately . . . I'm a sort of VIP bus driver for a general. From New York to Los Angeles or London with USO stars or senators. Not very inspiring, but it's the job I got after I was shot down. Anyway, it gets me home to New York often." Philip was curious about the "shooting down" part of the story, but he decided not to ask. The captain was behind the bar mixing drinks.

"Switch on some music, Philip."

"How?"

"Over there." Inside a long cabinet, Philip found a lavish phonograph setup with records already stacked on the spindle. He turned the knob, and by the time Johnny had brought him a martini, there was rhumba music.

Philip wasn't sure what he should do next. Sit down in one of the armchairs? Should he start to drink before the captain?

Johnny pushed aside one of the drapes, which hid a glass door. "Come on out on the terrace." When their eyes had become accustomed to the outside dark, he closed the drape. "Blackout, you know."

The terrace was sixty feet square. It led all around the penthouse, like a garden, with wicker furniture, shrubs, and two small trees whose leaves stirred against the navy blue sky. The moon was full and the clouds, silver-edged, scurried across the city. Below were Madison and Fifth Avenues and, behind the buildings, moonlight on the lake in Central Park. A slight breeze stirred from the west. New York was completely visible despite the blackout.

"Really something," said Philip.

"Except for the friggin' war," said Johnny. "Before, it was a fantastic view. You should have seen it with everything lit up . . . I took this place in 'forty, just before I enlisted."

"I was still in high school in nineteen-forty," Philip said softly.

"Where was that?"

"In an Army town. My dad is a Regular Army officer." Philip had often told this lie.

Johnny leaned his back against the balustrade and propped up his elbows. This boy's father an Academy man? Come off it, youngster, *pretty* youngster—pretty blond handsome youngster with your long legs and that skinny ass. But, what the hell? If he got his kicks out of lying, let him. No fun in calling him on it—he might get rattled and that would, well, dampen things.

Philip himself wasn't sure the captain had believed him. He liked it here; he'd have to watch it. No more careless fibs.

Johnny turned around to face the view. "Hey," he said, "come on over here and look at Park Avenue." Philip moved to the chest-high wall. High places got him in the back of his neck and arms, prickly and tense.

He stood next to Johnny and they both looked down at the cars with their tiny parking lights, scurrying up and down.

Johnny prided himself on his timing. This kid seemed simple . . . too raw for delicacy. He put his arm over Philip's shoulder, a friendly brotherly *chummy* goddamn hug. He said, "Something to look at, isn't it?"

"Yeah, something!"

There was that arm on his shoulder and the smell of

shaving lotion from the captain's face next to his. Philip had the *feeling* of the body next to him. . . . The arm tightened very gently. Philip moved closer.

He remembered the first time, exactly. They were twelve, thirteen. Basketball practice. Getting the word from the coach, a tall bespectacled math teacher. Philip stood behind Don Mulray.

Don was from Fort Early too, an Army kid like Philip. Don's father was a tech sergeant in regimental headquarters; he and Philip had been schoolmates since grade school. Don was about Philip's height, but heavy-chested with a dark Irish face and long black lashes. In school they'd kidded him about those lashes, said he looked like a girl. They kept calling him "Donna" until one day he trimmed off the lashes. Nothing changed for a while, but then Don grew tough. He was a top athlete, and Philip, who hated sports, was envious. Now he looked at Don's neck where the hair formed a V as it grew toward the nape. The skin was sweaty and the hair matted. The coach droned on, but Philip paid no attention.

He wanted to *touch* that hair. At first the desire was vague, then it became so strong that Philip reached out and felt the wet neck.

Don turned and whispered, "Yeah?"

"Nuthin'," said Philip.

"Then what'd you poke me for?"

"Tell you later."

Don shrugged and turned back to the coach, who was blackboarding a pass play.

"Well?" Don said after practice.

"Well, what?"

"What'd you want?"

"I forgot."

"You're nuts, buddy."

Philip was embarrassed. He walked home to the fort alone, although the Army boys usually went together, pushing, shoving, and wrestling through the quiet streets with their tree-shaded sidewalks. Within hailing distance of the fort's sentry post they would quiet down, and by the time they passed the guards they were perfect little gentlemen— there were wide leather garrison belts waiting to tan their butts. Their fathers, the sergeants of the garrison, were tough disciplinarians. Fort Early was Regular Army, peacetime old Army.

Philip cut across a meadow, circled around a cemetery (it spooked him even in daylight), and took the narrow church road toward Fort Early. He looked back at the residential road the boys usually took, but there was no one in sight. They were probably still sucking up to the coach. Philip didn't go much for that stuff, and anyway he'd never be a hotshot player like Don. He kicked pebbles along the sidewalk in front of him.

He wished he hadn't touched Don's neck. He didn't even know why he had, or why he'd liked it. Don must have thought he was screwy. But even now he could feel the wet hair and the hot skin beneath. His heart began to thump— he wanted to do it again. He held his hand to his face. The smell of Don was still there on his fingers.

The road from school to Fort Early led through Stilwell Park, named for a Revolutionary War general who had obviously done better than his British contemporaries. The pigeon-bespattered bronze figure stood behind a group of heavy trees and thick bushes in posthumous hiding, except for once a year when the Legionnaires hoisted a flag in his honor.

Philip and Don stopped there for a smoke. It took more courage for Don, who was in training; Philip had to hide his smoking only from his parents. The boys leaned their backs against an oak tree, pulled bent cigarettes from their pockets, and lit up. Philip, who knew how to inhale, dragged deeply. Don watched him enviously. Finally he said, "Hell, I'm gonna try that."

He pulled a mouthful of smoke into his lungs and burst into teary-eyed coughing. It struck Philip as hilariously funny. When he finally stopped laughing, he said, "Hey, Don, I thought you'd pee in your pants."

"If *you* can do it, it can't be that tough."

"Well, you sure looked like you'd choke, all right."

"Shut your smart mouth!"

Philip knew Don's temper was up, but he sank one more barb: "Bet you'd shit your pants if you took another drag like that!"

Don got to one knee and grabbed Philip's wrist. Philip yelped: "Hey, cut that out!"

"Hurts, does it? Well, I'll hurt you someplace else for that!"

"What? Leggo!"

"You know damn well what!" Don tightened his grip. As Philip tried to pull away, he began to twist his arm. Panicking, Philip pushed his cigarette at Don's hand.

Don dropped Philip's wrist and then slapped his face. It was not painful, but Philip's nose and mouth immediately went numb. Don was staring at the place near his wrist where a small red welt was forming. The sight doubled his anger. He launched himself at Philip, knocked him over, and climbed on top of him. He grabbed for Philip's crotch; *that* would hurt. Philip tried to fend off his hand but Don was too strong. The hand began to squeeze and crush. Suddenly the pressure let up a little. "Jeezus," Don whispered, "you've got a hard-on!"

Philip began to sob, mortified, frightened. Don eased his body from Philip but did not relax his grip. "Hey," he breathed through clenched teeth, "you like this, don't yer?"

Philip could no longer speak. He was passive, unable to prevent, unwilling to resist. Don's hand rubbed, kneaded, massaged. He was on his knees, staring at Philip's wet face. He leaned closer. Philip could feel Don's breath. They both found their climax.

On the way home neither one spoke, each made shy by what had happened. The next morning they avoided each other, but after school they met again, and their walk home led to the same clearing under the statue.

The walk soon became part of their lives, a day incomplete without it. Still, they were unwilling to acknowledge what was happening. Each afternoon they manufactured the fight which led to the moment they had waited for all day.

Something awakened Johnny, a fire engine or a police car twenty floors below. He squinted at the black-and-gold calendar alarm on the night table: Sunday the eighteenth, nine o'clock.

He stood up, reached for the Tahitian *pareu* next to his bed, and wrapped it around his middle, then took the old gold medallion and chain from the table and hung it around his neck. It was against Army regs, of course, but the hell with regulations. *They* couldn't keep his hands from shaking when he bounced his old C-47 through a fat cumulus cloud or tried to reach for the runway through pea soup. The medallion could; it had even stuck with him through a near-typhoon on that crazy-ass sail to Papeete back in '39 with his roommate from Yale. He'd bought it two months before in some pansy boutique in Carmel, but that had nothing to do with it. He had *decided* that this was to be his good-luck piece.

Johnny caught sight of himself in the mirror. Standing there in a New York penthouse, dressed like a beach bum.

What a joke! Hero pilot who has soft bowels through

most of his flights . . . Swashbuckler who likes the boys . . . The impeccable personal pilot of *the* famous General Tommy Rankin. Any half-assed private detective could have blackmailed him, security clearance and all.

What the hell? As they said, there was a war on, chum, and everyone had to jazz it his own ding-dong way. The last thing he needed was a lot of introspection. What he *did* need now, right now, stood right there on the bar.

"Breakfast on the terrace, sir?" Roberts was accustomed to the sight of his employer, barefoot, in a loincloth, with a glassful of tequila in one hand, the neck of the bottle in the other.

"Fine."

"How about the young gentleman?"

Oh, Christ, the *kid*. Philip. "Is he up?"

"Not yet."

"Well, let him sleep."

"Very well, sir."

Johnny tossed off the shot of tequila.

Out on the terrace, the morning sun was summer-warm, and the sky was clear over that peculiar yellow New York haze. Johnny gulped some orange juice, ignored the Sunday papers, and waited for Roberts to bring ham and eggs. He tried briefly to remember Philip's face, then gave up. He would see him soon enough.

God, it was a nuisance when they stayed overnight. Mostly they turned out to be bores and then how to get rid of them? One thing he did remember: the kid had a forty-eight-hour pass, so Uncle Sam would solve *that* problem.

Johnny never had wake-up hangovers, no matter how much he drank. They came an hour or so later, and he felt the onset of one now. I'll be feeling you, in all the old familiar places—a headache, the stiffening neck, the heavy arms. Besides, he had dreamed through the goddamn crash landing

34

again. Not the slow-motion bullshit; that only happened in movies. Not even the details—*nose high, wheels up, no flaps, stick all mushy like he was flying through warm water. Copilot howling like a baby, his balls shot off: crrrunch*—none of that. Just the panic. It usually stayed a few minutes after he woke up, when he was defenseless. More of the hair of the chihuahua.

Another shot and he began to feel better. Well, almost. Something kept nagging. Guilt? Good Christ, not that! About some hick kid he'd laid? The hell with that noise, the boy was old enough to take care of himself. And *he'd* seemed to want it pretty badly, at that.

Roberts arrived with the tray, and Johnny reached for the Sunday papers. He'd get rid of Philip as soon as possible, before lunch. It would be easy enough.

T HEY were already in the hallway when the phone rang again. It was the third time in twenty minutes, and Philip groaned, although after nearly two years with Johnny he should be used to it. It was a wonder they ever got out of the apartment.

"For Christ's sake, Johnny!"

Johnny shrugged. "Can't help it, m'lad, people do call . . . I'll take it in here, Roberts."

Philip followed him to the phone and stood nearby, his features tight. The party meant nothing to Johnny, the bastard, but for Philip it was an occasion. Christ, it ought to be, after the way he'd been hidden away all this time—local movies, dinners in small neighborhood restaurants, no big parties until this one. ("It's just that I can't bear being a *couple*. You understand.")

Philip understood more than Johnny thought, and as he recalled their most recent argument on this subject, his lower lip went out in a pout.

Johnny hung up the phone. *If he knew how he looks when he does that, he wouldn't.* No matter. This party would be his last gift to Philip Ross. Susan Ahern's lousy party, then he'd show him Elmo's, where the little snot could push all he wanted . . . A bon voyage party, and never mind that Philip didn't know it. After all, he was sending him off with good clothes, a Johnny-made vocabulary. And maybe some pocket money.

As they finally stepped into the elevator, Johnny put his hand on Philip's shoulder. "Better to get there late, Susan's parties are monsters. You'll see." Philip shrugged off his hand.

For those in the fashion business, Susan Ahern's annual parties were essential. It was vital to be asked, devastating to be overlooked or dropped from the previous year's list.

There were other great fashion editors, charming, talented, authoritative. But Susan, as editor-in-chief of *Ambience*, was at the top. It was she who coined the words, pegged the moods; whose opinions became dogma.

Fashion seemed to be her entire world. ("If I had lived marriage the way I live the business," she had once said, "I'd be a very dull lady still married to my first husband.") Nonetheless, her circle included bankers, actors, politicians, painters, and relatively few fashion people.

Tonight over a hundred people were crammed into the Terrace Room at the St. Regis. Only the tops of the velvet drapes and the gold-leafed ceiling remained visible. It was a pressure-cooker party, as Johnny had known it would be, the kind where everyone tries to stay in the middle. The lanky hostess was at dead center, the favorites grouped around her, and then there were the outer circles. At the kind of party Johnny liked best, these splinter groups would be jelling around several *types renommés*. Not at the annual Ahern. Here, the designation of a guest's rank was by accolade. If the hostess waved, one moved to mid-pie. Those whom she ignored shuffled around the edges, sneaking occasional glances at the seat of strength and at the new arrivals, much like a pitcher trying to keep batter and base stealer in sight.

Fortunately, Johnny was a favorite. Susan waved and he made his way toward her, Philip in his wake.

"My dear John . . ." (She never called him Johnny.) "What fun to see you!"

Johnny kissed her cheek and introduced Philip, who was scrutinized, evaluated, and smiled upon. (Score two for the smile, Philip dear, then minus one because it's one of her *tentative* smiles.)

He looked around at the inner group; Philip ought to be impressed. Doe Perrin, beautiful, Ahern's assistant on *Ambience*; Eric Marshall, Yale forever, publisher of *Now!*, the weekly fashion-cum-everything magazine; Paul Bender, president of Torrey Blake's, Fifth Avenue, gray-haired, gray-faced, super-tailored, overslim . . . And then there was James Farrow: couturier.

Farrow, who had been staring at Philip, turned to Johnny: "You are the *most* impossible man!"

"Oh?"

"You take attractive people like this young fellow and positively *hide* them away until Susan gives her party!"

(Cut it, you old queen!) "My dear James, you must leave me the right to a few secrets."

He moved toward Doe Perrin; Philip shrugged apologetically and followed.

Farrow's practiced eye had missed nothing. The boy in gray chalk-stripe flannel with a white shirt, black twill tie, and red foulard pocket kerchief; the same for Evans-Greene, only the suit was navy, the tie cream-colored. Same tailor, same haberdasher. Evans-Greene might as well drop the pinstripe sister act—anyone could see the boy belonged to him.

Fiona Evans-Greene had first brought Johnny to Farrow's salon when he was fifteen. Exquisite, even then; six feet tall with a Michelangelo-David face and gray eyes. Fiona was a *cliente supérieure* who spent a fortune on clothes. A great beauty, an excellent horsewoman, a flirt, and an all-time bitch. She and her husband, who was if possible more patronizing than Fiona, had arrived at a cease-fire if not a truce. Their indiscretions might scandalize the older Newport group, but they'd spiced many a house party in Southampton and Palm Beach.

Johnny was devoted to his mama, and if his parents made him insecure or resentful, he never showed it. His manners were courtly, oddly adult, and he smiled easily.

Farrow, enchanted with Johnny, was trapped between his appetite and his pocketbook. Johnny tempted him, but the danger of offending Mrs. Evans-Greene outweighed temptation. Instead, Farrow became an expert on Johnny's life, building a mental dossier through the years. How could he have missed the advent of this sulky blond *número* in the pin-striped suit?

Philip *was* sulking. Johnny was treating him like a ventriloquist's dummy, never giving him a chance to speak to Farrow. Pretty goddamn rude, and he'd even been slow in introducing him to Mrs. Ahern. If Johnny was ashamed of him, why had he brought him? Philip was in no mood to speak to this Doe Perrin Johnny had stuck him with. She was very pretty, but not one of the magazine faces he recognized, like Farrow. *They* were the ones he wanted to meet, and here he was talking to this girl. He answered her questions automatically.

"Yes, it's good to be back in civvies . . . Oh, with Johnny right now till I get my own place . . . I have no idea just yet . . . Yes, you're right . . . *Right!*"

Doe Perrin was usually charitable, but this lad was a bit much, his eyes sweeping the room like radar antennae while she tried to make conversation. Johnny, who had given her the "Doe, darling, would you talk to Philip for a minute?" routine and disappeared, was too far away for an SOS signal. She was cooked. Oh well, anything for old Johnny, and for

Johnny's chums. She had known many of Johnny's chums, and once, long ago, when they were kids in Southampton she had really *known* Johnny. A *long* time ago.

Now, she was running out of gambits. Isn't this a mad crush party? . . . Wasn't it hard to find an apartment? . . . Hopeless. Young Mr. Ross was monosyllabic.

She took another look at Philip and decided she wasn't being fair. He was probably very shy, very impressed. She tried again.

"Philip, I expect you *know* many people here, but in case there are some new faces . . . this is my bailiwick."

That did it. Now she had his unswerving attention. She began to point out who was who, enjoying his expression as he matched famous names with unfamiliar faces. He soon dropped all pretense of recognizing anyone, and the more ingenuous he became, the more Doe congratulated herself on her patience. Philip was a pretty nice kid, after all.

Nearby but out of earshot, Johnny was smiling at Farrow. "James," he said. "Sorry I had to run away before, but I had to say hello to Doe . . ."

"Ah, yes. I understand completely."

"Well now, what do you mean by *that?*"

"Not a thing, my dear Jonathan." Farrow could make "hello" sound like a double-entendre, but this time he had used the snide tone simply from habit. Johnny assessed Farrow's mood and decided to proceed.

"James, there's something I'd like you to do for me."

"Oh?" (Very un-Johnny that, asking a favor. Must have something to do with that sweet blond number.)

"The young man with me," said Johnny. (There we are! Oh, James, do you know people or do you *know* people?) "He's been back from the Army for a while now, staying at my place until he can find a flat of his own."

41

"I'm sure there's no rush about *that!*" said Farrow. This time there was no doubt as to his meaning. Johnny ignored it.

"The boy wants to learn a business and I know he's nuts about fashion. He reads every magazine and talks nothing but clothes. When he got wind of Ahern's party he drove me up the wall to bring him."

"I must admit that I haven't seen you around these velvet pits lately," said Farrow.

"I'm no good at discussing hemlines."

"What would you *rather* discuss?"

Again Johnny bypassed combat. "The thing I suggested to Philip—"

"Who's that?"

"The boy I was *talking* about."

"My dear, you failed to introduce me."

"Oh, did I? Sorry."

"Quite all right."

"Anyway, I suggested to Philip that he might learn the dressmaking business."

Actually, the whole thing had come to him on the way to the party. It seemed crystal-clear: Philip and his goddamn social ambitions. Well, if he got into fashion he would meet enough people to supply him with droppable names for the rest of his life. His taking a job would also break their stalemate, and without unpleasantness. Johnny had no idea whether Philip had any talent, but what the hell did that matter?

Farrow's eyelids drooped like bamboo shutters. Chances were that Johnny would now try to sell him on hiring Philip Ross. Actually, not that bad an idea. Farrow's old-crow clients would adore him; he could use a fresh face.

"Well now, Johnny, if you're thinking of my salon, forget it. I'm through training bloody amateurs. Why should I pay someone to learn my style so he can walk out on me and sell my ideas to some kike on Seventh Avenue?"

Johnny's voice was soothing. "I don't think you'll find Philip unethical."

"How the hell do I *know?* Anyway, business is rough enough without adding to my overhead."

It didn't look good, and Johnny *had* to convince Farrow. Impossible to take another month, week, *minute*, of Philip in the penthouse.

"All right, James, I'll pay for his apprenticeship, have his weekly salary sent to you. You pay him—he doesn't have to know it's coming from me."

Farrow's eyes unveiled for a second. This was more like it. He'd get the boy gratis, and something on Johnny Evans-Greene along with it, a rare pleasure. (Oh Johnny, poor Johnny, too bad. Love, oh careless love.)

"Well, Johnny, I really haven't any room for him, but . . ." At last, a cautious smile. "Send him over to see me. What's his last name?"

"Ross."

"Jewish?"

"No."

"Excellent. Have him phone me . . . What'll you pay him?"

"Seventy-five a week, I thought."

"Fifty," said Farrow. "Don't spoil him."

Philip could see at once that El Morocco was as different from the Stork as the party he'd just left was from any other party he'd ever been to. Here there were no youngsters, no out-of-towners, no tourists. The people who stepped out of their limousines and into Elmo's were rich, successful, sure.

Carino, El Morocco's grim-faced maître d', was the neme-sis of the cafe-ambitious. He greeted Johnny with a baleful but respectful look of recognition. (It was said that Carino *never* smiled, not even at the Duke of Windsor.) Once a signal as to their place in the pecking order had been discreetly conveyed to the captains, Johnny and Philip were piloted to a banquette near the entrance.

Philip inclined his head toward the distant dance floor. "You in trouble here, Johnny?"

"What do you mean?"

"Hardly a ringside table."

"Sonny, you've got much to learn," said Johnny, and ordered a bottle of Perignon. "In a good supper club the best tables are near the entrance."

"Even in a dancing place?"

"You've been seeing too many William Powell movies. In real life, the *customers* are the attraction. A man walks in, the first faces he sees are *famous* faces. He's cowed. He ends up tipping the maître d' and taking any goddamn table they assign him."

The champagne arrived, and as he sipped it Philip looked around like a medical student observing his first operation. They were seated next to the Duke and Duchess of Trent. Johnny watched and waited. Philip had scouted only the tables in front of them. Now he turned to Johnny and froze in mid-word. He had spotted the ex-king. It was lovely.

"You were saying?"

"Ah, Johnny," Philip's voice sank to a whisper, "that's the *duke* next to you."

"Yes, I know."

"Christ . . ."

"No, not Christ. His name is Albert Thomas—"

"You're making fun of me, goddammit."

Johnny stood up and moved away from the table, brushing his royal neighbor's elbow almost by accident. The duke looked up: "Johnny, what a nice surprise. How are you?"

"Fine, sir, and good evening, ma'am. I see you're both well."

"We're on our way to Palm Beach."

"Have a fine trip."

He bowed to the duchess. Philip was mesmerized.

"Relax," said Johnny in a low voice when he sat down again. "Old friends of my parents."

For one guilty moment Philip thought of his own parents. He had not seen them since he was discharged. In a skimpy and vague letter some weeks before, he had told them he was still in New York, that he would contact them, that he was looking for work. He had used YMCA stationery and given no return address. He dreaded having to see them, but it would eventually be unavoidable. Only not now. Not yet.

In the meantime, after all those stinking, stupid years of pride in his sergeant's stripes—"Noncoms are the backbone of the service"—his father had finally made warrant officer. Though he could now proudly wear an officer's uniform, he was still technically lower than the lowest shavetail.

Fuck him, thought Philip, looking around at the well-tanned, well-dressed, and well-heeled.

They were joined by Doe Perrin and a tall, chinless, blond man in his early thirties with a hooked nose and longish hair who wore a tightly cut English flannel suit with slanted hacking pockets. His stiff-collared white shirt was fronted by a Racquet Club tie, carelessly knotted.

His response to their introduction was delivered in a high nasal voice with a broad British "a," although the rest of his accent was American. After that, he neither spoke nor responded. He was quite drunk, but Doe seemed unconcerned. She launched into a long conversation with Johnny about Southampton. Philip tried to follow, but the names and places were unfamiliar. The chinless man was staring at the navy blue ceiling, so Philip watched the other tables: a blond

dowager and the queen who was her escort for the evening—
grotesque until they rhumbaed, when they were perfection. A
tall, balding businessman with some international playpeople
who ignored him as he yawned openly—he waved for the
check while the others were dancing, signed it, and left without saying goodnight. When the dancers returned to the
table, they were surprised and angry with each other. Obviously the man was important to them. They called the
maître d', who shrugged, unable to say where the tall man
had gone.

The Trents left, and a movie star Philip recognized instantly took their table. The star was handsomer off screen
than on, but looked out of place away from gladiatorial costumes and Roman chariots. The woman with him seemed
*hausfrau* for El Morocco and for her aquiline escort; she must
be his wife.

A tall slim young man with slick black hair and a girl's
face stopped at the table, exchanged banalities with Johnny,
and left.

"That's Don Jeffson," Johnny said. "A half-assed socialite
who's been trying to get by in Palm Beach and Newport. He's
too broke to manage it, though, and now he's on his way to
the Coast for a screen test. If he makes it he'll have some
cash, and out there he'll be the goddamn social nabob. Last
time I was in Beverly Hills anyone who could get into
Morocco was considered society."

Philip grabbed at the chance to get back into the conversation. "With all the movie people and things, I should
think Hollywood would be pretty blasé."

"Are you kidding? Most of the so-called stars go straight
from Cleveland into movies. A Beverly Hills evening is not to
be believed—you can bear me out, Doe—they play *games*,
stupid party games like Twenty Questions. Everybody has to
see the host's latest movie and then they all yawn and go

home at eleven. The only amusing people are the European writers and directors and the stage actors. At least they can *talk*. Oh, and Flynn's bunch. They're a drunken crowd of bastards, but at least they make some waves."

Someone nearby said: "What d'ye mean, drunken bastards, you drunken bastard?"

Johnny looked around, straight into Errol Flynn's smiling face. The two men fell into each other's arms like sailors on shore leave. They talked for a few noisy moments; then Flynn looked over at Doe, whispered to Johnny, shrugged, and left.

"Christ, I thought someone wanted a fight," said Johnny. "It was only Flynn. He asked about you, Doe. I won't tell you *what* he asked."

"I get the drift."

"Well, how about it?"

"Pimping, Johnny?"

"Matchmaking."

Philip was impressed. What in hell was this one doing with old chinless? And how *about* Flynn? All suntanned with a ruffled dinner shirt and a ring in his left earlobe.

Doe's companion came to life. He wanted food. Johnny poked Philip and they said goodnight. Chinless handed Philip a limp hand, but did not remember his name.

Ever since Philip was a kid, he had always awakened early. Growing up, he'd *dreamed* reveille, bugle and all, and he still felt guilty about oversleeping.

This morning, as usual, Roberts had breakfast ready for him in the living room. Their conversation was always minimal; Roberts lived in a sterile half-world, unquestioning and unquestioned, a modern-day eunuch.

Philip was surprised to see Johnny not only up but fully dressed, hours before his usual eleven o'clock. Also, he seemed uncommonly cheerful.

47

"Hey, kid, hangover?"

"Nope," said Philip. "Never happens."

"Wrap yourself around some breakfast, sonny, and I'll give you some good news."

"Oh?"

Roberts brought the ham and eggs. Philip looked up at Johnny between forkfuls, expecting him to continue; Johnny lit a cigarette, poured some coffee, shifted in his chair.

"Yesterday someone paid you a big compliment."

"Who?"

"Someone who wants to offer you a job."

"What kind of a job?" Christ, some creep with a factory who wants a salesman . . . Underdone eggs. Damn Roberts.

"A very glossy job. Wait'll you hear."

Johnny poured it on. Farrow had been charmed by Philip, was "dying" to hire him. "Of course, dear boy, I said you'd ruin his goddamn business . . ."

Philip stopped eating. This was no factory-flunky job. But how much would it pay? He wanted a place of his own, and that took dough. He was sick of hanging around the penthouse day after long day. "Sounds great, Johnny, really great!" Could he ask about the dough?

"Fine, then. And listen, he'll pay seventy-five a week." The hell with Farrow.

Philip's eyebrows shot up. Seventy-five a week would do it.

"You think he really means it? Or was he loaded?"

"Farrow loaded? Never!"

"Well, then." Philip hesitated for a second, then plunged on: "I've been in your hair around here long enough. Of course, you've been terrific to put up with me this long, but now I'll be able to afford a small place of my own."

"Not at all. Happy to have you here." You little son of a

bitch, you ungrateful little son of a bitch, you wanted to get out all along.

Johnny began to laugh. The joke was on him, but he enjoyed it. He was, after all, something of a ridiculous man.

"What's so funny, Johnny?"

"Nothing, kid, nothing!"

P

HILIP," said the girl in the black dress, "*he* wants to see you!" She tilted her head in the direction of the gold-trimmed door at the back of the salon and continued sorting through a circular telephone file. Her desk, like all the furniture in the room, was imitation Louis XVI. Even the switchboard was camouflaged behind a tufted gray satin screen.

Not that James Farrow *liked* Louis XVI furniture. On the contrary. His own home was Victorian, very *millefleurs* and fussy. But as he often explained, Louis XVI was *the* perfect approach: it calmed the spoiled and impressed the nouveau-riche.

The furniture, the beaten-silver plaque outside, the heavy mirrored doors which led to the little gray-carpeted stairway, all whispered: *It's expensive here . . . It's awfully, awfully expensive here . . . We don't really need you here . . . It's up to you: if you want to be a Farrow client, you have to pay for the privilege . . .*

Not that money alone was enough. The British receptionist made that perfectly clear:

"Madame?"

"I am Mrs. Kornman."

"Yes?" A cold smile.

"My friend Mrs. Lewis is a client of yours . . ."

"Which Mrs. Lewis? Mrs. Wethrall Lewis? Mrs. Rodney Tomkin-Lewis? Mrs. Cabot Lewis?"

"Mrs. Irving Lewis."

"Mrs. . . . !" Fractionally raised eyebrows, a slightly incredulous air, despite the fact that the mink-caped, face-lifted Mrs. Lewis is remembered instantly. ". . . *Irving* Lewis? Let me check, please."

Slim hand to antique white phone. "Accounting, please." A long pause. Mrs. Kornman uncomfortable, embarrassed, angry but holding her temper nonetheless.

"I see, a *new* client, thank you . . . Through that door, Mrs. Kornman."

All in accordance with Farrow's policy: "Kikes we need because they're quick money. But too many of them can ruin the atmosphere, so keep it down. And once they're inside be sure they don't *cluster!*"

He only spoke this way to the old-timers who had been with him from the beginning and to a few like Philip whom he trusted—if you could call Farrow's confidence "trust." At the very beginning, of course, the salon had been restricted, but now there were certain carefully selected Jewish names on the appointment sheets. It had proved to be a financially sound piece of subversion.

Two years had passed since Philip had first entered Farrow's private office, a small red plush room, in total contradiction to the gray hauteur outside. The floor was covered with Persian rugs, and a petit-point sofa took up one entire flower-papered wall. The other wall was filled with still-lifes, trompe l'oeils, and miniature portraits all in ornate gilt or velvet frames attached to red or green satin ribbons. Masses of vased carnations, garnet roses, and anemones mushroomed on end tables next to small antimacassared upholstered chairs. A long Oriental coffee table, inlaid with mother-of-pearl design, blocked the way to the couch. It overflowed with sketches, swatches of fabric, red crystal Venetian glasses full of hatpins, an enormous pair of brass-handled scissors. Farrow chain-smoked Gauloises, filling the room with nose-biting fumes. His short cigarette holder stayed clamped in his teeth, while he cut swatches with both hands, attaching them to sketches with the glass-tipped hatpins.

Farrow sketched each day of his life, pouring ideas onto paper—new shapes, new proportions, hairdos, hats, jewelry, shoes, make-up. The stream was unending, and at the end of the day as many as sixty croquis might go into the atelier, the workroom on the fourth floor, to be cut into muslins, the pristine cloth in which new ideas were tried out. Other croquis were put in front of quivering milliners, dour little shoemakers, or tight-faced coiffeurs who were called into the small room. By the end of the day the smoke had staled into near-solidity.

It all built toward two climactic days of the year, one in spring and one in fall, the openings. Clients were seated according to ironclad protocol on rows of tiny gilt folding chairs. Farrow, watching from behind the draped exit from the models' room, would wait until every last piece of gossip was exchanged, every mirror returned to its purse, every coat draped over the chairs, before signaling for the lead model to open the show.

Late-comers were barred with scant apologies. The invitations said "Four P.M. sharp," and Farrow intended to be obeyed.

Couture was a battle of wills: the couturier versus the millionairess, the man with the needle against the woman with the checkbook. The contest was not unlike lion taming —lose control and you were devoured. The lions would change your designs, protest your prices, disorganize your fitting schedule, and bully your vendeuses.

The way Farrow controlled his clients was as symbolic as the lion tamer's chair: he could bar them from the salon.

In New York it was easy to threaten the socially prominent. "Ross," Farrow had once said, "remember that top socialites are the top social climbers." Leafing through *Town & Country, Bazaar,* and *Vogue,* he'd read aloud the names of the prominent women whose parties, weddings, children were paraded in print that month. "Publicity hounds, every one of them," he said. "Nothing to sell but their own goddamn faces."

Philip had remembered, all right, and after two years he was still amused by Farrow's bullying of the very clients he used as bait.

Now, he closed the door, sealing in the smells of cologne, smoke, and coffee. He stood just inside Farrow's studio without speaking; Farrow, perfectly aware of Philip's presence, paid no attention. He sat on the sofa, concentrating on a sketch. Finally he looked up, jerked the cigarette holder from between his teeth, and said, "Shit!"

The outburst was part of the pattern. Dozens of previous meetings had begun in silences punctuated by epithets. Philip sighed, shifted his weight from one foot to the other, crossed his arms over his chest, and waited.

Farrow poked his cigarette into a butt-laden ashtray, causing a shower of sparks. He gestured with the bent end of the half-doused cigarette.

"Is it or is it not your job, my *dear* Ross, to keep track of our textiles?" Pause. "Well?"

"Yessir." One of Philip's first assignments had been to keep exact records of the bolts of woolens, silks, cottons, and linens in the vaultlike stockroom on the fourth floor. Textiles arrived from all over Europe and the Orient. Each length of goods was meticulously recorded. Whenever any of it was cut into clothes, the tally showed exactly how much had been used. There were brocades worth forty to fifty dollars per yard and some heavy Swiss cottons which cost even more. The House of Farrow was heavily insured against loss by fire, but no insurance policy could compensate them for the loss of unfilled orders.

The textile room was as carefully tended as a great wine cellar. Silks could yellow or rot. Woolens might discolor or become moth paradise. A false count of goods could lead to serious financial losses if it took months to replace special designs and weaves.

Philip anticipated Farrow's next question. The sketch Farrow held up was "swatched" with a bright red French wool Philip recognized. Farrow was probably furious because the fabric was no longer in stock and the style could not be cut.

"Where in hell *is* the red Lesur twill?"

(You used it to cover those cutesy pillows in your Radio City chorus boy's apartment, *sir*.) "Mr. Farrow, it's exactly where you told your chauffeur to deliver it."

Farrow jumped to his feet. He was a tiny man, though overweight; balding and heavy-lipped. Over his thyroid-thickened eyes was a fringe of dyed hair brushed forward, Nero-style. His chest was tightly girdled in a high-buttoned Edwardian coat over a double-breasted brocade vest, and his chin almost covered the immense knot of his wine-red bengaline tie. Despite his laughable getup, dumpling size, and quilt-soft body, he cowed many taller, harder men.

Philip, watching the anger rush to Farrow's face, was worried. "You may not recall, sir, but I believe *you* used the red twill. Do you remember now, Mr. Farrow?"

Farrow stood quite still.

Philip stumbled on: "I checked it off the inventory last week, sir . . ." He ran out of steam. The pause lengthened, then Farrow began, slowly and softly, in the strong Cockney accent that came back when he was angry:

"You foul . . . *dirty* . . . miserable . . . little cunt! You pig of a . . . little kept boy! Were you really going to teach *me*

55

. . . that you were such a smart little . . . bloke and that I was a stupid old fart?"

Farrow stepped around the coffee table until he was directly under Philip's nose. There were beads of perspiration on his bald pate and Philip could smell his sweat-heated cologne. They stood toe to toe. Then, abruptly, Farrow went back to the couch and sat down, his features suddenly relaxed.

"Okay, Ross, let's forget it. Bring me the sample chart."

Philip said, "Yessir!" and turned to go.

"Ross . . ."

Philip stopped.

"You're a shit, Ross, but you're bright!"

"Thank you, sir."

Philip left the office.

Farrow dropped the sketch on the table, clamped the cigarette holder into his mouth and leaned back against the heavy bolsters, closing his eyes. That had been a bloody foolish indulgence, letting fly at Ross. And then to top it off with Lombert's final remark: "You're a shit, but you're a bright boy." Ross had said, "Thank you," just as *he* had, years before.

"Jake, you're a shit, but you're a bright boy."

"Thank you, Bryan."

Thank you for being released, for allowing him to forget Jacob Rubin? It was Bryan Lombert's final generosity. They had not spoken since then, twelve years ago.

Maison Lombert had dominated Paris couture in the thirties, not so much despite the fact that Bryan Lombert was British as because of it. Lombert, a tall reed-thin Old Etonian who had once been the youngest Guards officer in the BEF, was uniquely qualified to cater to the mighty. He understood their tastes, their lives, their obligations, and he was gentle and discreet. His own taste was impeccable and he had the wisdom to hire fine craftsmen, who adored him.

In 1920 he had opened his London salon, a solid success, and then a branch in Paris. Like Worth, who preceded him, and Balenciaga, who followed him, Lombert was a foreigner. He was accepted by the chauvinistic French because he was a success. (Foreigners who succeeded were part of Paris. Foreigners who failed were, *après tout, des étrangers,* and what can you expect, *mon vieux?*)

As for Jacob Rubin, *he* was an apprentice tailor at Thompson's in Savile Row. His way out and up made its appearance one morning in the fitting room, in the person of the Honorable Derrick Chatfield (Eton, Sandhurst, and the Guards). Chatfield had arranged his body in an elegant Edwardian stance in preparation for a tiresome hour of being pinned, ripped, and smoothed into the season's wardrobe. Little Jake was on his knees, working on the drape of a trouser leg.

"I say, Jake, old chap. Something deucedly private I wanted to ask you."

"Yessir?"

"Well, y'know, I could stand some, ah, services. So could some of my friends." He touched Jack's mouth with one long, signet-ringed finger. His meaning was clear. Jake said nothing. Chatfield looked back at the mirror. "You Jews," he said, "are so, ah, sensuous . . ."

Jake was delighted. He knew exactly what he wanted— and, now, how he would get it.

He did not have long to wait. The latest toy of an extraordinary group of young gentlemen, he was careful to make his bid before the novelty had time to wear off:

"Mr. Chatfield, sir, do you know Mr. Bryan Lombert?"

"Lombert? Rather! Known him for years. Same regiment, you know. Why?"

"I'd like a job at Lombert's."

"Happy to ring him, old chap!"

First he got the job he wanted; then he got rid of Chatfield. It was simple: he threatened to expose him. (There had been several Guards scandals, and Chatfield gave him no trouble.)

Lombert's salon was in a charming Regency maisonette just off Carlo's Place in Mayfair. The workroom was on the fourth floor, and Jake simply walked in and took over. The ancient Hungarian who ran the shop never stood a chance. He quit within a month. Lombert disapproved of Jake's maneuvers in getting rid of the old man, but did not try to block them. His new employee was superb.

When Lombert opened the Paris branch in 1930, his three gentlewomen-vendeuses kept the London salon serenely on its course. Clients flowed steadily past the crests with the royal warrants at the entrance. The seasonal purchases of the royal family, London society, and county families were predestined. One went to Lombert's for one's ball gowns, daytime frocks, and country suits. One could even trust dear little Mr. Rubin with a decent pair of jodhpurs, my dear!

A few outsiders, the wives of wealthy businessmen, plucked up the courage to make appointments. They were treated courteously, but their fittings were never scheduled when royal personages were in the salon. The vendeuses often asked Mr. Rubin to handle these new clients. He had such a way with them.

There came the day when Jacob Rubin asked Mrs. Ffrench-Raynor, the head vendeuse, if she would be kind enough henceforth to address him as "Mr. Farrow." When she expressed mild surprise, Mr. Rubin explained that this appellation would make it easier for him to deal with the "new ladies." Mrs. Ffrench-Raynor could not for the life of her understand why, but she was perfectly willing to do his bidding, and she instructed the rest of the staff to follow suit.

Jake (soon to be James) Farrow developed a great following. He was known in St. John's Wood, Manchester, Leeds, Nottingham, and Wolverhampton as the key man at Lombert. ("Ask for Mr. Farrow, my dear. He takes great care of me. Tell him I sent you!")

The next time Bryan Lombert came to London, Mrs. Ffrench-Raynor informed him of Mr. Rubin's request—and of his success with Maison Lombert's new clients.

"*Dear chap,*" said Lombert to Jake, taking in his double-breasted chalk-striped flannel, wide tie knotted *à la* Prince of Wales, and brown suede shoes. "Of course we shall respect your wishes. Farrow it shall be, and a dashed good idea it is, too. Just don't bring me *too* much new business, dear boy, because the season is upon us and we shall have to serve our old clients."

"That's a promise, Major." Jake always used Lombert's Guards title. "No one will be neglected."

"Jolly good!" And that was that.

Lombert returned to Paris, leaving "Farrow" to supervise the new collection. He also instructed his accountants to augment Farrow's salary with sales commissions. Farrow moved from Whitechapel to Golders Green. He was free . . . finally.

"Farrow"? Why not Farrow? A bloody private joke, that name. Was he not the *fegele* in the Whitechapel ghetto, the Yiddish word for "queer"? "Fegele" literally meant a small bird. Fegele, the queer, the sparrow, had become Farrow. Fuck them all! Fuck their beards, the yarmulkas, their prayer shawls, their bagels and kishkas, their Talmudic smart alecks, their waving hands; fuck their contempt! The yid from Whitechapel was Mayfair now.

Despite the continuing emphasis on Lombert-Paris, Lombert-London grew rapidly under Farrow's management. In 1936 the last of the original vendeuses followed Mrs. Ffrench-

Raynor into retirement. James Farrow became managing director with a sizable salary, a home on South Audley Street, and a wardrobe from Poole's and Turnbull & Asser.

Farrow quickly tightened the slack discipline at the old London house. Profits were up, and Lombert-London often subsidized Lombert-Paris. Bryan Lombert, delighted with his protégé, decided to let Farrow design the London collections, based on an outline of ideas he sent from Paris. Farrow knew tailoring and he'd taught himself to sketch by copying from *Vogue*. The croquis of each Lombert collection contained a decreasing number of pages marked B.L.

Farrow was careful to keep Lombert's royal clientele happy. He continued to show the conventional styles suitable to their anachronistic life and tasks. "Dear Mr. Farrow" could, at the drop of a royal eyelash, produce critiqueproof costumes for ceremonial visits to hospitals or the launching of warships. The little tailor, dressed in morning clothes, sometimes appeared at the household entrance of the Palace himself, carrying gray Lombert cartons.

The Palace! The fegele had flown high as a hawk. ("Jakele . . . you remember me? Sammy? From the old days? Well, I hate to ask you a favor but—" Click. *Fuck you, Sam. The fegele tells you to go stuff yourself up yourself.*)

The manufacturers' wives from the Midlands and from St. John's Wood found the path into Lombert's strewn with ever-increasing obstacles. Appointments were difficult to get, prices astronomical. The new Farrow-trained vendeuses were young and patronizing. Nevertheless, these clients kept coming—and paying. Had they drifted away Farrow would hardly have cared. His eyes were fastened on a new group: the Americans.

There were an odd lot, these mink- and lynx-coated ladies with the twanging accents. They were naïve and socially insecure, but they had the strength of money and the noninvolvement of foreigners. A rich American client could seldom be made to take second place. ("Sorry, madame, but Her Grace has reserved three o'clock and I shall have to ask you to come at four . . .")

The response to each snub was to "up the ante," as they would put it. ("Gee, Mr. Farrow, I'm really pushed for time, we've gotta meet some friends! Lookit, I'll make it worth your while if you can squeeze me in!")

It was all very profitable, and, after all, Farrow was hardly cheating Lombert, who was getting paid in full for each purchase. Within two years Farrow had added large earnings to Lombert-London, all in dollars. Several American clients suggested an idea which Farrow considered so important that he went to Paris to present it to Bryan Lombert.

"Show in New York?" said Lombert. "My god, Jake, that would be quite a project!"

"I could prepare the whole thing, Bryan." (He had waited patiently until Lombert had suggested the first-name basis.) "Three of our New York clients, Mrs. Debenham, Mrs. Stuydam, and Mrs. Calhoun, have promised every facility in America if we do the show for their charity—I think it's called Episcopal Children's Hospital. They'll pay the fares, all shipping costs, insurance, New York hotel bills, the whole blasted thing."

"Um, well, it sounds all right. Of course, I've met Dorothy Stuydam—she's a great friend of Mrs. Kennedy, the American ambassador's wife. And I believe the Debenhams were very kind to the Prince of Wales on his last American tour . . . But dammit, Jake, I can't leave Paris. I'm in the middle of the collection, I've lost my *première*, and the atelier's in a mess."

He paused, rubbing the narrow bridge of his curved nose. He fiddled with his cigarette case, pulled out an Abdullah, and lit it. Finally: "I like your idea—now try one of mine.

Why don't *you* take the collection to the States?"

"Oh, I don't think so, Bryan. They expect to see you!"

"Nonsense, dear boy, you *are* Lombert-London, aren't you? I won't hear of any objections. After all, you're the one with all those dollar clients, I'd only get lost trying to know one from the other . . . Consider it settled. Lombert's Mr. Farrow is going out to America—and I hope you do a dashed sight better than Wales did. He just kept falling off his bloody horse!"

Farrow's big plan came to life as he leaned over the *Queen Mary's* railing, looking ahead at the hazy Atlantic. He was responsible for forty trunks of gowns, hats, shoes, and jewelry. There were ten London mannequins in a string of first-class staterooms and a crew of seamstresses and wardrobe mistresses in tourist class. He felt a sense of adventure and none of regret, though he knew that he was done with London forever.

A week later, in his suite at the Plaza, Farrow made his decision. He would accept Mrs. Debenham's offer.

"I assure you," she had said in London, "there'll be no problem. I'll be happy to back your house here in New York; just give me the word!"

She was a slight woman in her middle forties, golf- and tennis-trim, with tanned, leathery skin and ice-blue eyes. Her movements were deceptively nervous. She fluttered her hands, shifted her feet, fiddled with her bracelets, purse, coffee cup. She seemed vague and disorganized. But when she spoke she changed: her voice was emphatic, deep, and commanding.

In London, Farrow had thought her typically American. After a week in New York, he was no longer sure of what was typical. He had met dozens of society women who were like their British counterparts except for their nasal English —and, then, they treated him as a superior being, a great artist, an authority rather than a merchant-supplier. He was toasted at four luncheons, eight "cocktail" parties (the new rage in New York), five private dinners, and one huge charity ball.

The week had been crowded with work and interviews, entertainment and new faces. Anyone else would have been exhausted, but the little Londoner seemed to gain momentum from adulation. The press never stopped phoning. At first there were lady writers from the New York papers, kindly, henlike women with spectacles or pince-nez. With them came burly photographers who seemed to resent pointing their Graflexes at anything less dramatic than a murder or a fire.

"Okay, now, pal, er, Mr. Farrow. Now, hold up that gown and point at it!" (Flash!) "Arright, now, act like you're sketching—here, get me some paper someone . . ." (Flash!)

Then the interviews:

"Yes, Miss Clovis?"

"Tell me, Mr. Farrow, how does the Queen choose her accessories?"

"Sorry, but I can't talk about the royal family. You do understand?"

"Of course, Mr. Farrow. How about the Duchess of Kent? Does she still speak Greek?"

"As I said—"

"Of course. I'm being a naughty girl . . ." (Giggle.) "What do you think of American women?"

"Well, from what I've seen, they're marvelous-*looking*. Superb."

"More so than Englishwomen?"

"I didn't say that, Miss Clovis."

"Oh, I'm being naughty again, aren't I?" (Another giggle. Pencil flying over paper. She looks innocent, the old hag, but watch yourself, Jake.)

Now the fashion-magazine editors: imposing, majestic, surrounded by small swarms of debutantish assistants. Having seen the collection in London, they now wanted to photograph the styles on American society women, a risky business considering the cost of the gowns and the figures of their wearers. Farrow offered seamstresses for each sitting. The *midinettes* would guard the gowns with their lives. Each costume was fitted to one slender mannequin for the forthcoming show, and they were virtually impossible to alter. The society women who could wear them at all grew purple-faced from holding their breath.

The big night finally arrived—the great fashion show for "Episcopal," as the charity was usually called. The Grand Ballroom of the Plaza was filled to bursting with New York's ball-gowned and white-tied Six Hundred. They were enthralled. It was a fashion show in the classic couture manner, with gliding walk, runway pivots, and a bride's costume as the grand finale. The flower girls and trainbearers in this last number were the children and grandchildren of the socialites, a clever piece of last-minute theater conceived by Farrow.

One of the children was Mrs. Debenham's youngest daughter, Julia. Seconds after the applause had finally ended, her mother rushed backstage, flanked by Julia's governess, who took charge of the little girl. Mrs. Debenham was radiant.

"Congratulations, Mr. Farrow. It was *colossal!*"

"Thank you, Mrs. Debenham. They were a generous audience . . ." It was his mock-meek act, a direct imitation of Bryan Lombert's way of accepting florid compliments.

"Have you thought any more about my offer?"

"Well, Mrs. Debenham, I shall certainly have to sleep on it. May I give you my answer tomorrow?"

"Of course, Mr. Farrow. There's just one thing . . ."

"Yes?"

"Under no circumstances must I be identified as the backer."

"Of course, Mrs. Debenham. I understand completely. If we reach an agreement, your name will be kept in confidence."

He did not blame her. Association with his defection would ruin her in Paris and estrange her from her London friends. A single gaucherie of that magnitude could effectively block the offender from European society.

Emily Debenham was, of course, playing for high stakes. The Debenhams had already pulled off one coup: hosting Edward, Prince of Wales, at their Long Island estate. If Emily were to control New York's top couture house, she could manipulate from behind the scenes. She could also schedule her fittings to coincide with certain Newport *grandes dames* who had not taken Emily and Jim Debenham to their hearts.

The Debenhams were not a bad match. He had supplied the East Coast credentials (Exeter and Yale, the Social Register), she the money. It came from her father's construction company in Cleveland, Ohio.

Kindly and large (despite the years of squash at his club), Jim Debenham was always on the defensive about his wife's background. He got loaded easily and often, and was usually a good-natured drunk, but he could read a snub into the most innocent remark about, say, the Middle West. He was as anxious to back Farrow as she was.

"Goodbye, then, Mr. Farrow, until tomorrow. Oh, and one more thing . . ." She busied herself with her gloves. "The salon *will* be restricted, I take it."

"Restricted?"

"Oh, I forgot. You don't call it that in London. I mean no *Jews!* They're so pushy—and they do tend to lower the standard, don't they?"

"Well . . ."

"I mean, most of the shops are Jewish, of course, like

Bergdorf's, but it's a bit different with couture, don't you think?"

"No doubt, Mrs. Debenham, no doubt."

"You Europeans are lucky. Your Jews are so different, like the Rothschilds. We met some of them in Deauville, and they were divine. But it's different here, isn't it?"

"Yes, well, until tomorrow."

Far from resenting Mrs. Debenham's anti-Semitism, Farrow welcomed it. At least he knew where she stood. New York was straightforward and naïve compared to Mayfair; he would do splendidly in the States.

That night Farrow slept soundly.

His transatlantic call at 8 A.M. the following morning was plagued by static; bloody receiver sounded like a tin box full of pebbles.

"Bryan, it's Jake!"

"Jake, how are you? And how did it go?"

"Marvelously. They loved the collection—"

"When will you be back?"

"That's why I'm calling, Bryan."

"Can't *hear* you!"

"I said I called to tell you that I shan't be back." (Very slowly now, and loud.) "I *shall not* be back in London. I'm staying in New York!"

"Sorry, Jake, I can barely make you out. Glad all went well, I'll see you soon. Call when you . . ."

His voice faded into a faraway, crackling shout.

Farrow jiggled the phone and asked for his head model's room. Moira was older than the others, had worked for Lombert as long as Farrow. When she came into the suite, he handed her a penciled Western Union form which she read, reread, and then passed back to him.

"You can't mean it, Mr. Farrow."

"I certainly do."

66

"But—why?"

"Because I'm starting my own couture house here in New York."

"Well, all right! But you can't just leave Mr. Lombert in the middle of the season."

"I'm afraid that's the way it's got to be."

"A rotten thing to do, don't you think?"

"Oh, come now, Moira. What if a man you were madly in love with offered to marry you here and now?"

"That's different."

"Is it? To me, a couture house is like that."

Moira, who had been pacing, stopped to look at the short man with the touch of Cockney in his voice. "I suppose," she said slowly, "you really do care that much about being on your own."

Like everyone at Lombert, she had always considered Farrow the real head of Lombert-London. It surprised her that he thought of himself as an employee.

The next transatlantic call came from Paris. It was so clear that Bryan Lombert might have been calling from the Savoy Plaza across the square. He was quite calm.

"Hello, Jake . . . ?"

"Yes, Bryan."

"Got your cable, Jake. You're a shit, but you're a bright boy! Goodbye, Jake!"

"Thank you, Bryan."

That was all they had said.

Philip had nearly finished setting the sleevehead. He had basted it into the armhole with long stitches, leaving the fullness toward the back of the shoulder. He stepped back from the dummy to check the fall of the sleeve. It swung forward quite well, almost as if worn by a live person, but it was not yet right.

The canvas-covered dummy was stenciled "Debenham Sr." It had been padded with cotton and muslin to resemble the exact measurements and proportions of Mrs. James Wyckfield Debenham. Each Farrow client had a plaster and cloth lookalike, carefully updated with the rise and fall of her waistline, bust, and hips. Measurements were taken twice a year. One New York society matron, whose dummy ballooned and shrank fantastically from month to month—depending on her diet and sex life—was the joke of the workroom. The dummy was inevitably referred to as the Bullfrog, and its owner's dimensions gave rise to more than one workroom lottery.

Philip, reaching up to smooth the Debenham sleeve, tried to "wish" it into the right direction by gentle pushing. Dammit, it still curved outward a touch, as if the arm was asking a question.

For a year, Philip had apprenticed among the body and breath odors of four elderly Italian tailors. They were the aristocrats of the fourth-floor workrooms, far above the seamstresses, who were "only" dressmakers and handled "soft" clothes. Tailors were temperamental, arrogant, and clannish, and they made sure that Philip knew his lowly rank. They had apprenticed eight full years, and now this—little boy— was being allowed to get by with one year. They shrugged their Neapolitan and Sicilian shoulders and bemoaned the demise of their art.

The year was a depressing one for Philip. If this was couture he might as well be a salesclerk; his co-workers would at least smell better and speak English. (It was two years before he realized that Farrow had been right: tailoring was the foundation of couture, dressmaking only its froth.)

Mrs. Debenham was his client now, and she allowed no one but Philip to fit her. They spent hours in the little rooms where the mutual torture of fittings took place. Some women were easy, too impatient to be picky. Others fussed, returning ten and twelve times. Since each fitting cost the house money, Farrow scanned the weekly schedule with skeptical eyes. (Mario, one of the older tailors, had been accustomed to taking as many as fifteen fittings for Mrs. Debenham. Philip usually managed to satisfy her in three. "Of course," Farrow said, "Ross hasn't a clue about tailoring, but the old cunt believes in him and it saves us a *lot* of money.")

Philip had decided to let the sleeve go when Farrow's high-pitched voice startled him.

"Christ, Ross, what are you trying to do? What is this, a bloody sausage?"

He tore out the basting stitch, pulled the sleeve off the suit and threw it in Philip's face.

"Here! See if you can butcher it all over again!"

Philip grabbed at the cloth. There was a hush in the workroom. The tailors looked up, grinning, and several seamstresses in the next room giggled.

Philip, cheeks flushed, held his temper. He hated Farrow for humiliating him, but he knew the man was right. Ten minutes later the sleeve was finished and perfect. He handed the suit to one of the tailors and told him to go ahead and sew it. The man barely looked up. Behind Philip's back he moved hand under chin in the old Italian gesture for "screw you."

Farrow's chauffeur, Porter, was a large swarthy man who could give Swedish massages and handle a car in the crush of a Broadway opening. They said he was an ex-con who had been Farrow's stud in the thirties. Farrow dressed him in an old-fashioned gray tunic, breeches, and leather puttees to match his gray 1939 Rolls.

This afternoon, Porter's instructions were to bring Philip

to his employer's town house near Sutton Place. In the car, Philip worried about the summons. He had never been to Farrow's home. Porter, as usual, was silent.

A Japanese manservant opened Farrow's front door, showing Philip to a glassed-in veranda with a crescent-shaped couch. Furniture and walls were covered in a poppy print fabric, and there were real poppies in vases all around the room. Below was a small garden where trees and bushes shut out the neighboring yards. The sun was low. Shafts of light stabbed through the treetops and kindled both real and printed flowers into glowing color.

The Japanese set a pastry tray and a small stack of magazines in front of a poppy-upholstered armchair, then left the room. Philip picked up a recent edition of the *Tatler* and put it back down. The room was very still.

Farrow came into it so quietly that he startled Philip, who got quickly to his feet. "Sit down, Ross. You must be tired."

"Not too bad."

"How's it going in the tailor shop?"

"Okay, I guess."

"They're a bunch of bastards, you know."

"Oh, I'll get along." After the blowup over the sleeve, the tailors had given Philip a bad time. What the hell did Farrow expect? Of course they were pricks!

"I daresay things will smooth out before long, Ross."

The Japanese brought tea; Philip and Farrow ate and drank in a silence which apparently only Philip found uncomfortable. He broke it to compliment Farrow on the loveliness of the room.

"Yes, it is, isn't it?" said Farrow, as if he had barely heard, in between sips of tea and bites of pastry. The pauses grew longer and even more discomforting. Then Farrow did something that really startled Philip: he smiled.

Philip had never seen this expression. Farrow's round little face was suddenly punctured by a round little hole, ringed with teeth. Philip's surprise passed into easiness. Farrow was trying to be friendly! If Philip was to be fired, it would not happen in Farrow's sitting room.

He smiled back: "The new collection is beautiful."

Farrow nodded, acknowledging not the compliment so much as its accuracy. "Yes, and we've sold a lot. That brings me to something else . . ."

He stood up and put his hands on his large hips, flaring out his jacket. The gesture was graceful despite his bulk. "I think you've about had enough tailoring, Ross, and you certainly know fabrics and the way we keep records. It's a bloody shame to let you piss your time away in the workrooms any longer. You're a pretty little bastard—I could use you in the salon . . . The point is, I think you could learn to sell to the bitches. They'd come, just *looking* at you!"

(Impossible to be casual.) "I'd love the chance to handle clients."

"Fine," said Farrow. "But no bullshit! I mean no taking tips for special fittings or for rushing clothes through the workroom . . . And keep your cock in your pants!"

Philip, too elated to be embarrassed, smiled foolishly.

"Although," Farrow went on, "I guess we needn't worry much in that department, need we?"

"No, sir," said Philip, answering automatically.

"You bet your little tight ass we don't," said Farrow. "Because we both know, don't we, that our little Ross is a bitch, not a bastard."

Farrow reached suddenly for Philip's face, gripping it underneath with his fingers, his thumb in the cleft of his chin. There was surprising strength in that fat wrist. Philip jerked away and stood up.

"What *is* the matter with you, Philip? I'm just trying

to be nice. ("Philip"? That was new. Until now it had been "Ross" this and "Ross" that.)

Philip mumbled, "Well, I know you are . . . I appreciate . . ." (Here it comes . . . He wants to play games, and Christ, he's ugly!)

"Then why don't you sit down?"

"Well, I don't want you to misunderstand, Mr. Farrow . . . You see, I'm really very *fond* of you and all—I respect you—"

"What has respect to do with it? We're not at work now."

"Well, sir, that's just it. I, um, don't quite know how to explain it. I'm not—"

Farrow was fed up. He jumped to his feet, hands at his hips again. "Stop the nonsense, Ross. Don't play games with *me!*"

"I don't know what you mean," Philip said lamely, shaken by the sudden harsh edge in Farrow's voice.

"Just cut the crap. Don't tell me you weren't giving it to Evans-Greene!"

"Johnny and I are friends. *We* can be friends, I—"

"Friends? He was laying you—that's how you're friends —and then he dumped you in my lap!"

"I thought you *wanted* to hire me!"

"Who the hell told you that?"

"Johnny . . . He said you needed me, you—"

"Good Christ!" Farrow slapped his forehead. "*Needed* you? What the fuck did I need you for? You didn't know a goddamn thing about this business!"

"Well, then . . ." Philip was stunned. "Why did you hire me?"

"I didn't. Johnny did."

"Johnny?"

"Yes, you imbecile. Who do you think's paying your salary?"

If Farrow thought this would crush Philip, he had miscalculated. Minutes before, Philip had been tempted to accept Farrow's pass because he was scared of getting fired. Now he was free. He *couldn't* be canned, so long as Johnny was paying his salary. Great Johnny, fabulous Johnny! Some day he'd repay him.

Farrow was still waiting for the results of his thunderbolt when Philip walked calmly to the door. He waved " 'Bye, Mr. Farrow. See you tomorrow."

He was taking a risk, but not a big one. It also occurred to him that Farrow would not want the story of this afternoon to get around.

It was 10 P.M., and they had been at it since early after-noon without a break. Farrow stood in the middle of the salon, flanked by two long tables covered with costume jewelry, gloves, and shoes. He was surrounded by the entire sales and production staff. They were assembled for the final run-through of the fall collection, accessorizing the clothes and creating the final image for customers and press.

Most European couturiers, afraid of style piracy through photographs of sketches, barred the press from their openings.

Not Farrow. "There are," he said, "hundreds of rich women in cities all over America who have become Farrow clients because of some story they saw in their local paper. They arrive in New York from Detroit, Omaha, Dallas, or Seattle, lunch at the Colony, have their hair done at Arden, and then try to get an appointment here. Which," he con-tinued, "is much more difficult than booking a restaurant or a hairdresser."

The head vendeuse, Mrs. Locke, a fast-talking, stocky woman in her fifties with pitch-black Levantine hair and the suggestion of a mustache, acted as press attachée. She ar-ranged for eight-by-ten photographs of each important cos-tume. These were handed to the press along with mimeo-graphed press releases describing Farrow's current trend. Since Mrs. Locke frequently fell in love with her own prose, the releases were couched in curious language. A gathered chiffon skirt became "a cloudy suggestion of charm," a navy coat "the epitome of Nelson's grandeur." Unhappily, most reporters were so in awe of a Farrow opening that many of these phrases reappeared in the local stories they wrote, and ladies in Milwaukee or Savannah were left to puzzle over "the Gothic arch of a midriff" reportedly crucial to a new Farrow style.

There were one hundred and ten costumes, representing every conceivable category. Dresses for city wear or the country, cocktails or dinner, balls and weddings. Suits, theater suits, coats of all types. Farrow could dress a woman for a weekend in the mountains or sessions in the hospital, as mother of a bride, or as a more or less bereaved widow.

Currently the fashion magazines were in the throes of a love affair with Dior's New Look. The mood embraced full skirts, "wasp" waists and curved hips, ballet-shaped shoes, and skirts that all but touched the ankles. Gone were the knee-skimming narrow skirts, open-toed platform shoes, wide padded shoulders, and upswept hairdos of the war years, of Crawford and Betty Grable and the Hollywood Canteen.

Farrow had designed special petticoats and crinolines for the bell-shaped gowns. Shoes, sketched by Farrow and executed by New York's leading shoemaker, had lowish spiked heels with round toes like ballet slippers. Hats were small, and worn on the back of the head. They were conceived during stormy sessions with a wispy milliner who had come close to collapse because of Farrow's acid tongue. The little hatter had rushed more than once from Farrow's office, covering Philip's suit with tears and make-up. ("That bitch! That miserable Cockney bitch! How *dare* he speak to me like that!")

Now, all the fights were forgotten. Philip, who had taken

the brunt of Farrow's temperament and the mounting strain over the months, now took pride in the presentation that was taking shape. Every sketch, muslin, fabric swatch, accessory, had combined to make a cohesive fashion story: there was, no question, a distinct *look* to the clothes. The individual ideas had become a James Farrow Collection, a great designer's work.

"All right, all right, let's get our butts moving."

A model scurried into the fitting room for her next change, and Farrow beckoned to Philip, who was holding a stack of cardboard sheets, two feet square. On each one was a sketch of the next costume, a swatch of fabric, and the model's name. When the girl stopped in front of Farrow, he squinted at her.

"The little red cloche," said Farrow, not taking his eyes off the girl.

Philip selected a hat from the table and tilted it back on the model's small head.

"The emerald pin and earrings."

Philip located them on the opposite table, handed the earrings to the girl, and held up the pin.

"Dead center, just above the yoke," snapped Farrow.

Philip attached the pin.

"Take it off, take it off, we shan't need it. Give me a scarf, someone, a jade green one." He snapped his fingers, still without taking his eyes off the mannequin. Handed a green satin scarf, he draped it into the neckline of the dress, puffed it out, and said, "That'll do . . . Mark it down, Ross!" Philip took the card, sketched the accessories, and described their colors in his small, precise handwriting.

Each mannequin was assigned a number in the rotation of the showing, and the sequence was posted on a blackboard.

| 1 Diane | Red wool coat #4 |
| 2 Dee | Red suit #83 |
| 3 Mala | Gray flannel suit #18 |
| 4 Frances | Blue wool sharkskin #6 |
| 5 Diane | Camel hair coat #12 |
| 6 Dee | Camel hair dress #3 |
| 7 Mala | Four-piece red tweed costume #384 |
| 8 Frances | Gray tweed suit #8 |

Diane was this year's lead model, the girl who would open the showing. She was the Farrow Girl of nineteen hundred and fifty, tall, tiny-waisted, and long-legged. She walked like a ballerina, with pointed toes and an odd hesitation in each step. As usual, this year's number one was a brunette: Farrow, who was superstitious, never used blondes or redheads as lead girls. Diane, a former dancer who had been retrained by Farrow, would within a year be photographed by every fashion magazine—not because she was particularly beautiful but because Farrow, with unfailing instinct, had selected the girl who personified her time. With her fine arched nose and serene eyes and mouth, she looked graceful and vulnerable. Actually she was a tough Brooklyn dame who could cuss like a trucker and fight viciously for costumes which looked like show stoppers. The success of a collection was measured by the number of styles that were applauded, and Diane made sure most of them were hers.

Shortly after midnight Farrow said, *"Basta!"* and everyone in the room sagged. Diane, dressed in a half-slip with a scarf tied over her breasts, sat like a dancer in a Degas painting. She rubbed her feet, a cigarette dangling from her mouth, and muttered under her breath.

Farrow said, "Tired, sweetie?"

She arched her classic eyebrows and said: "Crap!"

78

Farrow guffawed. He left without bothering to say goodnight.


As usual, the opening was a *succès fou.*

By 6 P.M. Farrow's staff had restored the salon to some semblance of order. The debris had been swept, plucked, and vacuumed away. Some of the damage was permanent: burning cigarettes had been ground into the gray carpet by women who would have fired their maids for leaving fingerprints on a mirror. The little gold chairs were stored once again in the basement.

Now, after all, they were just chairs. Three hours earlier, New York's wealthiest women had fought for them. The ten on the little balcony at the side of the salon enthroned Emily Debenham's special friends. She alone could assign them and she did so with care and venom; it was her only remaining prerogative as an original backer.

The salon was ready, its banquetted alcoves and little fitting rooms poised for sales appointments. There had been *ten* rounds of applause (five for Diane's costumes), followed by long and feverish "bravos" at the end of the show. Farrow, who had been hiding backstage, appeared briefly and allowed himself to be kissed and congratulated. After a few minutes he was whisked away by Porter.

Philip was the last to leave. He double-checked his list of appointments for the next day, cleared his desk, and closed the door to his little office, a fitting room which had become the Ross Room. He locked the front door. Farrow had finally given him a key, though with the reluctance of a prime minister conferring an unlikely cabinet appointment. ("Here, Ross, take this key. Only Mrs. Locke and I have keys, y'know. Don't *lose* the goddamn thing.")

The curb was blocked by a line-up of limousines, thanks

to a cocktail showing in the art gallery next door. Philip threaded his way through people who were looking for their chauffeurs. A young girl waved at him: "Mr. *Ross*, waitaminnit!"

Mrs. Debenham's daughter, Julia. One of his clients, and a goddamn snob. Usually she barely spoke to him.

The people with her climbed into a Rolls and left the door open, waiting. "I've got a great big favor to ask you," she said. "You'll hate me when you hear . . ."

*Right*. "Anything I can do, Miss Debenham?" Farrow would have been proud.

"That little gray flannel. Is it finished?"

How the hell do I know? Somewhere in the workroom. "I think so," he said.

"I've simply got to have it by tomorrow morning," she said. "I'm off to California for a week and I *couldn't* do without it."

"What time are you leaving?"

"Nine o'clock."

You *could* have called earlier. "You mean you need it tonight?"

"Um, yes," she said, nodding her head and looking contrite, like some teenager begging for movie money. "Would you be a darling, and bring it to me?"

Don't put on that act with me, lady. When you're in the salon it's "I want this" and "I've got to have that."

"Where do you live?"

"East Sixty-eighth Street, Seventeen East."

"Your mother's house?" He knew the address well. He had sent many cartons there.

"Right!"

"It's near me," said Philip. "I'll get the dress and drop it off."

"Gosh," she squealed, "that's *marvy!* But lookit, it's a

brownstone and there's no one to open up. I'll be home by nine, nine-thirty. Would you like to drop by for a drink?"

"Fine," he said. That's more like it. I've never been asked inside your creamy house, and if I had it would be as some sort of delivery boy, no drink included.

"See you later, then." She followed her friends into the Rolls, and Philip turned back toward the dark salon. He climbed to the workroom, located the dress (fortunately it was finished), made out an invoice, and packed it into a gray Farrow box.

The street was quiet now. The gallery crowd had left. Philip, feeling the usual letdown after an opening, found himself looking forward to his drink with Julia Debenham although he knew that it was being offered only as a courtesy for delivering the dress. He crossed Madison against the heavy flow of homebound traffic in the east lane and continued toward Park Avenue. There were dead leaves on the sidewalk; the fall-stripped trees made him think of Fort Early. A chill breeze whistled around the corner from Park Avenue and he turned up his suit collar, wishing he had taken an overcoat.

On Park, he automatically looked up at Johnny's building. The penthouse was dark. Johnny was in France or England; he had not heard from him in months.

Philip's apartment was a so-called one-and-a-half in a converted brownstone like many that had been hastily renovated for young couples who could afford one-fifty a month in rent. There was a creaky little self-service elevator that could hold five people, according to the certificate, but was actually crowded with three. The outside of the building looked new, but the plumbing was old. In the morning, the tap water had bad breath.

His place was tiny: one large bed-sitting room, a small kitchen behind a venetian blind, and a modern bathroom.

After many battles with the landlord and his own conscience, he had installed a window air conditioner. He was paying for it in monthly installments.

He had furnished the place slowly, beginning with a large convertible couch in brown velveteen, a housewarming gift from Johnny. The rest he added piecemeal: two armchairs, a beige corduroy from a Village shop and a white leather from Bloomingdale's (which he often regretted because it constantly needed cleaning); a long-haired Mongolian sheepskin rug and a brown-and-white cowhide. The walls were stark white with two Picasso "Dove" posters and three Miró prints. He had decided against hanging drapes. At night he closed the venetian blinds, always open during the day.

All the lamps worked from one switch near the entrance, so that he could light up the entire room with one touch. He hated coming into dark rooms.

Lately the luxury of living alone had begun to pall. Some Sundays he was perfectly happy to read the newspapers and drink cups of coffee, undisturbed by a single voice. But there were too many Saturday nights when he had failed to make any plans and craved company. It was lousy going to a movie alone and returning to the empty apartment.

Occasionally Diane had invited Philip to her place on West Fiftieth Street, but the model's friends were mostly scruffy young theater people who talked backstage gossip and Sardi's until Philip could have screamed with boredom. He concealed his feelings poorly, and Diane's invitations soon stopped.

His life was so different from the one he had envisioned when Johnny first told him about the Farrow job. Glamorous people? He'd met plenty of them, but his private life and theirs never touched. And Farrow's salon attracted few young clients. Most of them preferred ready-made things from the Fifth Avenue stores.

Philip had once suggested to Farrow that they needed a younger clientele. Farrow snorted, but later he called Philip into his room and said, "You know, Ross, you're quite right, we do have a bunch of old farts in the salon. But we can't lower our prices, and that's the reason. Besides, young people today are too impatient for fittings and I can't really blame them. Fittings are a bloody nuisance for the client and they cost us an arm and a leg. Christ, I wish we could *afford* younger clients. Until then, Ross, you'll just have to put up with the poor trade I can drum up for you . . ."

It was nearly time to go to Julia Debenham's, and Philip wondered if he should change. The hell with it—he was too tired. He would dump the carton and get out fast, delivery-boy style. Still, Julia *had* mentioned having a drink, so there was a certain social something about it.

He went into the bathroom to shave.


Even at night the Debenham house was imposing, with whitewashed front, black shutters, and a black brass-trimmed double-winged front door. There were boxes of flowers in the windows and a basement delivery entrance. The house was completely dark.

Philip rang the bell, and after a while he could see light in the curved-glass transom above the door.

"Who is it?" Julia's voice.

"Philip Ross."

The door opened, and Philip stepped into a dim hallway with a black-and-white checkered marble floor. The light came from the open door of an upstairs room. Julia held a glass full of liquor. She was wearing a man's bathrobe with the sleeves rolled up.

"Sorry I'm such a mess, but I just got home. I had to get out of my cocktail rags."

She led the way up the semicircular staircase. He followed, carrying the carton, climbing cautiously; he could barely see the marble steps. When they reached a small sitting room, she took the box from him and threw it behind a black leather couch. She waved her glass: "Have some?"

"A little scotch, please."

She poured a large shot from a decanter and refilled her own glass. "Look, I was about to take a shower. Why don't you just relax, okay?" She headed into the next room, moving very deliberately, like someone walking on a swaying train. Soon Philip heard the sound of running water. He sat down and sipped at his scotch. Soon he felt sleepy; he was very tired, and the scotch was hitting home.

When Julia came back she was still in the robe and she was drying her short black hair. She wound the towel around her head like a turban, got herself another drink, and stretched out on the couch.

"Gee, that feels better. Cheers!"

She raised her glass and Philip returned the salute without saying anything. They both drank quietly.

"What's your story, Philip? That *is* your first name, isn't it?"

He nodded. "Don't you want to try on the dress?"

"The heck with it," she said, and Philip's face flushed with irritation. It was obvious that she couldn't have cared less about the dress. After all the trouble he'd gone to, finding the thing and wrapping it and writing out the bill. And he wasn't *seeing* any of the house, just this room, which looked as if everything had been tossed together for a rummage sale.

"Like my story"—Julia went on, although he had not answered her question about himself—"it's simple. I'm here. I'm bored stiff. Got out of Briarcliff a year ago and since then it's been ghastly! They trot me to Newport and Palm Beach just like they did when I was a kid . . ." Her voice was a monotone, aimed at the ceiling.

"Dad and the old lady are up in Newport to close up the house, and I'm running off to California to visit my roommate from school. She's in Bel Air, and that's not so much either. I've been there. At least it's better than here. This girl, my roommate, her people are in movies, she's Jewish. Anyway, right now she dates Don Jeffson and he's doing movies now. I knew him when we were kids in Palm Beach. It'll be kinda fun—I hope."

Her voice remained on one level and muted, as if she were in the next room and he listening to her through the wall. Jeffson's name rang a bell. The boy he and Johnny had met in El Morocco that night . . .

Julia stopped talking and gave Philip a careful look. He was even better than she remembered. Lord, he was *beautiful*, stretched out that way in the armchair. His legs were long and she could see the line of his thighs under the cloth of his trousers. When he sipped his drink his lips nibbled on the glass . . .

Julia was not really drunk, just high, and the hot shower had set everything in motion. Hot pants, she thought—even though I'm not wearing panties. She giggled. If she hadn't seen Philip on the street she'd have ended up rolling in the hay with one of the fatfingers from the party. Yuck! But now Philip was here, and the house was empty. She'd gotten rid of the one maid left behind, the cute little trick Pop had the hots for. She was probably getting laid right now . . . She wondered whether Philip was shy or just tired.

Philip finally tried to make conversation. "Your mother is my client now, you know."

"I know," she said. "Your client, my pain-in-the-rear."

That stopped him. He had no intention of asking her what she meant.

"You never did tell me about yourself," she said. "We got off the subject."

Philip glanced at some oil miniatures on the wall. Ghastly! "There's really not much to tell. I've worked at Farrow's since I got out of the Army."

"How'd you get to Farrow? Try other places first?"

"No, a friend got me the job. Johnny Evans-Greene. Do you know him?"

"Sure. He was sort of like a young uncle when I was little. He was in Palm Beach a lot." Johnny Evans-Greene? How did *they* get to be friends? Johnny played it both ways, everyone knew that. She had to try something.

"You know Don Jeffson?"

"I've met him once."

"Well, *he* was a friend of Johnny's. A . . . close friend."

"Oh?" Johnny hadn't told him.

She could see no reaction on his face. Perhaps she was wrong. Of course he *might* be a fag—he *did* work in a dress-making place. But he didn't look it or sound it, and even if he *was*, he was just too great-looking to pass up. She wanted to touch him. She got him a fresh drink and when she handed it to him sat down on the arm of his chair and leaned her elbow on his shoulder.

"Some room this, isn't it?" she said, looking around. "It used to be my bedroom, all frilly and girly. But I've been away so much they turned it into a spare guest room with stuff from all our houses."

She touched his neck. "You're hot," she said. "Take off your jacket." She helped him out of it.

There was a television set, the mirror kind, facing the couch. She lifted the lid to tune in a program, fiddled with the buttons until the picture finally held still. They moved to the couch and sat quietly next to each other until the sound finally came up.

"Turn off the light," she said. She looked blue-green in the reflection of the set. She pulled up her bare legs, hugging them.

The television actors were having an argument.

*"I don't know what you want of me—"*

*"Want? I want nothing, I do deserve some decency!"*

*"Decency? Is that what you call it when I have to give up my job because you're bored?"*

*"Not bored, darling, not bored. Just tired of this dreary little company town and all the dreary people in the company . . ."*

Television fascinated Philip. The only person he knew who had a set was Diane—he'd seen it in her apartment (with all the theater kids grouped around, blasting the actors on screen). He began to get involved in the play.

Julia leaned against him until her knee touched his legs and her elbow was against his side. Her cologne was body-strong. "Come on," she said softly. "Relax, Philip."

He smiled, but he didn't know what to say. Then her nose was next to his ear and he could feel her breath. She kissed his cheek. "Do you mind?" she asked. He shook his head.

*"Never knew what it would be like to be cooped up like this. With the whole board of directors telling us how to live!"*

*"Well, isn't that too bad? You're the one who wanted me to make it big, who thought it would be just dandy . . ."*

Julia laced her fingers into Philip's, then moved her hand to the inside of his thigh. Her touch was not unpleasant, and he even began to feel something.

"Come here," she said. She took his glass and set it on the floor, then pulled his head into her lap. Her robe was half-open, and he liked the feeling of her warm skin under his neck. Her fingers played with his face, stroking his nose, eyelids, mouth.

"You know you're really gorgeous, Philip."

She leaned close. Her eyes were speckled green and her breath smelled of scotch. The cologne was even more powerful now. She bent lower, touched her lips to his mouth, but he did not react. She kissed him softly, moving from lip to lip, and he let it happen. His inertia excited her. Her tongue was out. He wanted to bite it, the way one wants to slap a wasp but dares not. Her robe slipped open. She pulled up one of her legs and turned his head down.

For a moment Philip kept his mouth between her legs, then he panicked. He rolled away onto the floor, spilling the glass she had put there. Christ, he'd made a royal mess of things. Now he'd have to explain, and fast. "Look, Julia . . ." he began, still on the floor.

She pulled up her legs, wrapped the robe around them, then poured herself a drink and finished it in one gulp. The television play had been interrupted for an Ivory commercial.

Finally she spoke: "Are you trying to tell me this is not for you?"

Philip shook his head. There was nothing he could think of to answer. He was furious with himself.

"All right," she said. "I got your message, loud and clear!"

He scrambled to his feet, stood in front of her shaking his head. He felt like crying or getting sick. She handed him his jacket and he struggled into it as quickly as he could.

"Excuse me," he said, and moved quickly to the door. She stared at it for a moment when he had gone, and then laughed. "Just my luck, just my fucking luck! Greaseballs or fairies . . . Julia, you really know how to pick 'em!"

Philip stumbled down the dimly lit staircase. At the bottom, he looked back up—she was standing at the top. "Just my fucking luck!" she shouted, and heaved her glass at him as he ran for the front door.

He kept running, all the way to Fifth Avenue, as if Julia Debenham were chasing him.

Not hungry, the hell with eating. Just want to sit. Cigarette, maybe—where the hell are they? Must have dropped the pack on her couch.

Got to wash my face, hands, get the stink off. Funny how perfume can be nice one minute, then the next . . . All that softness, like slime and jelly—it's just so goddamn wrong. Like touching a dog's pecker . . .

Got to shower!

She's no different from the smelly girls back in school— you passed by their locker room and it stank to heaven. Or a woman scratching her leg through a nylon stocking—drive you up the wall.

Hope Julia doesn't make trouble. It was crazy, just crazy, throwing that glass . . .

Julia is like a swamp! Julia smells . . . bbbrrraaach!

Farrow's black moods became more frequent.

When he called Mrs. Dawson Tibbetts a fat pig to her triple-chinned face, she walked out—for good, she said. Her vendeuse, who had come to Farrow from Balenciaga and had brought Mrs. Tibbetts with her, threatened to quit.

Farrow had no choice but to invite Mrs. Tibbetts to lunch at Pavillon. He explained that he had been "under a strain," and she began to thaw. But when she stuffed herself with crêpes farcies, rolls, butter, and gâteau maison, he came within a hair of telling her to lay off the calories.

Later he told her mollified vendeuse: "I fed your blubbery friend, we'd better charge her 10 percent extra. Besides, it takes extra cloth to dress her. . . ."

Philip rather liked Mrs. Tibbetts. She always asked him if he was eating enough.

Now that Philip was in the salon most of the time, he learned fast. He read every fashion magazine and society column, followed marriages and scandals, regattas and auto races. He knew that you could sleep your way to London in a bed on TWA. You stopped in Shannon, had Irish coffee for breakfast, and landed in London slightly loaded. It was the way to fly to London.

He hadn't done it.

But he knew all about it.

"This is our model 'Admiral,' Miss Milter."

"Very nice."

"It's a simple Navy-style coat—don't you love that curved princess seam?"

"Mmm."

"We think it looks very nineteen-fifties!"

"Yes."

"Now, while Diane changes, here is Bonnie in a little red dress we call 'España.'"

"Nice."

"I think it would be a marvelous color for you."

"Maybe."

"You looked marvelous in that flamenco-red suit last year."

"Yes."

"Do try it on. I have a model suit in your size."

"No, I've got to go now!"

"All right, Miss Milter."

"Thank you, Mr. Ross."

"Thank you! I'll take you to the door . . . A pleasure."

"Goodbye, Mr. Ross."

"Good day, Miss Milter."

(Damn the bitch, she always comes to look and never buys, except that red suit last year, and that was a payoff from some guy. Have to find some way to dump her.)

"Mr. Ross?"

"Yes?"

"This is Edith Milter. I've decided to get the red dress. Could you schedule a fitting for me?"

"Of course, Miss Milter."

(What do you know?)

"Mr. Ross, we've got a little problem here . . . We have an outstanding bill with Mrs. Turner Cattlin."

"So what?"

"It's four months past due."

"What of it? She's good for it."

"Not for a while, according to the Knickerbocker column. They're getting a divorce—here, look at this item."

"Gawd . . . Didn't see the afternoon papers. Now it's too late. Write her a letter anyway, the usual."

"Mr. Farrow'll hit the roof!"

"I suppose so . . ."

"Mr. Ross, I just can't take it any more!"

"What is it this time, Miss Dorch?"

"Mario. He won't fit Mrs. Delmar's suit. It's still awful. The skirt hangs crooked, and she's been raising hell!"

"I'll talk to Mario, Miss Dorch."

"Eh?"

"I said, 'What's the trouble with Mrs. Delmar's suit?'"

"Wha' trouble?"

"The vendeuse says you refuse to fit it."

"Refuse? Do you know how many times I open up that skirt? Six times! In four months!"

"You mean she got the suit four months ago?"

"And she's gotten fat from stuffing herself."

"Well, that's different. I didn't know."

"Now you know."

"We'll charge her extra—but try once more, for me, okay?"

"Well, jus' once more."

"Ross, er, I wanted to talk to you. Sit down."

"Yes, Mr. Farrow."

"Well, as you know a lot of our clients are slow about paying their bills."

"Yes, I know."

"In fact, I've had to ask Mrs. Debenham—this is confidential, of course—to advance some money a few months ago."

"Oh?"

"Yes, well, she did. But I am amazed that she has not bought anything from this collection!"

"I've tried calling her. Her maid takes the messages, that's all."

"That won't do, Ross, it won't do at all. I think you're just lying down on the job."

"I don't see what else I can do."

"You can get some flowers and your pretty little arse and hustle both of them over to Mrs. Debenham's house with my compliments and find out what the *hell* is going on!"

This time the Debenham house was fully staffed. A lace-aproned maid opened the door, took the flowers, and showed Philip into a cream-colored salon off the entrance hall. As he crossed the checkerboard floor, Philip looked up the stairs, but Julia's door was closed. She was probably still in California.

Emily Debenham had stayed remarkably slim, but there were signs of age which no amount of care could hide. Much had changed since the days when she had launched Farrow. The novelty had dimmed long ago, and time had slowed her ambitions. The Debenhams were now securely entrenched —they had pushed hard, and New York social standards were slipping.

She liked Philip Ross but she had dodged his calls. She was angry at Farrow for reasons of her own. Besides, Jim had set her a deadline.

"Em . . . we don't need this Farrow thing any more. If he's doing as well as you say, I'm sure he can buy us out. Personally, I think he's a fraud and my accountants do too."

"Accountants?"

"I've had Thomas Lane Livesey look him over, discreetly. They say he's in trouble."

(Oh my Lord, now what? There's that twenty thou more of my own Jim doesn't even know about.)

"And as for that last twenty of yours—"

"How'd you know, Jim?"

"I know, never mind how. Anyway, I doubt you'll see it again!"

"Nonsense."

Farrow had called a week later. He wanted to borrow a red beaded ball gown she had bought from the last collection, a fifteen-hundred-dollar extravagance. (She had sworn to skimp on something else.) He promised to return the dress quickly.

The following Friday night they attended a charity ball for King's Hospital, where there was to be a James Farrow fashion show, a rare event.

The red gown was in the show, of course. The program

notes read: "Red beaded gown, donated by Mrs. James Wyckfield Debenham for the permanent collection at King's Center Museum."

"Donated?" Was he kidding? Permanently? She had called him the next morning but he was "unavailable" and had not returned her call. She could hardly ask the museum to send back the dress without a great deal of embarrassment.

She had no intention of buying anything from the new collection, although Farrow had eventually called to apologize about the King's Hospital business. Also, there was Jim's warning. She was cordial, nonetheless, when she saw Philip.

"Good morning, Philip. Thank you for the flowers, they're lovely. Berta is putting them into water."

"Not at all, Mrs. Debenham. Mr. Farrow sends them with his best. He asks when we may expect you in the salon? The new collection is lovely, and some of our fabrics are already getting scarce."

"Well, Philip, I've been rather busy . . . but would you give Mr. Farrow this note from me?"

She handed Philip an envelope, heavy beige paper with dark brown trim, addressed in brown ink in her large handwriting.

"Good to see you, Philip."

Then she preceded him out of the little room.

Philip was in no rush to get back to the salon. He had been brushed off, and telling Farrow would be a pain. Then he thought of the envelope, and smiled. He knew now how it would go.

"Did you see Mrs. Debenham?"

"Yes."

"Well? Yes, what?"

"Yes, nothing. I saw her. She gave me . . . this!" He would hand Farrow the envelope and get out fast.

94

Something was very wrong, and Philip knew he would
have to watch out.
For what?
For himself.
Screw Farrow!

# BOOK

# 2

Leon Fassman was shown to his favorite table in the Colony. It was near the entrance of the bar and usually seated four. For Leon it became a table for two.

The maître d' pulled out his chair and a waiter automatically brought a glass of Byrrh with a twist of lemon. Leon checked his watch (it was twelve-forty) and then stared at the tablecloth while he fiddled with the red-and-green rosette in the lapel of his double-breasted pin-stripe suit. (The rosette was the Italian star of solidarity given for helping to introduce Italian textiles to Seventh Avenue.) At forty-four, Leon's figure was still trim and his hair just beginning to gray.

"I'm waiting for Mrs. Ahern," he told the maître d', who was hovering nearby.

For Leon, New York was the only city in America. Good restaurants in New York might look like good restaurants in London, or Rome, or San Francisco—but the *people!* He thought of Brennan's on Royal Street in New Orleans, full of crimp-curled matrons and their crew-cut, bloated husbands. In San Francisco: the Fairmount's Victorian glory spoiled by clusters of drunken conventioneers. And Chicago's Pump Room looked like an overdressed PTA meeting.

It was their voices that bothered him the most. Elephantine, middle-aged men stood next to each other in hotel elevators, shouting at each other as if they were on neighboring mountaintops.

"Hey" (pause), "*Sam!* How's it GOIN', boy?" (Playful punch in the ribs.)

It puzzled Leon that they would not change, improve, *smoothen.* After all, *he* had begun nowhere, a nobody starting at the rock goddamn bottom, without a proper education, a little Jew boy from North Philadelphia.

He'd gotten out of Philly as soon as he could, and he would always be appalled at men who, growing up with every advantage, seemed willing to stay on in their home towns, never entering the big life except as spectators on vacations or at conventions . . .

Leon looked at his watch. Where the hell *was* Susan? She was usually prompt.

Susan would be amazed if she knew what it had been like for him all those years. The reeking shop, the bent women who sewed those *shmattes* on old-fashioned belt-driven machines. The stench of machine oil, rancid bodies, moist woolen sweaters. Cracked foggy windows, patched with cardboard, bare fly-smeared light bulbs. Tall band-saw cutting machines, those razor-sharp knives which could take off a man's hand at the wrist if he slipped while pulling in an eight-inch-high lay of stacked woolens.

Leon had cut and sorted the bundles, his shirt sweat-drenched from armpits to belt, fourteen years old and supposed to be proud because this business, this contract shop, would be *his* one day: the sewing machines bought with finance-company loans at twice their real price (by the time they were paid for, they were worn out). The furniture in the steel-enclosed "office"—a roll-top desk, an ancient Underwood, a swivel chair with peeling leather.

He had watched his father argue over prices with the jobbers who called themselves manufacturers and who came down from New York to give them work. With each new style a new battle, ten styles each month, six months a year.

The rest of the year: "Sorry, Fassman, we got no work!" while the sewing operators went home to their kids and husbands. They damned you for not having work for them, then when you needed them they refused to come back unless you raised their rate per dress. They were not yet unionized, but they might as well have been.

"So what do you think, Mendel?" The man from New York; slicked-back hair, parted high.

"It's a complicated style!" His father, hands raised in horror.

"What's complicated? Two side seams, two sleeves, two darts?"

"Hold it, look at them pockets. You gotta press each one separate before you set them . . . I don't think we can make out for less than twelve a dozen."

"Are you *meshugge*? Twelve a dozen? A dollar apiece? I'd get thrown out on my ass if I pay you that! Mendel, I give you work when the whole business stinks, don't take advantage."

"I give you my word, I can't do it for less."

"I'll give you nine dollars, Mendel, no more."

"So make it ten."

"Well, all right, ten dollars a dozen. And don't stick me later when you're ready to deliver and give me heart attacks like you did last week about your goddamn presser being sick and you can't ship goods we need desperately."

"That was *one* time. How often has that happened?"

"All right, Mendel, shake."

And Mendel Fassman and the production manager shook hands. Another battle over the price of cutting, sewing, pressing, and trimming a new style was over. There were four hundred pieces in this lot, a few days' work. Better than closing the shop, although Mendel Fassman knew that at eighty-four cents a dress he could not possibly break even. He would have to make it up somehow. He'd skimp the dresses, squeeze out a few extra pieces from the fabric they'd send him. Then he'd peddle them to the women in the neighborhood. It was wrong, but he had contracted to manufacture and deliver four hundred dresses—and four hundred dresses he would deliver. If he sold forty extra ones on the side, that was *his* business. Maybe three bucks apiece, one hundred and twenty dollars.

Leon watched his father from the doorway. A bottle of schnapps came out of the roll-top desk, and *l'chaim!* To the deal! All very friendly on the surface but most of the production managers had to be paid off. So the "agreed" price had another 10 percent deducted. There was barely enough to pay rent and installments on the machines, even with the cheated-out extra dresses.

Fassman's contract shop was like hundreds in Philadelphia, Jersey, downtown Manhattan, and Brooklyn. Sweatshops they called them, and sweatshops they were. Small-time salesmen in New York opened fly-by-night firms. Stores canceled orders on a whim or haggled over prices. Textile jobbers overextended credit and raised the cost per yard in return. At the end of the line, there was a contractor somewhere in some slum who actually manufactured the dresses so that everyone—store, salesman, textile house, and the bank —could be paid. Pressure, pressure all the way. And sweat!

Leon had hated every minute of the years he worked for his father.

"That your *boychik?*" The production man.

"That's my Lennie! Come here, *Leon,* meet Mr. Finkel from the Sally Hartford Company in New York."

"Hi, Mr. Finkel."

"You're a lucky kid, Lennie, to work for your poppa. He's

a good guy." (A wink at Mendel Fassman; the envelope with the fifty bucks' kickback already secure in the breast pocket of his jacket. Sure Mendel was a good guy or else no work for Mendel! Scrawny goddamn little *mamser*, that Fassman kid . . .)

Susan Ahern cruised serenely into the red plush lobby of the Colony, a warship slicing through a fleet of fishing smacks. She acknowledged no one until she shook hands with Leon and boomed, "Hello, awfully sorry, Leon. Meeting with the publisher—the beast! No raises for my baby editors, I'm afraid."

In one fluid series of motions she slid into her chair, shrugged off her rust melton jacket, and stripped off her gloves. She pulled a gold cigarette case and lighter from her purse, arranged them in front of her on the table, and listened to the captain's cocktail suggestion. Leon cast an appreciative eye over her cream-colored crepe shirt with huge antique cufflinks, tucked neatly into a gray flannel skirt.

"How *is* Sandra?" Susan asked.

"Great. She sends her love, and she told me to listen to you."

"About what?"

"Tell you later. What about lunch?"

Diet-conscious women at neighboring tables cringed. The impeccable Susan Ahern ordered vichyssoise and eggs Benedict; had a thick dressing on her salad; ate rolls—with butter. They noticed, too, that she said very little, concentrating on her food and enjoying herself immensely. The owner of the Colony paid his respects, but others who said hello or waved were given no encouragement. Giving all her attention to the people she was *with* was part of the Ahern style.

Coffee came and finally she asked Leon what was on his mind. (She always pronounced his name the French way,

*Lay-on.* She also called nylon *nee-lon* and Cadillac *Cadee-yack.* Affectation? Tongue-in-cheek? Eccentricity? Who knew? Even those who worked with her were never sure. She could say: "You know, don't you, that the *turtleneck* is traditionally part of the entire American visual structure and very, *very* important to the entire *scheme* of things?" and they would wait for the signal to join her in a hearty laugh. Often she remained straight-faced, leaving the listener to fumble.)

Leon said: "Susan, give me a straight opinion about something I'm planning. Before I go further, I have to tell you that Sandra thinks I'm off my rocker, and I know that even an old friend doesn't disagree with a man's wife. But it's different with the three of us, right? Sandra respects your judgment, and this is purely a *business* decision."

(Oh my Lord, is he kidding? *Il blague le cher Leon!* So honorable, *so* straightforward . . . But—go against Sandra? *Merde!* Well, we shall see . . .) "What are you hatching, Leon?"

"James Farrow."

"What about Farrow?"

"I want to make a deal with him. I want to manufacture his designs as ready-to-wear."

"Why?"

"Because, for one, I'm fed up with Paris. Everyone drinking at the same water fountain, getting the same ideas from the same couturiers. Another thing, I think it's *time* to popularize a New York couturier."

(And it is, but that's not all our Leon has in mind. Poor love thinks he'll have better *entrée* if he ties up with Farrow. Funny, he's so bright but sometimes so childish. Can imagine how Sandra feels about it . . . But he's obviously made up his mind!) "Well, now Leon, you're right, of course. It is rather awful in a way to sit in Paris and have everyone there from Ohrbach's to Zuckerman and *know* they can all copy the same things. But that's the nature of your business. You're involved in ready-made clothes and even at your prices you have to produce a few hundred of each style to make a profit—"

"What has that to do with Paris?"

"Well, there is that sense of *assurance,* isn't there? With everyone around and all our little luncheon sessions at the Berkeley and cocktails and chats at the Plaza Athénée or the Ritz? We all seem to more or less *agree* to like certain styles and to ignore others. After all, I always tell you which ones I want to photograph for *Ambience,* don't I? And the Magnin people let you know which styles they bought . . . So there is that interchange of thoughts, rather like a medical convention, don't you know?"

"Of course it's reassuring to check around but—look, I don't want to sound conceited, but after all, it's been a lot of years; I think I know what I'm doing."

(A lot of years, Leon? Nineteen thirty-five, seventeen years . . . the Lombert opening, a party at the Ritz . . . Paul Bender, the Magnin people, *Bazaar*'s Mrs. Snow, Mrs. Ballard, all the usual types. And young Leon Fassman, André Armand's new right-hand man. In his twenties, slim, Broadway-style clothes, *très* Jimmy Walker, all nipped in the middle with a narrow tie, pinned shirtcollar, skinny pants . . . the Beau James look. All the old retailers worried that the firm would go downhill because Leon looked so young and— *crude.* He really wasn't, though. Just a bit rough, very New Yorky, and trying too hard not to seem Jewish. Of course no one was anti-Semitic. That would have been too bourgeois for words, and anyway, half the retailers were Jewish. But, there were Jews and there were Jews, and Leon was *very* Jewish, or perhaps it was just very New Yorky. There was this whole life in New York she knew nothing about: Jack and Charlie's and Reuben's and West End Avenue, the Catskills, Jolson . . .)

"I'll have peach Melba," she told Leon. He ordered only coffee for himself. Susan always drank tea. With milk.

"Of course, Leon, if anyone knows the *métier* it's you! But you'd still be going to Paris, wouldn't you?"

"Wouldn't miss it. But this is different . . . has nothing to do with the things I buy from the collections."

(Of course you'll go to Paris, Leon! Where else can you be so sure of yourself? That last time, in Maxim's they nearly turned handsprings for you. And the *baronne*, your *commissionaire*, that spectacular party . . . Dear, silly Leon, you deserve it, of course. You've worked hard and spent a lot of dollars there and Paris owes you a great deal. And here? I can't blame you for running away to Europe twice a year from those insufferable asses in Southampton who won't even have a Rothschild in their stupid club . . . America is so—*parvenu*. Paris has been good for you, and Italy—well, there are all those *marcheses* and *contes* and *commendatores* and *dottores* who just worship you. Don't you know New York can never be that way for you?)

She asked: "Why Farrow?"

"Who else? Mainbocher would never consider a deal."

"You're right, of course."

"So it's Farrow. He has top clientele, a top name, and he's broke."

"Where did you hear that?"

"A little bird called Sol Barnett told me."

"Barnett?"

"My accountant."

"That's interesting." That Debenham girl, the nympho, had spilled the whole thing to Doe one night, and Doe, good girl, had of course told Susan all about it.

Leon continued: "It's hard to believe, but the man has

lost a lot of money during the last couple of years. I can't understand it. His collection looked great and you gave him more pages—"

"Of *course* his collection was great. Farrow is one of the world's best. He's wonderfully original, genuinely creative, and has marvelous taste. We'd be fools not to give him good coverage, you know that." (But all the things you don't know . . . like the time he called Laura Tibbetts a fat pig . . . And "borrowing" Emily Debenham's dress for that charity thing and not returning it and last month he threatened to bar us—bar *Ambience*—because we wanted to photograph one of his styles for the *cover* and he was afraid it would be copied. And those prices! Two thousand for a little dinner dress! Most of his old clients are fed to the teeth with being kicked around. Canceled fittings if the Great Man *decrees* they fit well enough . . .)

"Tell me, Leon, are you discussing a very long-term deal?"

"He wants a five-year contract."

"*Five years?*"

"He can ask, can't he?"

She waved for more tea without waiting for Leon. "He can ask, but you won't sign it, will you?"

Leon laughed. "*That* crazy I'm not. I'll offer him a one-year deal and he can take it or leave it. I'd rather pay more and stay flexible."

"Very sensible of you." (So you haven't completely lost your mind . . . And anyway, it wouldn't do any harm to shake up the Paris crowd a bit. Good for the business, and also a chance to do some editorials for Armand-Klein. Not that you ever ask for payoff editorials in return for advertising. But we could do a whole group of exclusive Farrow-Armand-Klein pages, beat *Vogue* and *Bazaar* to the punch, *and* settle all of *Ambience*'s old obligations to Armand-Klein.)

"Well, you know, Leon," she said, "I am not at all sure that this is such a bad idea. Frankly, we would support it, editorially. And if it's only a short-term arrangement you can always dump him if anything goes wrong. Just what are Sandra's objections?"

"She thinks—" he stopped and shook his head, looking at the tablecloth—"she thinks I'm ambitious, you know, the society way."

"Ridiculous!"

"Of course! That's what I'm trying to tell her. Would you—well, I know it's a nuisance—but would you tell her you think it's okay?"

"All right, Leon, I'll call her. But I can't guarantee anything. And if anything goes wrong, don't blame me—and let's hope Sandra won't."

Sandra Fassman was large enough to fill up most of the love chair next to the telephone table. She had just hung up after speaking with Susan Ahern. A frustrating twenty minutes. Susan had actually liked the Farrow idea, and there had just been no way to *penetrate* to her. She had disappeared behind that patented screen of mock-dramatic language.

As for herself, she'd had no convincing answer when Susan asked her why, since it was only a one-year deal, she was so rattled. Sandra could hardly tell her she thought Leon was lying to himself.

There would never again be a man like her husband, certainly not for her. He was a *man*, and he was a *mensch*. Easily upset by minor failures, but wonderful when things got rough. Of course he was vain. (Ambitious, really.) But usually he was honest about his vanities . . .

If he had only said: "Look, Sam, we don't make it into the Racquet Club, at least this way we meet a few dames whose husbands are members. I always wanted a tie with tennis racquets on it to go with my Italian decoration . . ."

Well, they both would have roared with laughter, thus admitting the *unsound* part of the Farrow deal. That would have been fine with her. But this big phony act of being cool and calculating, making a "pure business decision," that was so much bunk. She knew her husband too well to buy it!

Leon swiveled in his chair, something he did only when he was extremely nervous. He hated chair-swiveling, pen-gnawing, desk-drumming, and all other involuntary executive self-revelations . . . But, after all, the Farrow deal was a special thing, worth a swivel if anything was.

*Had* Susan spoken to Sandra? He dialed his home, using the private line which by-passed the switchboard. No answer. Sandra was probably shopping and the maid out buying groceries. Dammit! He let the phone ring on and on before giving up.

The goddamn phone! What it used to mean to him in the old days, when he was a salesman and his fate hung on the other end of the line! . . . Back in the thirties all switch-boards had looked like snakepits, and their operators like adenoidal contortionists.

His romance with Sandra dated back to a phone call from Bondley's Fifth Avenue, about the new copies from Balenciaga.

"Where *are* those dresses? Mr. Fassman, the ad is running Sunday and we've spent a fortune on artwork . . . Now I know you—"

Leon finally interrupted her. "Now you listen to me for a minute, Miss Stirling. No use you getting into a temper, the garments will be there in time for the ad if I have to carry them on my back!"

"Well, I should certainly hope so, Mr. Fassman. And let me just say that *if* you let us down . . ."

Leon reassured, soothed, placated. He had met this girl only once, two months ago when she became the buyer. Before that she'd been tucked away as an assistant, never came to Seventh Avenue. That's all he needed—a tough buyer, at Bondley's yet!

Armand-Klein had supplied Bondley's since Armand-Klein was founded. Thirty years of continuous business through a depression and a war. He'd joined the firm in twenty-nine, that lousy year when *everyone* sold off price—everyone but Armand-Klein. They made the best and sold it to the best; that was the premise of the firm. André Armand and Murray Klein, the elegant Frenchman and the meticulous little Jewish tailor, had the finest ready-made dresses in the high-priced field.

It had been hard to believe at first that he could fit into their operation. After years of shlepping cheap rags in canvas bags to every store from Ohio to Florida, peddling schmaltzy junk, overtrimmed, cheated together out of skimped and sleazy fabrics and shipped in haphazard confusion, he had been almost ulcerous. But it was better than his father's shop, and he had learned a lot.

He'd listened to the lies of hundreds of garment peddlers in the cigar-staled washrooms of swaying Pullman sleepers, had fenced off bosomy buyers in hotels that reeked of bacon. He had sold one hell of a lot of merchandise he detested for bosses whom he despised.

When he walked into the thick-carpeted showroom at Armand-Klein, he knew that this was the dress business as he had always imagined it: dignified and tasteful. Mr. Armand himself had interviewed him. Leon still had the sheet of embossed stationery telling him to report to work . . .

Anyplace but Armand-Klein and that snotty new buyer

would be told off, and not gently. But at Armand-Klein everything was done with the style that characterized the firm. Collections were shown without comment. Salesmen never applied pressure, and no buyer was ever hounded by telephone or mail. Each season Armand-Klein announced that the new line was ready, and that was that. From the tiniest specialty shop to the big department stores, everyone was treated the same, and an order for four dresses was processed as carefully as a commitment for five hundred. Complaints from customers were never ignored. So where did this Stirling girl get off speaking to him as if he were a wash-dress salesman?

Just to make sure, Leon called the shipping room, where an indignant clerk told him the Bondley delivery would be made on Thursday, *of course!* After all, didn't they have an ad running this Sunday? (Yes, they do, and that little Bondley biddy knows what she can do with her dresses . . .)

"Talking to yourself, Leon?" It was André Armand's accented basso.

"That new buyer at Bondley's," Leon said. "She's so nervous about that damned Balenciaga ad she's been driving me nuts, afraid we'll let her down."

"Oh, well," Armand shrugged an elegant shoulder, "she'll learn in time that we just never"—he sounded like a Paris policeman trying to recall a difficult address—"do the unplanned!" He patted Leon on the cheek. "Don't be upset, *mon petit*. By Monday afternoon she will love you or hate you. Depending on how well she does with the ad."

André Armand, who had been a great maître d'hôtel until Murray Klein persuaded him onto Seventh Avenue, knew that clients were usually impatient before hors d'oeuvre and cheerful after dessert. It was the way of the world, and Leon would learn.

By 3 P.M. the following Monday, Sandra Stirling was

cheerful *and* charming. "If I can only get some more twelves by tomorrow I would appreciate it *so much*, Mr. Fassman." The ad had pulled. The dresses had sold *very* well. Armand-Klein was marvelous, Mr. Fassman was a prince, and the god of all dress merchants was in his crepe-lined heaven. As she paused for breath, Leon took sudden advantage of their *détente* and asked her to dinner.

The evening began with a standoffish and shy fifteen minutes at Sandra's apartment on West End Avenue. Then Leon taxied her to the Waldorf, where they had a reservation in the Sert Room (he had checked and rechecked it). He tipped the maître d' at once, and after all the phone calls, the man knew his name. "Mr. Fassman" was shown to a ringside table. He hoped Mr. Fassman liked the table. Thank you, Mr. Fassman.

"So did you get the twelves?" Leon asked her.

"They got into the receiving room just before closing, thanks. We'll need 'em tomorrow."

"Is the ad running?"

"*Tribune*," she nodded.

"It's the third ad."

"Yes," she said, "it's a good item. We'll ride it till the end of the season . . . and happy to mark down what's left."

"You've already sold two hundred of the dress?"

"Two-fifty. Just marvelous!"

Leon knew they really should not be talking business. This was a date, a *social* date; but the fact was, he knew nothing *about* this girl and it was hard work finding other things to talk about. Long minutes passed, uncomfortably.

Then they danced, and their troubles were over. She was nearly as tall as he, strong but soft and easy to lead. By the time they walked back to the table there was a flood of things they wanted to tell each other. He called her "Sam," and she giggled. And as easily and naturally as they had danced and talked, after dinner they went back to Sandra's apartment and Leon spent the night. There was no sense of adventure, guilt, daring. It was self-understood, friendly, warm, and—*right*.

Six months later Sandra quit her job and they were married. The day before their wedding she moaned: "A girl changes her name from Stirnweiss to Stirling and what does she end up with? *Fassman!* You can't win!"

André Armand, in impeccable pin-stripes, gave Sandra away in his penthouse on Central Park South. Murray Klein was there, as sentimental as a mother of the bride. Leon's parents were reluctant witnesses to the *goyish* wedding despite the (*reform*, wouldn't you know?) rabbi. Sandra, whose parents were dead, was backed up by her older sister, the matron of honor.

They were still newlyweds, married only a few months, when Leon took full charge of Armand-Klein. His two old bosses waited a decent interval before offering him the presidency. A brand-new wife *and* job would have been a bit much all at once.

Then one morning they called him into André's office. They were unusually formal. They offered him a cigar, then the job, and seemed completely surprised that *he* was surprised. This boy who was virtually running the show and who was like a son to them?

Armand shrugged at Klein and Klein shrugged at Armand.

As for Leon, it had simply never occurred to him that the two of them were ready to retire, and for the moment it panicked him. Of course he knew how long he had been running things, but they were always—*there*. "Murray, André, *why?*" he asked.

"Because," said Armand, "I am tired and so is Murray. Because we know you can handle things. Because I have no children and because Murray's sons want no part of the rag business. They're busy doctoring and lawyering. Enough?"

"Enough!" said Leon. He could hardly wait to tell Sandra.

The news that made his seem all but insignificant came two days later, at Sunday breakfast. It crackled in over the radio, an evil instrument fate might have invented to interrupt their happiness. *Japanese bombers . . . striking without warning . . . hundreds of casualties . . . burning . . .* It was too unreal. The peaceful Sunday papers seemed a mockery, their headlines already obsolete.

The cozy morning was brutalized, but it was not until the next day that they knew their entire life was, too. The President was to address a joint session. The United States was at war.

Four months later it was only a question of time. Leon had barely taken charge of Armand-Klein. He was thirty-three years old and married, and there was no immediate question of his being drafted. All the same, he wanted to join the other men going into the service; Sandra could certainly look after Armand-Klein while he was gone.

Sandra, realizing that the penalty for marrying a *man* was that he would behave like one, was careful to avoid influencing him one way or the other. And then, at Leon's request, she telephoned her old boss, the former general merchandise manager at Bondley's, now a colonel in the Quartermaster Corps. After one interview and several weeks of time, an envelope arrived from the War Department notifying Leon that, based on his civilian experience, he was qualified for a commission in the Quartermaster Corps.

Two days later, he set out for 90 Church Street to report for his physical.

The snow crunched under Leon's feet and the chill night wind cut his forehead. He turned up the collar of his new officer's coat, which seemed strange and stiff. He had arrived at Camp Ryder late that night after hitching a ride on an Army truck from Hagerstown, Maryland, the nearest bus stop. The wintry mountains gleamed moon-white all around the post, a new installation for the training and indoctrination of administrative personnel. A small U-shaped valley, about a half-mile wide, had been turned into an Army town with two-story barracks, wooden buildings, and right-angled streets. At night only the lights of the guard posts and the smoke of kitchen fires gave evidence of life in the valley.

At Fort Dix, the clerks had looked at Leon's brand-new uniform and QMC insignia with a certain patronizing hauteur. There were hundreds of new "straight" commissioned officers on their way to posts like Camp Ryder, where they would be taught the rudiments of soldiering, although many would spend the rest of their Army careers as accountants or attorneys or uniform buyers. Some of these new captains and majors knew less about soldiering than infantry pfc's. They had to learn how to salute, march, and tell a lieutenant colonel from a lieutenant general.

The sleepy-eyed sergeant looked at Leon. "Here it is, Lieutenant," he said, his finger tracing down a list of names. "Fassman." He sounded surprised, as if Leon had been caught in an unexpected truth. "Barracks 10K."

Lazily he got to his feet behind the wooden desk in the bare orderly room and preceded Leon onto the snowy street. He pointed toward the far end of the post.

"Just go two blocks down this road to K Street, then right. It's the third barracks on the left." He saluted and stepped quickly back into the warmth of the room, without waiting for Leon to return the salute. Leon, who had not noticed this lapse of military courtesy, picked up his Valpack and started off for the barracks which would be his home for the next six weeks. Inside, a stumbling, yawning pfc checked off his name and led him to a bunk on the second floor of the dark building. It was 2 A.M., 0200 in Army time, and reveille was at 0600 . . .

Leon did not bother to unpack. He took off his uniform, hung it on the rack behind his bunk, and slid between the ice-cold sheets. He was fast asleep within seconds, oblivious to the forty snoring men whose breath he could have seen by the cold light on the moon.

Nothing had prepared Leon for this form of existence. Like most poor kids he had never been to camp, had never known the outdoors. Nor had he ever been in close contact with men outside of his own realm. The new men around him were strangers, not because they were *goyim* but because their attitudes were strange. They seemed to be more lethargic, patient, unconcerned than he: they cared less, strove less, worried less than he did. Leon had always been suspicious of men who were content just to *get by*, taking such an attitude as evidence of laziness. But these men seemed to achieve just as much as he did.

The officer in the next bunk, a tall and sinewy man with a hangdog face, was the first of the older trainees to speak to Leon.

"Mah name," he said, "is Ware." He did not extend his hand, but merely raised it in a token wave.

"Fassman's mine. Leon."

"New York?"

"Right." New York? Did that mean, "Fassman, a Jew from New York"? Leon hoped he was imagining things, but his uneasiness grew when Ware seemed to discourage further conversation.

The next few days came and went like speeded-up scenes from a silent movie. Gruff Regular Army sergeants began with the "position of a soldier." Then came close-order drill, barracks procedure, nomenclature, and field stripping of the rifle and forty-five automatic, military courtesy, Articles of War, guard duty, general orders. Subjects were rotated at three times the rate of regular infantry training for these noncombatant trainees, who as a result learned the vocabulary of soldiering without grasping any of its skills. Nonetheless Leon, who had expected the Army to be dull, was fascinated and rather pleased with himself because he was learning fast.

Ware remained distant, and Leon concentrated on his other neighbor, Corbett, a pudgy lawyer from Baltimore who spent most of his time complaining. At first Leon felt sorry for him, but by the end of the week Corbett irritated him unbearably.

"I tell you, Fassman," Corbett said after staying out of a field exercise by faking a sick call, "I've had enough of this shit. For Christ's sake, I'm joining the Judge Advocate General's office. I wish to hell they'd stop wasting my time here."

Leon, exhausted after a day of marching, crawling, and climbing, said, "Corbett, we're all here to learn. After all, you'll be an *Army* lawyer!"

"What's the difference?"

"Maybe if you'd stop goldbricking you'd figure it out."

Corbett shrugged and left.

Ware, seated on his bunk with a *Reader's Digest*, looked up and smiled, and after dinner he walked alongside Leon back to the barracks. When they had stomped the snow from their boots and stowed their mess kits, Ware said, "Hey, *Lee*, I know it ain't regulations, but I got me a bottle in my kit if you want a nip."

He fished a hip flask from his foot locker, unscrewed the cap, and handed it to Leon.

"Ain't no one watchin'. Bottoms up!"

Leon took a drag. It was bourbon, something he had hardly ever had, and it tasted wonderful.

From then on Ware and Leon were friends. On their first pass, they went to the local movie. It was a war film full of technical mistakes. Spotting the errors made Leon feel very soldierly, the way salutes from enlisted men on the post did. He returned each one meticulously, feeling lordly and, at the same time, a little guilty for liking the whole business.

Three letters from Sandra had finally arrived at the end of Leon's second week. Each one began with news of Armand-Klein, which apparently was flourishing. Leon was not surprised—Sandra was a great businesswoman. There were fabric shortages and OPA restrictions, but a good firm could sell anything it produced because merchandise was scarce. Sandra would be fine, he'd bet on that, and so would Armand-Klein. The fact was, he really could not have cared less right then. If someone had told him a few months ago that he could go through two weeks with hardly a thought for the firm . . .

The personal parts of Sandra's letters were strangely stilted. Sandra had never been a love *talker*, and she now could not write of love. Yet Leon could read beyond the words to her loneliness. Sandra had always said everything physically. For the first time since leaving New York, he felt the pain of needing her.

It was August 1944, and Leon was on a highway in Normandy. The jeep hit a pothole, and he cursed the hundreds of tanks and trucks which had cracked the paving since the invasion.

His driver, a corporal, didn't seem to mind the jouncing. Leon envied him for being nineteen and tough.

"Nice country, Captain. Just like my part of Connecticut."

"And where's that, Corporal?"

"Mystic, near the Rhode Island state line."

They passed the burned-out hulk of a Tiger tank. The hatch was open—maybe the krauts had got out. Nothing like Connecticut, even if it reminded the corporal of home.

They arrived at the Quartermaster Depot, where Leon was on temporary assignment, checking shipments of new uniforms for the shower platoons, which deloused and re-uniformed troops from the front.

The Twenty-eighth Division was two days from Paris, and the Red Ball Highway, which cut across Normandy, was a stream of highballing supply trucks. Leon, sent into the line with a Division G4 so he could learn combat supply close up, learned the smell, the shock, and the messy vagueness of combat. Dead Germans in careless heaps; dead Americans in carefully covered rows. Brown dried blood on riddled jeep carcasses, frantic ambulances slithering over mud-covered pontoon bridges, GI's slogging along, heads lowered. Crash-landed B-17's in belly-flattened fields, and rows of clanking tanks which left pulverized pavement in their wake.

In small towns behind the line, GI's scoured for Cognac and girls, or watched USO movies in music halls. They read *Stars and Stripes* and hoped they would never be assigned to Patton, who could chew out dogfaces for failing to salute after a night on patrol.

Leon was part of this world. The inhabitants spoke their own language and concentrated on the business at hand, day by day. Home was far away, a glorious place but not for now. Letters from there seemed unreal—like America itself, an invented place one saw in movies. Leon was not really home-sick. He liked getting letters from Sandra, but he read them hastily. It was important to know that she was *there* and that she was *his*. What she had done and whom she had seen did not really concern him. He wrote one perfunctory letter each week, but he said little because of censorship and because he could not share his life.

By Christmas, it looked as though the Nazi offensive had collapsed. The three trucks in the small convoy behind Leon's jeep were transporting C-rations to the Armored people up ahead in the Bulge. Machine guns were mounted above the truck drivers' heads, but it was cold and they were unmanned. Quartermaster troops had lousy aim anyway.

Leon was huddled in the jeep's right-hand seat, his nose tucked into his trenchcoat collar. But his helmet was a wind trap, and he was freezing.

"That's better, Major!" his driver shouted over the slip-stream. The moon had finally broken through the clouds, illuminating the snow-covered highway a half-mile ahead. They had just left the protection of the woods. Ahead was one long open field.

Leon and his driver heard the low-flying plane at the same instant, but it was an instant too late.

The snow in the roadway ahead suddenly puckered, and even as the driver swerved the jeep off the road, they heard the jackhammer of the plane's guns.

Leon was standing in his seat, holding onto the wind-shield with one hand and waving at his trucks with the other, exposing himself like a maniac signaling the obvious: Get the hell off the road!

The two front trucks headed for the field, churning into the snow, but the third truck skidded crazily—the driver had panicked—and was now stuck fast, its rear still on the road. Leon ran toward it, stumbling in the deep snow, yelling, "Take cover! Take cover!" but even then he could hear the roar of the German plane making its next pass, its bullets hitting the stalled truck. Why didn't the driver get out, damn him? He was up into the cab of the truck before he saw that the kid had been cut on the cheek just below the helmet line and knocked out. Leon pulled his hands off the wheel and managed to get him down onto the running board and into the ditch just as the plane made a third pass and shattered the truck's windshield to smithereens. Leon could see the first flame and then the gas tank blew, showering the snow around him with small black fires.

The plane did not return. The men scrambled quickly from cover to help Leon with the boy. As if he had done this every day of his life, Leon yanked the sterile gauze out of his kit, dusted it with sulfa and pressed it against the bleeding cheek. He held it there while the others got the jeep and the two trucks back on the road. Then they bandaged the wounded soldier as best they could and loaded him into the back of the jeep. They met some MPs a few miles ahead and followed them to the nearest Armored medics, where they unloaded the wounded kid.

Leon's Bronze Star came from Corps a week later. His men had told the story. When he read the citation he thought: Five points for the medal, five points closer to home! Sam, your boy's a friggin' hero!

After the years in uniform it was a chore to select tie, shirt, and cufflinks, suit, shoes, and socks. All that time he had looked forward to civvies, and now each morning, when he saw his uniform in the closet, he was almost tempted to put it on.

One day he slipped on the blouse. He buttoned it, belted it and checked himself in the mirror. Three rows of ribbons, major's leaves, five overseas stripes. Then he quickly took it off, like a kid caught trying on his father's clothes.

He had expected it to take some time for Sandra and him to get reacquainted. As it turned out, they clicked as if a three-year war were a two-day business trip. And Sandra was happy to hand the business back to Leon.

For him it was brutal. For three years he'd worked with young men, and Armand-Klein was now top-heavy with men in their sixties, prewar garment veterans who still believed that "personality" could "sell anything," who seemed flabby-brained and lazy. Shortages during the war *had* enabled Armand-Klein to sell whatever it could make. Now that the soft days were over, Leon desperately needed talented people, driving people.

Just before shipping home to the States, he had visited Paris; sad, beaten Paris with its bicycle-riding girls, wood-burning cars, and decimated couture. Several designers were reopening their ateliers, though. Lombert, for one, planned to show the following spring: muslins had been cut and already were being sewn in unheated lofts by shivering *midinettes*.

"We should go to Paris, Sam. But it's no good putting together a great collection if we don't have a great sales force."

"I know," she said, "but the men have been with the firm forever. What can we do?"

What Leon did was to dismiss three fine old gentlemen as soon as he could. He flattered their age-stiffened egos and provided for their financial needs, but he dismissed them. The three men, too old or too vain to see the truth, could brag about their "retirement."

André and Murray both came in to Armand-Klein to welcome Leon home. He was afraid they might be upset by his house-cleaning, but the two men never questioned it. Nor did they seem to have interfered with Sandra's wartime management. Murray's five grandchildren were his sole concern, and André would soon retire to France.

Leon set about recruiting his new team. He placed a carefully worded ad in the *Times*:

An Exciting New Marketing Team now being formed by a distinguished fashion business firm. We need bright young college graduates who are anxious to take responsibility. Call or write ARMAND-KLEIN, INC., 549 Seventh Avenue, New York City. LOngacre 3-9940. Ask for Mr. Leon Fassman.

The ad drew an avalanche of responses from out-of-work veterans. The first man Leon hired was an ex-pilot named Howard Sands.

"Jesus, Howie," said Tom Brett, watching his roommate towel away leftovers dots of shaving cream, "you've got to be kidding."

"No, I'm not," Howard said. He pushed a comb through his stiff black hair and started putting on his clothes. "I'm going to work for a garment firm. Armand-Klein. Classy, glossy outfit, let me tell you, and it pays well, too. When I see this guy Fassman today, he'll tell me more about what I'll be doing, but it sounds plenty exciting."

Once Howard left, Tom poured himself a beer and settled back on one of the bolstered studio couches. They were lucky to have found the one-room apartment on Forty-eighth east of Lexington. The two of them had given the building superintendent and then the rental agent hard cash and heartbreaking stories—in 1946, New York had too many ex-servicemen and too few apartments.

Fortunately, Tom and Howard were flush, loaded as only ex-pilots could be. Their terminal-leave pay had been handsomely augmented by the winnings from a huge transatlantic crap game which lasted through a flight from Scotland to Washington. The pilot and co-pilot of the troop carrier wallowing its way across the Atlantic had even taken turns joining the game while the plane droned along on automatic pilot.

For six weeks they'd done nothing but drink, screw, dance, and loaf. They went to Brooks Brothers and emerged wearing slim flannel suits, flaring button-down collars and reversible Burberrys. Howard had gone to UCLA and Tom to Arizona State, but now they looked like Yalies.

It was Howard's idea.

"You'll see," he said. "All the good jobs will go to the Ivy League boys, and we might as well *look* Ivy League."

Tom laughed, but the Brooks look helped Howard get his job. Who would have guessed it paid to look like Greenwich, Connecticut, on Seventh Avenue?

Leon found his new assistant's tight, rugged face, Madison Avenue clothes, and easy West Coast manners an attractive combination. Even better, he liked Howard's drive and willingness to learn. Witnessing every letter, phone call, showing, negotiation, he soon began to grasp the intricacies of Seventh Avenue.

Leon had also hired another veteran, Randy Kirsh, an ex-officer in the Signal Corps who was detail-happy and meticulous, but above all liked to look at a problem as if no one had ever come up with a solution before. He saw how the pieces of garments moved through the factory, where the time gaps were, which phases took how much time, and slowly—on paper—worked out a new plan that would lop 20 percent or more off production time. Randy was a natural-born efficiency expert. When he outlined his new and very workable plan, Howard was impressed, but it was Leon who was really attentive. There was no logical reason why Randy's plan wouldn't work, saving both time and money in the production process.

Meanwhile, Howard experimented in his own way. He developed an offhand sales approach for the showroom, never talking "fashion," but suggesting instead specific *uses* for each style. ("Marvelous little dinner-at-home dress, but not right for formal parties . . .") Buyers loved the new angles this kind of thing gave them.

When Tom Brett landed a job with J. Walter Thompson shortly after Howard started with Armand-Klein, the two of them moved into a duplex in Murray Hill. During the winter months it was a weekend hangout for masses of pretty girls. In summer, Tom and Howard rented a cottage on Fire Island. More weekends. More girls. Winter or summer, Sunday nights found the whole cast at P. J .Clarke's on Third Avenue.

Sunday mornings were for nursing hangovers and reading the papers. For both men, this meant work. Howard counted credits in the magazine sections, pored over ads, worried over why Saks had bought Maurice Rentner's styles and not Armand-Klein's or why Ben Reig had an editorial in the magazine instead of them. As for Tom, now an advertising man, he was personally affronted by every ad he disliked (and he liked few ads). "Look at this shit, would you? They call this *advertising?* Christ, if I had my way!"

They eventually tried skipping everything but the funnies, but it was no use. They settled for limiting the Sunday-morning "work" to a half-hour, and by the time they had their first Bloody Marys they had usually calmed down.

"Jesus," Howard said one Sunday morning. "I don't know how I ever read the Sunday papers before. Guess I really just looked at headlines, sports, and entertainment.

But they're *loaded* if you know where to look." Tom taught him to read V*ogue, Bazaar,* and *Ambience* like a pro: Why was *who* on the cover? Was it a "legitimate" cover or was it a payoff to an advertiser? How could you tell? Easy: How many ads had been bought by the manufacturer of the dress on the cover? Who really paid for ads? Often it was everybody but the manufacturer of the dress. There were plugs for synthetic yarns, airlines, hotel chains, cameras, and perfumes tucked into the copy. Did stores pay for magazine ads in which they were mentioned? Hardly ever. Many manufacturers gave free ads to prestige stores as bait for other stores. Certain manufacturers had free editorials although they were cheap schlock houses. Their styles in the photos looked fashionable—but then, they were made especially for the magazine in order to get the free plug. The few plugs Howard missed were spotted by Tom.

The magazines devoted two special issues a year to Paris, and the "Paris" pages were free of payoff, as if the magazines were doing penance after months of sin. The French couturiers, who never advertised, were hero-worshipped, their names used in bold type. Identical styles were often photographed by rival magazines, although the magazines insisted on exclusives from American houses.

Howard was quick to join his colleagues with cynical comments about the Paris issues and even the collections themselves, but the anticipation he felt when Leon asked him to attend the spring couture showings made him realize he was hardly immune to Paris excitement.

He was headed for more than one surprise.

Howard thought he knew Paris. He had spent several leaves there during the war, could find his way around easily. But from the moment he and Leon checked into the George V one Friday in February, Howard realized that this much more complicated Paris, where Leon was an old hand, was a stranger to him.

They had one free day before the showings. They shopped for belts and scarves on the Place Vendôme, lunched at the Berkeley, visited dozens of little boutiques to see if they could find style ideas. Then the Ritz for cocktails, where the bar was full of Seventh Avenue. At Maxim's, they were joined for dinner by a group of American manufacturers and retailers and several *commissionnaires*, the French agents who arranged entry to the couture houses.

By the time they returned to the George V, Howard was footsore and stuffed.

The first couture showing was a few blocks from the hotel. They showed their tickets to a guard and to a superior-looking girl at the head of the stairway. To Howard what followed seemed faintly ridiculous.

A room that should have held fifty was jammed with a hundred perspiring people, all reverently hushed, while fair-to-middling girls walked through a silent fashion show. Some of the designs were attractive, some were ugly, but all were received with worship. The believers were at the shrine, and lifelong enmities were possible over the placement of a single spectator's chair. Ninety-seven pairs of eyes were focused on three women: Mrs. Snow of *Harper's Bazaar*, Mrs. Chase of *Vogue*, and Mrs. Ahern of *Ambience*. Whenever these three seemed ready to applaud, the audience poised its hands like an obedient claque.

After the fiftieth style, about halfway through the show, Howard noticed that one famous editor was dozing. He watched her droop, then lift up sharply, then droop again, lower each time till suddenly her chin hit her brooch and she opened both eyes with a start.

The show ended with a pristine bridal gown worn by the least virginal-looking model. There was a hushed pause followed by thunderous applause and cries of "Bravo!" The couturier, a shy little thing with a pale face and startled gazelle eyes, appeared briefly at the entrance of the models' room, where he was immediately swamped by admirers. He retired in fear, but several undaunted ladies followed him into the dressing room. The woman next to Howard, an editor from a Chicago paper who had applauded and shouted with the others, shrugged her shoulders and said: "Between us, it was *mezzo-mezzo*."

"Oh?" said Howard. "I thought you loved it."

"It was all right, I guess." She began to elbow her way toward the focal point of attention.

Later that night, in the bar at the Ritz, Howard was unusually quiet.

"What's the trouble?" Leon asked.

"I just don't *get* it!"

"Get what?"

"This whole circus. Look, you can call me nuts, but we saw two big showings today. Some stuff was okay, but most of it looked—amateurish, sleazy, not as good as Armand-Klein."

"Oh, come on, now!"

"No, I really mean it."

"But didn't you see the new ideas, the new approach?"

"If you want the truth, no. There are a whole bunch of kids designing in America—like Rudi Gernreich and Ann Fogarty—who could give these couture people aces and spades when it comes to new ideas."

Leon had seen them featured in Lord & Taylor ads, and had not been impressed. "You got to be kidding," he said. "Cheap sportswear, or young kids' dresses, that's the thing they do, right?"

"What's price got to do with it? There's a woman called Claire McCardell who works for a sportswear firm. She designs modern clothes, the kind women will need: jersey knits and loose-draped things and lower heels. She shows dark stockings with her dresses and even some dresses that are cut just like men's shirts. And how about Trigère and Charles James? Their clothes aren't cheap, and they certainly look professional."

Leon listened, surprised at Howard's intensity.

"You know, Leon, those color combinations everyone was raving about this morning, like mustard and shocking pink, turquoise and yellow? Gernreich has been doing them for months. The full skirts and peasant blouses? Fogarty! And about those slim pants, well, they're cut like Levi's, and we all know American girls have worn them for years."

A tall, pretty girl stopped at their table. Both men rose and Leon introduced Howard: "Doe Perrin, she belongs to *Ambience*, this is my good right hand, Howard Sands." She smiled and shook hands.

"How about a drink, Doe?"

"Fine, Leon, but it'll have to be a quickie. We have to photograph all night."

"All night?" asked Howard.

"Oh, we shoot the collections at night so the couturiers can get their darned samples back by morning. It's sort of a rat race trying to beat *Vogue* and *Bazaar* to the punch."

"Every night?"

"So long as there are showings."

"Are the styles you're photographing that great?"

"All I know is, we're holding twenty pages open in the September issue. We fly the negatives to New York."

"But how about the styles?"

She shrugged her shoulders. "Some of them are all right."

"Good as McCardell or Gernreich?"

She raised both hands and laughed. "Mine is not to reason why. Mine is only to get my derrière over to the studio on the Rive Gauche and help the photographers. But I'll admit that for myself, I'll take McCardell."

She finished her drink and left. Obviously she was not sold, either. Howard wondered all over again what all the fuss was about.

As for Leon, he was irritated. How could Howard be so negative? Helluva lot of good it did to bring him to Paris . . . Still, you hired young men to bring fresh ideas into the shop, you might as well listen to them. Besides, he might not admit it to Howard, but there were plenty of things he resented about Paris.

His competitors were all there, of course, seeing the same collections. Even the cheapest manufacturers could swing the air fare and come away with the same styles.

Just then Harry Ray, one of the cheapest copyists in the business, tapped him on the back.

"Hullo, Leon."

Leon barely acknowledged him.

"How'd ya like the stuff this morning?"

"Okay, I guess." No use telling Ray that he had liked the collection. He'd only be cutting his own throat.

"See ya, Leon!" Ray moved on with a grin, looking all around the crowded bar, anxious to connect.

Christ! All of *Chinatown* was there, all the cheap boys, Thirty-seventh Street bums. Leon watched Ray seat himself at a table in the corner—all cheap manufacturers. Even the discount stores were there. And the chains.

Meanwhile, though, he would confirm his orders at Dior and Balenciaga. That should keep Meltzer and her design room busy for a while. She was a genius, that dame. Could do a Dior almost as well as Dior.

Mildred Meltzer had been an Armand-Klein designer for nineteen years, ever since 1933. A chubby little lady with dyed red hair and nimble short-fingered hands, she was skilled, efficient, cooperative, and an excellent copyist. She had never designed an original style in her life.

After all, that was not her job. The boss picked the fabrics and bought Paris models, which she copied or adapted, then approved or changed each sample. Also, the boss paid her a handsome salary. Not all styles were Paris copies, of course. There were always adaptations of Armand-Klein's old "bodies" that had been successful in previous seasons. There was one body, a prewar style, now ten years old. For many seasons it had been widened, narrowed, lengthened, shortened, but it had remained the same basic style all the while.

She loved to drape, smoothing the muslin into place and pinning it to the dummy. Her specialty was chiffon with hundreds of little tucks. She viewed "tailored" garments with some distaste, although she could tailor with the best of them. Tailored garments were so *sterile*, so "unfeminine."

Her sample room was a large, sunny area facing Seventh Avenue. It housed a small cutting table, five clothing dummies, racks of sample fabrics, and five seamstresses, "sample hands." All of "Mrs. Meltzer's ladies" were devoted to her, working late into the night when the pressure was on. She had also formed a reluctant business marriage with two old male pattern makers. It became positively loving every Christmas when she gave them ties, pipes, or schnapps.

She was a widow, a condition her *yente* friends found increasingly hard to take. How, they asked over bridge, could Mildred stay *alone* so long when so many fine men were available? The fact was, Mildred Meltzer was perfectly happy with her cozy apartment on East Thirty-eighth Street and her old Negro maid, who adored her. Her late husband had spent several years going about the business of dying, and she had no intention of ever nursing another *alte kacker*.

Mildred Meltzer might be queen among Seventh Avenue's old-time designers, but no one outside the business had ever heard of her. It had never entered her mind to want her name on Armand-Klein labels, or in the magazines. What for? She had enough trouble as it was, dodging women who wanted to buy wholesale.

"Sit down, Mildred," said Leon. She took the large leather armchair opposite his desk, a decision she regretted instantly. Her short legs barely reached the floor, and that made her uncomfortable.

Leon came to the point at once. "Mildred, you should know I've decided to sign a contract with James Farrow."

(Farrow, the *meshugge* couturier? Have you got trouble coming, Mr. Fassman!) "Yes?" she said, waiting. She was not worried. She would outlast all experiments. The things she'd had to do during the war when Mrs. Fassman was running the firm (a lovely woman that, a real lovely woman). She'd had to learn to skimp, because the government told them to skimp. And over the years she'd adapted some pretty awful dresses from Paris. She would be able to turn Farrow's pipe dreams into something Armand-Klein could sell.

"Now as you know, Mildred," Leon said, "Farrow is a difficult man. He's afraid we won't translate his things properly." He anticipated her protests, but she kept quiet, nodding her head.

"You and I know, of course, this is crazy, but I want to humor him at the beginning. So I said okay to something he wants, and I know from you I'll get cooperation about it."

"And what, for instance, has the Great Man to propose?" Mildred was no good at irony.

"He wants us to hire one of his people to supervise the

copies. You'll like the boy he's sending over—a very talented kid, Farrow's right hand for years. It's only temporary. Farrow can't manage for long without Philip Ross, that's his name."

She sighed. "All right, Mr. Fassman. Whatever you say." She dismissed herself by scrambling from the depths of the man-sized armchair, a plump little bug regaining its feet.

Howard felt sorry for Philip Ross, whom he found easy to like. *Everything* had hit the fan!

They had announced the Farrow deal to the press, advertised it in *Women's Wear*, written to the stores.

They had spent weeks with Philip taking the originals apart, seam by seam, using the closest possible fabrics, and reconstructing them for wholesale production. Leon, Howard knew, was very proud of the results. Even he could hardly distinguish between the original Farrows and the Armand-Klein copies.

Philip had worked hardest of them all. He had to approve each seam, each button, each belt, all the while guiding the crotchety pattern makers and cajoling Meltzer's sample hands. He simplified the complicated architecture of Farrow's styles; resisting compromise, he spent many nights alone in the studio, reshaping patterns and trying out muslins.

When he finished his work, the collection was intact in look and spirit. Farrow might be a bastard but he was an artist and it was obvious to Howard that no matter how much he despised the man, Philip would protect his work.

As a surprise for Farrow, a *beau geste*, they had arranged a special one-man private showing behind locked showroom doors. There were caviar canapés and a magnum of Dom Perignon, and Philip had even bought Gauloises. While they awaited the couturier's arrival, everyone—except Meltzer, who had claimed a headache—thanked Philip for his help.

Farrow was late, of course. Philip had warned everybody that he would be, had even told Howard that it was an act, that Farrow loved entrances.

When he finally arrived, Leon introduced everyone except Philip, to whom Farrow gave a perfunctory nod: "It seems I know Mr. Ross." Howard began to pour champagne and Philip passed the caviar, but Farrow waved both away as if refusing a bribe. "Let's get on with it," he said, and Philip went into the model's room to start the show. He had accessorized everything as Farrow did, had even sent the girls to Daché for the new Farrow coiffure. He was disturbed by Farrow's mood, but there was no time to worry about that now.

Philip had no inkling of what was happening outside in the showroom until the fifth costume, when the model came back into the dressing room and sat down. Philip said, "Hey, let's go," and handed her the next dress, but she shook her head. Was she ill?

"He's gone!"

"Who's gone?"

"Farrow. He yelled something just as I came out, and then he up and left."

Philip dashed into the showroom. It was true. Farrow was not there.

"It seems," said Howard, "that the *master* did not approve of our handiwork." It took Philip a few seconds to comprehend. Howard had said *our* handiwork; apparently Philip was not being blamed for whatever had gone wrong. That bastard. That lousy bastard, this was it!

Leon patted him on the shoulder. "Leave it to me, Philip, he won't get away with this."

Philip mumbled something and headed off for his little

studio, next to Meltzer's room. He stayed there, boiling, until Howard came in.

"It was really something," he said. "During the first three numbers, the two suits and the coat ensemble, Farrow *stared at the ceiling.* I swear, Philip, he didn't even *look* at the clothes. Then the fourth style came out, the red wool dress, and he *yelled:* 'I've never seen such shit!' Then he walked out. It was so fast we couldn't even ask him why or try to stop him!"

"Christ, Howard, I tried my best—"

"We know you did. No one is blaming you."

"What's Fassman say?"

"It's not what he'll say, it's what he'll *do.* He's advanced Farrow a big chunk of dough against the royalties."

"I didn't know."

"How could you, Philip? I know because I was in on the contract negotiations. If Farrow thinks he can get away with this, he's peeing upwind. I'll put my bets on Leon. He can be a pretty tough old bird!"

As if on cue, Leon looked in. "Hello, boys." He stopped Philip from getting up and propped himself against the cutting table. "Look, Philip," he said, "I know you're in a spot, because you're still working for Farrow—"

(Working for Farrow? Hell, he was probably still working for *Johnny.* He had refused to ask for a raise, because that would have meant *Farrow's* money, and he was not about to get his can into *that* sling again.) "No, Mr. Fassman, I'm in no spot, really. I did my best. I hope you believe that. As for Mr. Farrow, I did my best for him too, but he'll probably fire me anyway, and I shan't be sorry—for many reasons. It's hard for me to explain—"

"Well don't, Philip, I can guess. Meantime, how would you like to come to work for us?"

"You mean at Armand-Klein?" Perfect . . . "How about Mrs. Meltzer?"

"Your work would have nothing to do with hers. I've got other plans for you."

"Mr. Fassman, that sounds great. Can I let you know tomorrow?"

"Of course."

Leon beckoned to Howard and then left. On the way out Howard patted Philip's shoulder. He said, "I told you, buddy boy, he's a tough bird."

Soon, Howard was to find out how tough.

When he got to Leon's office, the phones were jangling. The lawyers and the press had been contacted and the calls were already coming in. The lawyers came first. Farrow did not have a leg to stand on. He had assigned his own man to supervise the samples and he had no contractual right to withhold approval of the results. This was a point Armand-Klein's lawyers had won months before, Farrow being too strapped at the time to argue. He had finally agreed to carte blanche approval, provided "a member of the James Farrow staff was assigned to supervise the preparation of the whole-sale collection."

"Howard," said Leon, "prepare a statement for the press, something about shelving our plans for the Farrow collection for now. No explanations, no comments. Got it?"

"Right."

"You can give it to them on the phone, then follow up with a printed release. They'll call Farrow and he'll probably run off at the mouth. All the better if he does."

"How do you mean?"

"If Farrow says we were incompetent, we shut up. With our reputation nobody will believe him, and besides, with the rumors about him, it will reflect badly on him, not us. If *he* shuts up—if his lawyers got to him on time—we're still ahead of the game.

"Next." Leon ticked off the moves on the fingers of his left hand. "Philip will take the job, don't ask me how I know, but I know . . . He can rework all the Farrow stuff. We let out the word that Philip was the *real* talent behind Farrow. *That* ought to make the cocky little anti-Semite howl!"

"Anti-Semite?"

"I'm only going by reputation. There are practically no Jewish clients on his books, you know."

"Then why?"

"Never mind, why. You're right, I shouldn't have even— oh, the hell with that. It's done and I'll undo it." Leon was grinning. "You know, Howard, I don't really mind making a fool of myself; I'd rather have it happen now than later, after going out on the limb for that little prick. If you're wondering why I'm not trying to patch up the whole thing or calling Farrow, that's why."

This was the last reaction Howard expected. Most people were set back by mistakes; this guy used them. Leon kept talking:

"The cash advance to Farrow is gone, we'll never see that dough again, so we write it off. We'll have Philip design special collections after this for a sort of couture division, the kind of new clothes you were talking about in Paris that day, but expensive and well made. We need a good name for this new division. *You* figure that one out . . . something like the Studio collection or the East Sixties collection or some such ritzy bullshit. Right?"

"Right. I'll get on it."

Howard left the office. Studio? Couture? East Sixties? Not quite right; should be ritzy but not cutesy, Leon.

First he'd call the press, then he'd sit there until he hit upon the right name. And he would enjoy doing *both*.

Why had it happened again? All *over* again, like some wild thing punishing him, and then it went away and he, Farrow, was alone. When he least expected it, when he had even *decided* to spend this *one* day without having it happen. Each morning there it was: gall, bitter anger, *hatred* for what? He never knew. Anything. Everything. He was like a dog jumping at a burglar who is not there, defending himself against—nothing . . . Ill? Was he really ill? Who had told him? Who knew him well enough to tell him?

Who needed anyone close, anyway?

Whores and pimps and cocksucking muscleboys who would squeeze his last buck, his last secret . . .

*His* work, kiked up by butchers on Seventh Avenue. And damn the old cunts who had put him in this bind . . . Especially the Debenhams, both of them, and their stinking millions. Over his back they'd climbed, and now when he needed them where were they?

If he could have shut up, just this once. The stuff was probably all right, and he just *could not* look at it. Ross wasn't creative-good, the little bastard, but he was *Farrow* good . . . All of them, when he walked in, peeing glory and champagne all over him. No control. No choice. He just *could not* stop himself.

*What, oh dear God, what'll I* DO?

The cage closed from outside. Each day he tried to hold it open, to breathe the air, to slip out and touch and taste, but he was shut in again.

*Fools, idiots, fatheads—you built it and you fucking well can't look in. I have been better always and I am still now and will always be better than you—*CUNTS!

# BOOK
## 3

P HILIP watched Howard light a cigarette as they finished
their breakfast. Sometimes Howard's face, with its high cheekbones, seem as drum-tight as a movie Indian's. His eyes were
deep-set, separated by a high straight nose with a narrow cleft
tip. His mouth looked pouty, but he smiled easily, flattening
his upper lip. If he had been a few inches taller, Philip might
have rated Howard as handsome—handsomer even than
Johnny, whose booze-splotched skin had bloated easily and
who had his on and off days.

Still, Howard held no special physical appeal for Philip.
There was something inflexibly male about him, without a
softening touch. Philip knew it would be hopeless; he could
always tell. Howard was not possible.

"Got to get back to the house. Want to come along,
Philip?"

"No, thanks, I'm off to the beach."

It was Saturday morning, and the weekend lay ahead of
Philip. Fire Island was waking up. Most people had arrived
from the boiling city the night before to find a crisp north-
west breeze clearing the sky. The *Times* forecast, "variable
winds with overcast skies," was wrong as usual. On weekends, the New York gods seemed inclined to be generous.

Like Howard, Philip was the color of a Waikiki beach
bum. They had spent each weekend on the same island, but
this was the first time they had met.

Howard's island was a bachelor heaven. Flat-bellied, oiled girls in two-piece swimsuits; barefoot, denim-shirted young men. The cottages they rented might as well have been mattress-padded, wall to wall. Freedom from work, bracing salt air, and a Niagara of booze encouraged easy sex.

Philip had drifted to the other end of the island, usually staying in Cherry Grove. The two boys who shared the downstairs garden apartment in New York (he had often noticed their little black name plate: "Sherwyn/Bates") had asked him to a cocktail party weeks ago. He'd found his neighbors charming and liked their guests, a mixed bag of fashion, decorating, and theater people, mostly male. Sherwyn and Bates, in their early thirties, had lived together since the war. Sherwyn was a slim six-footer with curling sandy hair and profuse gestures. Bates, balding and shy, with a chunky ex-athlete's body, seemed happy to let Sherwyn hold center stage. Philip was happy to find his neighbors *simpático*, a word he frequently used. (These days he often caught himself saying and doing new things he could not remember where he had picked up.)

The following weekend Sherwyn and Bates invited him to Fire Island. Their cottage sat on stilts, jutting out from high dunes like a platform. The bedroom was shared by his hosts. The living room faced the ocean through a salt-streaked picture window, and there was also a small guest room. They cooked on a wood-burning stove in the middle of the living room under a funnel-shaped chimney, which also heated the room on cool nights. The cottage was furnished with canvas-covered foam-rubber couches, bright deck chairs, and straw mats. They had no electricity, but there were kerosene lamps. The windows were draped in ticking. The outside walls were covered with graying wood shingles, and a sign over the door said "She-Ba's Palace."

The seeming informality, which began on the ferryboat,

was deceiving. Philip quickly realized that Cherry Grove social life was quite rigid. You went to the beach at certain hours; were careful about issuing and accepting invitations; wore special clothes at cocktails; dined at a set hour. The community was divided into the merely fey or gay, and the screaming queens. The queens were likely to appear in drag at the "wrong" time, away from parties. They were amusing, but too campy for real acceptance; they drank too much even by island standards, and could cause scenes. With the local cops always anxious to clamp down, no one wanted a scandal.

Queens or not, Cherry Grovers preferred their own company to that of the other end of the island. In Cherry Grove they could weekend without embarrassment, and the more conventional among them saw that the community's unwritten rules usually remained unbroken.

Philip, who ordinarily kept to himself, was quickly accepted as "desirable." After that first weekend, Sherwyn and Bates offered to rent him the guest room for the entire summer, and he accepted gladly. He began a superficial flirtation with Charles Malo, a young actor, slim and delicate and part-Spanish. Neither of them took it very seriously, and the affair never became physical probably because neither of them drank. Their friendship became a fait accompli nonetheless, and one invited them to parties together. Since they were not in love and since no one else attracted them, the relationship was idyllic. No jealousies, no quarrels. They never saw each other in the city.

Philip's hair, which quickly turned the color of straw, accentuated his tan. At twenty-nine, he was slim and narrow-hipped, his legs long, his features good. He was a beautiful man, yet was seldom approached by other Cherry Grovers: they sensed about him a distance from indulged sensuality, the removed air of the spectator, the observer. Circumstances had in fact isolated him. Since Johnny's departure there had been nothing other that the terrible time with the Debenham girl.

At night he often thought of Johnny or Don, projected fantasies in which one of them played the roles he most wanted to remember. The setting was nearly always the grass under the old statue, or the windswept penthouse on Park Avenue. Sometimes, as drowsiness crowded out his consciousness, Don, Johnny, and he would intermingle, a trio of touch and scent, dreamlike but quite real until the moment when thrust and tension would finally leave him. Other dreams came by themselves, in the middle of the night. Then he would awaken, spent and guilty for giving of himself more to one than to the other during the helpless puppetry of sleep-found sex.


Philip arrived at She-Ba one Friday afternoon to find Sherwyn beside himself with excitement. They had all actually been invited to a party at Millin's-Airs, the most lavish house in Cherry Grove. It belonged to Emil Zug, a well-known milliner. His custom salon on East Fifty-seventh Street barely broke even, though it attracted some of the country's richest clients; Zug had made his fortune by licensing his designs to a cheap mass manufacturer.

Sherwyn and Bates were enormously flattered, if puzzled, by the invitation. Why, even Philip had been invited.

The fact was, Zug and Farrow were legendary enemies, and when Zug discovered that Farrow's former assistant was on the island, he knew he *had* to meet him. (He also had to invite Philip's roommates and boyfriend Charles, which was a bore but could not be helped if he was to meet the kid who had put one over on Farrow.)

They spent all of Friday afternoon primping and deciding what to wear to the party. It wouldn't do to look like a sister act: white ducks and a red printed shirt for Sherwyn; yellow poplin bermudas, a coral cashmere sweater for Bates. They pooled their stocks of silk scarves, jewelry and beach shoes and selected each other's accessories. Sherwyn wore a bronze St. Christopher on a neck chain over his bare chest (shirt unbuttoned to the *third* button), and Bates tied a polka-dot scarf around his neck, cowboy-style.

Charles turned up in the light-blue terrycloth coveralls he had bought at the Squire on Lexington Avenue, where many Cherry Grovers got their beachwear. The color was perfect with his dark complexion. Philip, who without giving the matter any thought had put on a clean pair of jeans, bare-toed sandals, and a thick white turtleneck sweater, looked better than any of them.

They walked the quarter-mile to Zug's together. Millin's-Airs easily dominated the cottages around it. It was built on higher stilts, was larger (twelve rooms), and had its own electric generators, which were noisy enough to disturb Zug's neighbors.

The sun had set by the time they reached the house, and it was aglow with lights—an odd contrast to the candlelit cottages nearby. Zug greeted the four men as they entered the huge living room off the sundeck. He was tall and painfully thin, with a fringe of white hair atop a near mahogany face. His welcoming smile seemed to split the face in two, wrinkling the halves like the bellows of an accordion. He had long, simian arms and a powerful handshake.

Zug gave Sherwyn and Bates vague hellos before propelling them toward other guests. Then he steered Philip aside —barely acknowledging Charles, who was finally dismissed: "Do help yourself to a drink, Mister, ah . . ."

"Malo," said Charles, smiling apologetically and ambling off to find Sherwyn and Bates.

"I've wanted to meet you, Mr. Ross," said Zug.

"Oh?"

"You're a famous young man, you know."

"*Famous?*"

"Well, notorious may be the better word. You're the man who told Farrow to shove it."

"Well now, Mr. Zug, it wasn't quite like that. Mr. Farrow was simply too busy for the Armand-Klein project."

"Bullshit!" said Zug.

There was a pause. What the hell was all this *about?*

Zug suddenly continued. "Farrow was too fucked up for the Armand-Klein deal, that's all. It had to happen. Look, I know Fassman and he's a tough hebe—Farrow couldn't pee all over *him*. Anyway, you were a smart cookie to take over the whole thing."

Zug's bony hand patted Philip's cheek. Then he grinned and turned on his heel, leaving Philip perplexed and irritated. The man seemed to mean no harm, but then he didn't *know* Philip—everything he had said seemed presumptuous. Never mind how famous Zug was. The way he behaved smelled of Farrow, that whole Queen Mother act. Goddamn dowager bitches, both of them.

An hour later, circles had formed around celebrity guests. There was obvious rivalry over the size of these entourages, but victory eventually went to Garsett Bell, a decorator who had done dozens of homes in Nassau and Palm Beach and on upper Fifth Avenue, and now sat in a high-backed wing chair, holding court.

Runner-up to Garrett was an overage movie actress who adored Fire Island because the gay crowd dismissed her wrinkles and worshipped her. She drank a lot, and her coarse voice foghorned her presence.

Zug floated for a while from group to group, a mobile listening device. Finally he decided to sit down on a couch next to Philip and Charles, who had joined none of the circles. When Zug tried to resume their conversation, Philip barely listened. (Teach the bastard a lesson.)

The milliner was no fool. Furious, he immediately began to flirt with Charles, ignoring Philip. As shy Charles crawled into his shell, Zug became more and more aggressive. Finally, he grabbed Charles's hand and pulled him to his feet.

"I'll show you the rest of the house," he said, and began steering him toward the nearest door.

Philip had tried to ignore the whole performance. He was not jealous: Charles did not mean that much. But now he was furious that Zug thought he could steal Charles with a snap of the finger.

"That's enough, Mr. Zug," he said. "Leave Charles alone."

"Jealous?"

"No. Just leave him alone."

Charles was mortified. Zug was still holding his hand.

"Who the *hell* are you to tell me what to do in my own house?"

"Charles is *my* friend," said Philip. "Leave him *alone*." Their voices had risen; he knew he was making a scene, but he did not want to stop himself. The room was suddenly silent—even the Bell group and the actress had stopped talking—and everyone was staring. Sherwyn walked over to make peace.

Zug reached back and slapped Philip with his free hand. There was a split-second pause. Then Philip, aiming vaguely, hit Zug across the mouth with the back of his hand.

Zug let go of Charles. He put both his hands to his face, saw a little blood from his mouth on one of his hands, and collapsed against the end of the couch. Guests crowded around as he rocked, holding his face and moaning. Then he looked up and screeched:

"Get out of here, you cunt! Get out and take those other

cunts with you!" He sounded slack-lipped, his mouth was bloody. It was then that Philip saw Zug holding his false upper plate in his hand.

Philip and Charles walked out fast and kept going; the noise of the party and the electric generators was soon covered by the roar of the surf. A hundred yards farther on, Philip led Charles onto the beach through a gap in the dunes. They sat down on the sand and watched the high surf, ghostly in the moonlight. They could feel the reverberations as each wave broke. Looking south, they could see the electric lights of Millin's-Airs.

Finally Charles moved close to Philip and put his head in Philip's lap. He sobbed, "I'm sorry, Philip. It wasn't my fault."

"I know," said Philip. "I know." He stroked Charles's hair. Then he kissed him to soothe him. There was tenderness in the kiss. Nothing more.

Walking back toward She-Ba's, they spotted Sherwyn and Bates a little way ahead. They followed.

Sherwyn and Bates were solicitous. Zug had behaved abominably, and Philip was quite right to hit him back. Everyone knew what a pig Zug was, couldn't hold his tongue or keep his grubby hands to himself.

It had all happened, thought Philip, because Zug believed he'd told Farrow to shove it. The fact was, Zug was the only person he had really stood up to in his whole life.


Philip had hitched a ride in a small outboard motorboat, since there were no cars on the island, and it was too far to walk. The two young kids in the boat, local Long Islanders, had been fishing the bay. Knowing Cherry Grove, they were surprised to find this sunburned guy in faded jeans and a navy turtleneck living among the queers. They dropped him at Ocean Bay Park and Philip went in search of Howard's "brothel," as he called it.

The ramshackle bungalow was littered with the belongings of men and some girl visitors, but there were no human beings in sight. Philip called out. No answer. He decided to try the beach.

He found Howard, plus two girls and two men, huddled against a dune trying to light cigarettes in the wind.

Howard jumped to his feet when he spotted Philip and introduced his two roommates and the girls, all dressed in pants and sweaters, their bare feet tucked into the sand. After they walked back to the bungalow, the couples wandered off, and Philip and Howard headed toward the bay on one of the footpaths across the island. In a dockside restaurant they ordered sandwiches and beer and watched the water skiers. Philip half expected Howard to mention the Zug incident, but apparently Cherry Grove had kept its secrets.

They chatted for a while, uncomfortable, and then eased into talking shop.

"What do you think about Meltzer leaving?"

Philip shrugged. "I'm sorry she quit."

Howard watched his expression. He meant it. "Well, don't be. She could have stayed, it was up to her. Frankly, the stuff she was turning out can be done by any assistant."

"I just hope I wasn't the cause of it."

"What if you were? Look, Philip, the firm is changing, and if Leon had wanted her to stay, he'd have found a way to twist her arm."

"Yeah . . . I guess it's all in my lap now. Of course, I don't know much about the staple part of the line, the bread-and-butter stuff."

"Leon will tell you all about it, and I can help you. It's

just a matter of checking the sales records and spending time in the showroom. By now I can almost predict which one of our bodies will be next year's hot number."

Philip was not convinced. "How about fabrics and colors?"

"Leave that one to the boss, he's a genius for picking the big fabric. You help him with colors, you're good at them. Anyway, I can predict we'll sell a lot of black for cocktails, right?" He had made the inside joke. Black was as predictable for cocktail clothes as white was for nurses' uniforms.

"Guess you're right—and it's such a damn bore. Why not yellow? Or jade?"

"Keep dreaming."

Philip made a face. "It's just that I hate to admit women can be so dull."

"Listen, Philip," said Howard, "you go ahead and design all the new ideas you want for the *Armand* collection. That's why we started the division, so we could show some fresh stuff. Let's face it, they won't bring in the gravy, but we can use them to keep things rolling. The old Armand-Klein customers aren't dull, they're *old*. The Armand division is our insurance for the future."

"I suppose," Philip said.

Howard was enthusiastic. "The Armand stuff, your stuff, will be for selected stores only. The best stores. We've already got a date with Torrey's—they want to see the collection as soon as it's ready."

"Christ, I hope I don't have to be there when you show it," Philip said.

"Why in hell not? You designed it, didn't you? But it'll be great stuff."

Philip shook his head. "I hope you're not all disappointed, that's all."

"Come off it, chum."

They left the restaurant and then loafed along the shop-lined village street. Howard chattered away, but Philip was barely listening. He was thoroughly, *badly* frightened by the new responsibility and the real possibility of failure.

PHILIP arrived at the studio late. Cindy, his assistant, had made coffee, and he sipped it so fast he burned his mouth. The morning mail and a stack of phone messages were piled high on his desk. The walls were chalk-white squares of plastic; the floor, shiny black tile. Philip's desk was an enormous black slab of formicaed wood, and the chairs were chrome-trimmed leather. On the wall behind the desk were textile swatches and sketches, neatly lined up to show the progress of the collection. Alongside them were photographers' proofs and tear sheets from fashion magazines. Mrs. Meltzer's old room could have fitted into a corner of his studio.

Cindy's desk was at the other end of the room, near the sample machines. She was like her name, tiny and spunky. Philip had hired her straight from Parsons, and she worshipped him. She was there from eight-thirty each morning until early evening, handling Philip's letters and calls, draping, making patterns, and jollying along the sample operators. She also kept up a steady flow of coffee.

Philip checked his phone messages: Doe, Ellen Wilson, a couple of textile men—and Eric Marshall.

First he called Ellen Wilson at Torrey's. Their Armand Boutique was over three years old. A special section on the third floor, next to the French Room, it carried only Philip's styles and the scarves, shoes, belts, bags, and costume jewelry he had chosen as worthy accessories.

The boutique was small, but its volume was large and it earned a big profit. All styles in the boutique were made exclusively for the store: Armand fans *had* to go to Torrey's.

Torrey's was happy, Leon was happy, and Ellen Wilson, Torrey's better-dress buyer, had a flattering complaint: every time Philip spent a day in the boutique there were nearly twice as many sales. The customers loved his looks, manner, fashion suggestions. But Ellen always had a rough time persuading Leon to let Philip come to the store. He'd say that Philip was needed in the sample room, even on Saturdays. (He told Howard: "It's up to Torrey's to sell dresses, not our designers.")

Ellen's tone when she answered Philip's call was conspiratorial. "Look, Philip, I've talked that boss of yours into another one-day stand in the boutique. Do you mind coming on Saturday?"

"Of course not. Long as it's okay with Leon."

"Thanks. Anything I can do for *you?*"

"Glad you asked. I did some dresses in bright-yellow linen for Doe. Can you accept credit in *Ambience?*"

"Sure."

"One piece of each, that's all we'll cut. Just samples."

"Okay with me. We'll tell customers who call that we can special-order them, four weeks."

"*Five* weeks."

"Five weeks, then."

"Poor, deprived customers . . . Look, you can always say you're *so* sorry, you just sold the last one and you *can't get any more.*"

"Philip, you're in the wrong profession. You have all the instincts of a con man."

"Cheer up, it's publicity for Torrey's, isn't it?"

"Right."

"And you can always sell them something else, can't you?"

"Right."

"And how else can I make up Doe's pet ideas and get them into the magazine *and* have a store to sell them to?"

"Right!"

"Right!"

"Ellen you're a con man, too!"

"Right."

"*Ciao*, Ellen."

Philip put the receiver back in its cradle and started through the mail. He opened first a letter from his parents, who had retired to central Florida and a small house in a new development. They had finally stopped expecting a visit from Philip: his letters were full of excuses; he was always too busy, always "working on a new collection." They had not seen him since the war, almost ten years.

They wrote whenever they were lonely, and at least he answered their letters. Often, they enclosed photos. Their new house looked like all the inexpensive prefabricated "tropical retirement homes" he'd seen advertised in the Sunday tabloids. Then there were snaps of his mother in printed housedresses, or his father in a short-sleeved Hawaiian shirt, toasting the camera with orange punch.

No doubt their friends were all retired couples who, like them, had "saved up for a little home to spend the evening of their lives in peace and quiet." Philip had seen the phrase in ads published by the same Florida development company. It was probably repeated in every letter from Glory Groves, which was the name of the community. The very thought of visiting there was chilling. Nor had Philip invited them to New York; they would never understand his life, his friends, or the things that mattered to him.

Philip skimmed the letter. Nothing. His mother was "under the weather," but then, she always was.

He buzzed Howard on the intercom. "Care to guess who called at nine this morning?"

"Morning, Philippo. Who? Balenciaga?"

"Better. Eric Marshall."

"Jesus! Do you know him?"

"Well, I met him in Paris last season and we had a chat."

"That can be disastrous, you know."

"Don't think so. It was very pleasant."

"Just watch it, Philip . . ."

"I'll try."

Philip continued to stall on returning Marshall's call. He checked his schedule: Fittings. Lunch with Doe. More fittings. A particularly routine day.

Philip and Doe Perrin had a standing lunch date each Thursday. They had become close friends. Philip worked out special styles for her pages in *Ambience*—this month he had made two suits and two dresses, all in ivory wool, for a "White Winter" section. They looked marvelous, but Leon had shrugged them off. ("We'll cut a few pieces to cover the editorial credits, that's all. They're okay for publicity, but no use showing them to buyers. Nobody's going to *stock* white dresses, they get filthy in the store.")

Philip had passed on Leon's reaction to Doe, who was neither surprised nor concerned. It was routine for manufacturers to dodge special magazine styles.

Philip asked Cindy to confirm the lunch date.

"Done," she said.

"Then get me Eric Marshall." She did.

"What are you doing for lunch, Philip?" Marshall asked.

"Today? I'm afraid I have a date."

"With whom?"

Philip was so startled by the direct question that he answered it immediately: "With Doe Perrin."

"Mind if I join you?"

Philip felt trapped. "No, of course not . . . I'm sure Doe won't mind."

"Good. Where?"

"It's Doe's choice of places this week, but it's sure to be La Ronde."

"One o'clock?"

"Oh, yes. One is fine."

"A *tout à l'heure*, then." He hung up.

Although Eric Marshall was only twenty-eight, his face was already lined—each slight crease was set, now, where in middle age it would be a full-fledged wrinkle. His hair, brown and straight, fell forward over pale-gray eyes, deep-set, saved from total disappearance by long lashes.

Marshall's huge but slablike torso went straight from shoulders to hips, like a cowboy's. Although he weighed over two hundred pounds, he seemed lanky in his Brooks-cut jackets—he was six feet four inches tall. A Rhodes Scholar, he had won his rugby blue at Oxford as a wing-three quarter. He had once scored a hundred runs at cricket, and could drive three hundred yards off the golf tee. He was totally trilingual (English, German, French), with no detectable accent except in English, his mother tongue.

Those who knew his father found Eric less remarkable than most people did. How could the son of Ambassador Marshall grow into anyone *but* Eric Marshall? The forbidding gray-mustached ambassador—that *rara avis*, the American career diplomat with a great personal fortune—had never worked a day except in the service of his country. And certainly, by any standards, he was a remarkable man.

A widower, Ambassador Marshall took his only son's superior performance as a matter of course. He never praised achievements or complained about errors. The few times that Eric's grades were merely good, his father had expressed resigned disappointment.

By the age of thirteen, Eric had attended schools in Switzerland, France, and Italy. Finally he entered St. Dennis in Devonshire, one of England's ten oldest schools. It was there that he first grasped his own elusive shadow. The school was full of anachronistic trappings: formal striped trousers, cutaway morning coat, stiff collar, and top hat; thousands of vestigial taboos and customs, prefect-governed student body. Still, there was respect for the individual and isolation from parental influence. The austere, gowned masters were sentinels against influential fathers—the boys must find their own way. To Eric, it was blissful to be on his own and to know that bigger names than his father's had failed to intimidate the headmaster of St. Dennis. He learned rugby and cricket, boxed for the school, did so well academically that he passed his matriculation exams at fifteen.

Later, at Oxford, he grew curious about his own country. Other young men left to join the services, but Eric was an American, a supposed neutral. He loved Oxford and felt guilty about leaving Britain during a war; nonetheless he applied for transfer to Yale, the ambassador's alma mater. His bum rugby knee kept him 4-F, and the war ended while he was in his senior year at New Haven.

He had done as well in all areas at Yale as he had at Oxford, and his friends and professors speculated as to what career would be equal to his strength and talents.

He surprised them all by founding a magazine.

*Now!* was conceived during Eric's senior year. By graduation he had already quietly arranged for some financial backing from the bank that handled his trust fund. He got the rest of his capital from a few wealthy classmates, treating each transaction as a loan and refusing to offer stock in the magazine.

Next he teamed up with Corinne Marr, a fashion model who knew her way around Seventh Avenue. The magazine that resulted was unlike any other publication in the world. Eric saw to it that *Now!* stuck to certain guidelines:

It fascinated people to read about the famous, and celebrities loved reading about themselves, but anyone who exposed himself to *Now!* gave it a hunting license. No holds barred.

*Now!* never plugged a trend unless it was linked to someone famous. Often, the connection was pure fiction. (A movie actress was amazed to read in *Now!* that she had invented evening sweaters. Soon she believed it.)

*Now!* never yielded to pressure from advertisers. Those who threatened were told to take their ads elsewhere. (If *Now!* reaches their market, they'll buy pages in it even if they hate us.)

*Now!*'s bitchy gossip was counterbalanced by serious articles. (Some parts of *Now!* must always remain solid journalism.)

Above all, *Now!* was quick. (Better to be fast than accurate. *Now!* readers must always be first to know, even if the information is based on rumor. Readers forget errors, but they never forgive tardiness.)

Whenever *Now!* introduced a trend, it invented *Now!*-words which it used in every conceivable context, week after week. The unbelted chemise-dress was first presented with an article called "freeshape." Within two weeks everyone spoke of the freeshape look, the freeshape dress, woman, haircut, and even the freeshape car. Six months later, *Now!* decided that freeshape was *démodé* and began to use "reshape" to describe a more curvy silhouette.

Copywriters at advertising agencies all over the country changed "free" to "re," although the products they described remained unchanged. Last year's freeshape chair became this year's reshape chair, and everyone was satisfied. It was easier to change language than product.

The most obvious thing about *Now!*'s formula was that it worked. In a few short years, *Now!* grew from an experimental magazine for the garment trade into a famous fashion/

news publication with a network of photographers, correspondents, and stringers on every continent. Even the semiretired ambassador, who had publicly disowned his son's "gadfly gimmick" (*Time* 8/3/54), managed to convey his pride in Eric.

Eric was hardly famous, but his celebrity status certainly equaled or surpassed that of many people who figured prominently in the pages of *Now!* But unlike *Now!* celebrities, he guarded his personal life to the point of phobia. He never accepted invitations, and only a few intimates knew where he lived. There were many tales: he commuted by sea plane from a tiny island off New Haven, he kept a penthouse in the Plaza under a pseudonym; he was completely asexual, he was a closet homosexual; he and Corinne Marr were passionate lovers.

Corinne's private life was as much of a mystery as Eric's. Before *Now!* she had been a photographer and model, a favorite of Avedon's and *Harper's Bazaar*, on her way to a great career. Her camerawork had illustrated many of *Now!*'s early stories. She was not a creative photographer, but she was fast and ruthless. No one was safe from her telephoto lens. She trapped famous beauties at their hairdresser's, was fond of exposing sagging stockings and jowls.

In Paris she photographed new styles before the openings, shooting through open windows from nearby rooftops. As the couturiers were stringently protected by French law, this was a criminal offense; Corinne was begging for a jail term.

*Now!* went right on publishing bootlegged pictures of the Paris collections before other magazines had even sent their editors. Fortunately for Corinne, the French government could not disprove *Now!*'s claim that the photos had been submitted through a blind.

*Now!* interviews were without precedent. Designers, constitutionally vain, were trapped into indiscretions; socialites and society actresses, into wholly unintended self-revelations.

Favorite designers, on the other hand, were outrageously blurbed. When *Now!* decided that a designer was deserving, he was touted on page after page, in issue after issue. The writing style was *Nowese*, a breathless kind of present-tense prose freely borrowed from European periodicals.

*Now!* pets too often mistook momentary generosity for permanent accolade, considering themselves beyond criticism. Lulled by *Now!*'s latest flattery, a designer might express some opinions which ran counter to *Now!*'s theme of that month. The response from *Now!* was always the same. First the designer's assurance would be shaken with a few snide hints in the magazine. If he protested, *Now!* would move to open derision. If he banned *Now!*, he would be completely ignored, a condition few designers were successful enough to survive for long.

When Corinne Marr withdrew from *Now!* in 1954, there was much speculation about the facts behind her departure. Some said she had gotten fed up with all the bitchiness. Others insisted *she* had been the extremist, forced out by Eric as a result.

The rumors were laid to rest along with Corinne herself when she died of cancer four months later. The magazine continued without pause or change; *Now!* noted Corinne's passing in a brief obituary. Most of the "soft news" space in that issue was allotted to the beginning romance between a rising young politician and a fabled French beauty.

Death by cancer was not entertaining.


Eric read and initialed the copy for the lead story, checked make-up and captions. He returned two sketches for changes, then proofread his own page-ten piece. Boxed in a center column and signed with one of his many noms de plume, it was pure *Nowese*:

As the blood-red Ferrari comes to a screeching halt, the young man with the tousled hair laughs, the shocked passenger sits trembling. A *madman* . . . the man is *wild* . . . and yet his fashions are so—gentle, so serene—so filled with perfection, that balance demanded by *true* style!

Perhaps he is a *terror on wheels!* But to women all over the world he is the *Savior*, the one who can free them—this is ANTOINE VILLARD, the new young fashion *great* who is rocking Tout Paris (and Seventh Avenue, too). His collection, his serenely abandoned styles, his riotous colors are the answer everyone has been waiting for—all else is démodé— B. and G. and even She, the great one, C., must bow to this talent.

Antoine Villard. Remember it well: ANTOINE VILLARD.

The young driver jumps from the Ferrari, and all Paris is smiling with him . . .

v o x.

Eric checked the grainy photos of the Villard collection selected to prove *Now!*'s contention that it would be a year of *la vie légère*. The Easy Life. The country suit, a minor fill piece between two startling costumes in Villard's collection, would be enlarged five times over the other photos. Villard would blow his top when he saw the layout, but once he got used to the idea he'd be bragging about having started *la vie légère*.

Eric had seen designers take credit for a *Now!*-invented trend many times. Oh, well, Villard was good for a year or two until he got too full of himself . . . And wouldn't Balenciaga, Givenchy, and Chanel blow their tops when they read this piece! What had Corinne always called it?

"Puberty time." *Corinne!* He paused for only a second, then buzzed his secretary.

"Stuff's okay, put it to bed. I'll be lunching with Philip Ross at La Ronde if you need me."


For once, Doe was punctual. The waiter showed her to a table for three, which was curious since she and Philip always lunched *à deux*. She waited for him with her usual lightly concealed excitement.

Of course, she knew about him. And she was even more determined. Philip was everything she wanted: gentle and thoughtful, with charm and taste and beauty.

Whom had she known? The young men of good family she'd grown up with. Drunk and thoughtless. Or hyenas, playboys, cocksmen who prowled.

There had once been a boy, at *Science Politique* in Paris. They had adored each other but it hadn't lasted; since then there had been few others, mostly *work*. Editing was a full-time job, and Ahern a full-time boss.

The Perrins were proud of their daughter. For three hundred years Perrin women had never ventured beyond the "famous hostess" stage. Now, finally, one of them had made a real career for herself. When Doe's name on the *Ambience* masthead had finally been moved up to senior editor, three spaces under the great Ahern, there had been cables and letters of congratulation from Perrins all over America and Europe.

There he was now. Beautiful. "Hello, Philippo."

"Hi, Doe." His lips brushed her forehead.

"Who's joining us?"

"Eric Marshall."

"*Marshall?*"

"That's the second time today I've had the same reaction

—Howard Sands nearly jumped through the phone when I told him. Why does everyone get so jumpy about Eric Marshall?"

"Oh, come on, Philip, don't be naïve!"

"I'm not being naïve. I've met him, he was very nice."

"Okay, no comment. Here he comes."

Eric Marshall towered above the maître d', who had recognized him and was ushering him toward their table.

He smiled at Doe. "Sorry to butt in on your date, Miss Perrin. Glad you're here, though—I get a chance to see both of you. There are certain things I'd like to discuss . . . Martini, please, waiter! . . . How about you, Miss Perrin, Doe, may I call you that? A cocktail? Scotch? Scotch on the rocks for Miss Perrin . . . Philip?"

He had taken over, and it was obvious that Doe and Philip had capitulated. Flattered and curious, no doubt—exactly what he wanted. What was *their* story? They were supposedly inseparable . . . Great-looking girl, but then all the Perrin women were. Even her two dumb society sisters who spoke with potatoes in their mouths but were always rigged out in Balenciaga and Givenchy. Doe was different.

"Tell me all about the Armand Boutique, Philip," he said. "My editors say the clothes are marvelous."

Eric half-listened as Philip told him all the things he already knew. Ross would be no problem. Young, no name, doing some good work—good training, plenty of boy-style charm, working for an old firm . . . After Farrow, Ross *had* to be ambitious.

Doe was touting Ross, too, along with a few others, building him the way Snow and *Bazaar* had built Balenciaga; Chase and V*ogue*, Dior . . . Could be Miss Perrin had the idea that an American couture could be built. He'd have to check and see if she was on the Fashion Award panel, where she could really boost Ross. If he was right, she'd have to fight Ahern and the other old crones, plus Fassman and most of Seventh Avenue's old-timers, all the big manufacturers.

*Now!* could gain by all this. A fight was always good for readership, and this one would have larger implications than most. Corinne had nagged him for years to concentrate on Americans, never understanding that his worship of Paris was a matter of necessity, not devotion. Paris was the center of everything, and so long as Paris paid attention to *Now!*, the magazine had worldwide strength. But times changed, and perhaps Corinne's predictions would come true. It was happening in art and theater. New York was beginning to outrank Paris and London; the British wrote good plays, but nothing mattered until they clicked in New York. And these days every painter wanted a New York opening . . .

"One of my editors told me you make personal appearances at Torrey's," Eric said to Philip.

"Yes . . . Well, you see, Torrey's has the Armand Boutique in New York, and I go there sometimes to help sell the new things. In fact, I'll be there two Saturdays from now."

"And how do they introduce you to the customers? As Mr. Armand? Sorry to sound stupid, but I still have a lot to learn about Seventh Avenue. My partner Corinne used to handle New York—"

"Funny you should bring this up," said Doe. "I've been meaning to talk to Philip about just that. I think it would be smart for Armand-Klein's to publicize Philip's name. He sells one heck of a lot of clothes when he's at Torrey's."

"Come on, Doe," said Philip. "I'm really not much of a vendeur. Ask Mr. Farrow!"

She shook her head. "You forget, Philip, I know how much you sold at Farrow."

"Can we order some lunch?" asked Eric. "You'll please be my guests since I horned in."

He had sunk his first stab. Now he would stall.

Through appetizer, main course, fruit, and coffee, every time Doe or Philip got back to the original subject, Eric changed it. He spoke of Paris, London, Rome. He gossipped about couture, discussed food and restaurants, anything but American designers in general and Philip Ross in particular. Finally, he asked for the check. "I'll pop in at Torrey's and look at your things," he said, then excused himself and left.

"What was all that about, Philip?"

"Haven't the faintest."

"He said he wanted to discuss certain things, but he never really got around to them."

"Maybe he decided against telling us."

"Maybe," she said. "But I have a hunch he got what he wanted."


Four days later the cover of *Now!*, graced in the past by Chanel, Conrad Hilton, and the Windsors, carried a photo of Doe and Philip lunching at La Ronde. It was a grainy, badly lit shot, but it was effective against *Now!*'s bright red title and *Time*like frame.

The caption read: "Doe Perrin and Philip Ross. America's young designers and editors. Tomorrow's Couture?"

And on page four, in the *Now*ese reserved for the lead story:

### AMERICAN FASHION . . . TOMORROW

Philip Ross, 32, is one of the designers who are turning American Fashion into a game for the young. Ross, trained by James Farrow, one of the world's greatest, has been brushing cobwebs out of the fuddy-duddy world of old-time Seventh Avenue. As staff designer at Armand-Klein, an Olympian name in American Fashion, Ross is proving what young spirits can achieve . . . with only the slightest guidance from Paris.

166

Said Ellen Wilson, brilliant young buyer at Torrey's, Fifth Avenue: "Philip's styles have just walked out of the store. We consider his Boutique an important moneymaker."

Ambience editor, socialite Doe Perrin, 28, is also part of the revolution. Her startling pages have put grande-dame Ambience into the hands of young readers. Having climbed within masthead proximity of the great Susan Ahern, Ambience's High Priestess, "Doe" (Dorothy van Slyke) Perrin is rapidly becoming the magazine's freshest new asset. "Doe," says Fashion Photographer Sam Melnick, "has the eye. She's there, she knows how it all works . . ."

Philip Ross and Doe Perrin are only two of the rising yeast of Fashion hopefuls who are turning stale bread into snappy gâteaux. Rudi Gernreich, the dancer-turned-designer, and a battery of other talents are launching new assaults on the Fashion Everest.

Can they do it without Paris? Most experts doubt it. Paris still rules, and Paris is Fashion. Can they do it without their bosses? Will Seventh Avenue finally realize that tomorrow's Fashion stars are right under their noses, nameless but not unknown? During one recent Saturday at Torrey's Philip Ross sold dresses to twenty starry-eyed women. Said one salesgirl: "When Mr. Ross is here, we might just as well take a break."

Yet, no one knows Ross beyond Seventh Avenue, where his name is becoming legend. Manufacturers and stores never publicize these young stars.

Philip Ross who designs, Doe Perrin who edits, Ellen Wilson who buys, they will have to give us the answers tomorrow. Should Paris be worried? Hardly. Not yet. But who can predict?


"Look, I still think you've got this thing figured wrong," said Howard. "You're taking it too personally. You don't know Marshall."

"And why shouldn't I take personally a deliberate attempt to interfere with my business?" asked Leon. "And where the hell does Marshall get off trying to make me look like a fool? And who in the hell told Philip he could give interviews, he's got no business talking to the press unless he clears it with me. Did you know about this?"

"I knew Marshall had called him, that's all."

"That's *all*? Don't you think maybe I should be informed when my employees get calls from *Now!*?"

"I was sure Philip could handle things."

"And did he *handle* things! Made us look like jackasses, like we'd fold up and die without him!"

"I'd be willing to bet you he meant nothing of the kind. You've read *Now!* long enough to know how they twist things."

Leon calmed down slightly. "Well . . . next time I see Eric Marshall he'll hear a few things from me."

"I wouldn't tangle with him, Leon. What I *would* do is to milk all we can out of that story."

"I don't get you."

"Look. You can't bury Philip's name now that it's been publicized. Why not use it on our labels and ads, even in the editorials? *Now!* has made him a name—why not exploit it?"

"For Crissakes, you want to create a monster? Next thing I know the *famous* Mr. Ross will want a partnership or he'll quit and join the competition!"

"I think you know Philip better than that, Leon."

"Now I know him. But he gets a swelled head, who knows what he'll be?"

"Take a gamble. You can always fire him."

Leon swiveled his chair toward the window and looked out at Seventh Avenue. Maybe Howard was right, maybe he was being old-fashioned. It would certainly give him pleasure to take the play away from Marshall . . . Use Ross's name and *Now!* would have to give them even more publicity, because they'd "discovered" him.

"All right, Howard," he said. "What do I do?"

"Put his name on the Armand Label—'Philip Ross for Armand'—and ask the magazines to credit the clothes that way. For the time being, we can skip using his name in our ads. Until you feel more sure."

"That sounds fine. And, Howard, while you're about it—"

"What?"

"Write to Marshall, thank him for the generous coverage. Tell him we're so pleased with Philip, that we'd had plans to use his name, long before their story."

"Well, I'll be—"

"You'll be what, Howard?"

"Nothing, Leon. Nothing."


It was nearly dark in Susan Ahern's little office, which was more like a charming sitting room. She had not switched on the lights, and outside the evening sky was turning dark. The Empire State Building towered to the south like a light-spangled obelisk. To the northeast, against purple-pink clouds, apartment buildings were coming to evening life.

Susan's staff had left for the day. Everything was still after hours of phones, voices, rattling typewriters. The twentieth floor, where twenty-five underpaid young women helped five great professionals to put together *Ambience*, was deserted.

New York, thought Susan, was the most exciting of all cities, the most strenuous, the most rewarding. And the most threatening. London was in decay, Paris in mothballs—no matter how hard they tried to perfume it with fashion and food. Was New York getting to be too much for her? She wondered how long she would be able to keep pace.

Her close friends were old friends, literally *old* friends. She had always felt young, she encouraged young editors, but did she know them? Were they part of her life, or was she just an observer, like some benevolent great aunt?

She was not annoyed by the *Now!* story. Knowing Eric Marshall, she understood what was behind the article. He was trying to provoke a brouhaha and she, for one, would never give him the satisfaction. She had already calmed down *Ambience*'s publisher and blunted the jealousies of her two other senior editors who were ready to slash Doe. She had even reassured Doe, who was mortified. Her guess was that the girl was genuinely shocked. Still, the whole thing might make her face up to her ambitions. Sooner or later Doe would aim for the top, and why not?

But not yet. Not now. Not until Susan was ready to hand over the magazine. Doe was good, of course. Her background was the best, and her taste could not be faulted. But what of her ambition? Would Doe have the strength to resist the cheap, the vulgar, the gimmicky, even if it meant a loss of revenue? Would she fight everyone, even the publisher, to keep *Ambience* unique, even at the price of being scooped by the young magazines?

Susan stood up, took her coat from the closet, picked up her purse and left the office. Waiting for the elevator, she imagined Leon Fassman's face when he saw Philip on *Now!*'s cover, and laughed out loud.

*Pauvre Leon!*

Ellen Wilson faced the president of Torrey's resolutely, and waited for him to speak. Paul Bender looked tough, even when all was well. He had high cheekbones, steel-gray short hair, pale eyes under bushy dark brows, a harsh mouth, and a tall, forbidding figure. He made her think of an elegant falcon, circling silently.

A circling falcon . . . despite the fact that she of all people knew how gentle he could be. Paul, though married, was her life, her love. She was his mistress. There was no way around it. The antique word accurately described her position. Their affair was in its sixth year.

No amount of rationalizing about an alcoholic wife or Catholic strictures could alter the facts. Paul could not and would not get a divorce. He would give of himself with all his heart and body and resources, but he would never marry her.

She was no longer unhappy, as she had been at the beginning. She had adjusted to the structure of their lives. During the day she was a buyer—a very good one—in the store he ran. Several nights a week he made love to her, and in every waking moment she was his beloved and he was hers.

It had all been settled long ago, and now she would not have it any other way. If this was all they would ever have, she accepted it and was deeply thankful for being loved by him.

Just now, though, she was in trouble.

"Don't you realize," Paul said, "that we have people whose job it is to take care of the store's public image?"

"Of course I do."

"Then how in blazes did this interview come about?"

"It wasn't an interview, Paul! It was just a phone call from some gal at *Now!* She asked about a lot of other things, all innocuous, like what colors we're selling and what fabrics. They call often with questions like that."

"Then how did the whole Ross matter come up?"

"I've been trying to figure it out. She asked how the Armand Boutique was doing, and I said fine. Then she asked if there was more sold on Saturdays, a silly question, and I said of course. Then she asked about Ross. It all seemed quite innocent. How she got the quote from a salesgirl I'll never know. The girls swear they spoke to no one from the press. But how would they know a customer from a reporter?"

"Well, Ellen, it's a helluva mess. I'm sure the Bergdorf people and the rest of them think we're out of our minds casting doubt on Seventh Avenue."

"We did no such thing!"

"*We* didn't. But the article implies that we're rocking the boat."

"They know better!"

"I hope so! But, worse, what about the Amalgamated people? How will *they* react?"

"I'll bet they'll think we're alive and creative."

"Creative or irresponsible? How our manufacturers handle their designers is none of our business. Although I will admit one thing"—his mouth softened almost to a smile—"I had a call from Tom Armbrust at Amalgamated, congratulating me on the article."

"You *see?*"

"I see that Tom Armbrust is an opportunistic son of a bitch who thinks any publicity is all right so long as they spell Torrey's right."

"Now, honestly, what harm was there in the article?"

"We've always let our manufacturers run their own show. We don't interfere. The article suggests that we're creating our own designer names and the manufacturers be damned."

"Well, isn't that happening already? Lord & Taylor is promoting a whole group of new designers, all American."

"They'll regret it. Wait till the manufacturers get on their hind legs. I mean the *big* houses—you can't just shove the top firms around."

"Maybe. Meanwhile they're selling a lot of clothes from the new designers."

"Inexpensive stuff, aimed at kids!"

172

"Not forever—"

"All right, Ellen." He smiled, but it was the boss's smile, not the lover's. "Now get out of here. And in the future please check the PR department before you make statements."

She left his oak-paneled office, smiled at his ancient secretary, and walked slowly to the elevator.

Of course the Amalgamated deal mattered, and not just to Torrey's. If the retail syndicate bought a Fifth Avenue store like Torrey's, it would be the crown jewel in their countrywide chain. And Paul, running Torrey's for a family estate, naturally hoped that Amalgamated would go through with the deal. She knew he wanted to open branches in the suburbs, redecorate three sales floors, bring expensive new machinery into their billing and merchandising operations, use new promotional techniques, pension off some staff members, and train new ones. Torrey's, though profitable, lacked that kind of capital. And the board had turned down Paul's request for a long-term bank loan.

The Amalgamated offer was lucrative, including a block of their stock and additional options as well as a fifteen-year contract. Paul had told her they were within 5 percent of a deal and Ellen was sure he would clinch it within the month. She was sorry he had been thrown off stride, if only momentarily, although she believed the *Now!* story would have no real effect on the deal. Obviously, Amalgamated had *chosen* not to find the article detrimental.

Paul looked tired. Once the deal was signed, they could go to Florida or the Bahamas (observing all the nonsensical proprieties, of course). They needed some sunshine, and more time together.

Paul watched Ellen's back as she left the office. She had wide shoulders, like a boy's, and a small rear, where he loved to put his hand and feel the muscles move. For a brief moment he was tempted to call after her, to pull her back into his office and *touch* her—a thing he had never done, and would never do. It was hard enough as it was to keep the two amazing relationships they had, professional and personal, from damaging one another.

He felt lousy, anyway. When he went for his checkup tomorrow he'd have to get a prescription for those chest pains and for something to help him sleep the nights he wasn't with Ellen. He was *tired* of being tired.

Dr. Sam Blyden dried his hands and tossed his paper towel into the basket. "Paul," he said, "you're in fine shape. You just need a rest."

"How about the chest?"

"I can't find a thing wrong with your heart, if that's what you mean. It's probably muscular."

"You're the doctor."

"First time I heard that was—God, I hate to think how long ago. Now get dressed before my nurse comes in and sees the great Paul Bender in his drawers. She has a low threshold for orgasm!"

Paul Bender reached for his shirt, wincing slightly as he put his arms into the sleeves.

The Carey town car Philip had hired for the occasion
pulled up in front of the Corhans' brownstone on East
Seventy-seventh. Their butler greeted Doe by name, took
their coats, and led them up the stairway to a large sitting
room where Dolores Corhan greeted them. She was in her
middle thirties, tall and supergroomed. When Philip was
introduced, she said, "Doe told me she was bringing you.
That was a smashing picture of both of you on the cover of
*Now!*"

Philip grinned. "Do you read *Now!?*"

"My dear, everybody does. Even my husband enjoys it,
and he doesn't give a rap about fashion . . ."

Within twenty minutes all the guests had arrived, an
even dozen. They all knew Doe, who introduced Philip to a
novelist and his socialite wife, and to two handsome young
couples Philip recognized from the columns. There were
two people Philip knew: Don Jeffson, the pretty young
socialite actor from that night in El Morocco, and Julia
Debenham, Don's date for the evening. Philip said hello
to her, then reminded Jeffson that they had met.

"You were on your way to Hollywood. Johnny Evans-
Greene introduced us."

Jeffson, flashing very white teeth in a saddle-tanned face,
was cordial. "Johnny? He was in Los Angeles last month,
saw him at a party in Beverly Hills. The old boy looked a

bit beat up, but he's okay, I guess . . . Same old Johnny, you know."

"Adore your Armand things, Philip," said Julia. "Bought a *ton!*" She was wearing a dress from the boutique.

Philip had not known that Johnny was back in America. He wanted to find out more, but decided against asking. Instead he said, "What's your latest, Don?"

"Well," Jefferson said, "I've got two films in the can. We'll just have to see how things go once they've been released."

"I heard they're marvelous," Julia said. "They were produced by a friend of mine." She mentioned a Hollywood producer better known for his New York/Palm Beach/Acapulco social climbing than for making successful films.

"Meantime," said Jefferson, "I've got me a house in Malibu and an old Bentley and this wild gal here, if she'll only come to visit me."

Julia giggled. "Better pay off the house before you have guests," she said.

"Don't be old-fashioned; that's what I want you *there* for. To pay off the house *and* the Bentley!"

She loved it. "You're impossible, and the worst part is I know you mean every word you're saying."

"Sure, baby!" He turned on another dazzling smile.

They all found their way downstairs to the dining room, which was separated from the floodlit garden by a glass wall. The effect was startling, as if they were dining outdoors. Philip's place card was next to Doe's. "Dolores only separates married couples," she said. "She usually allows lovers to sit together."

Later, during dinner, Doe suddenly said, "Speaking of lovers, I had no idea Johnny was back in the country."

How had she meant that? Was she implying that Johnny

was his lover or did she just mean he was a loverboy? Maybe Doe was high . . . They'd had only two drinks before dinner; more likely, she was jealous. He was sure she knew the whole story, had known since Ahern's party, long ago . . . Best to leave it alone.

Doe, apparently, was not so inclined. "How long has it *been* since you've seen Johnny?" she asked.

"Not since I went to work for Farrow."

"That's quite a while . . . Do you miss him?"

"No, not really. My life is so different now. Look, Doe— let's drop it."

"All right, darling."

"Don't be mad, okay?"

"I'm not mad."

But the two of them were like automatons for the rest of the evening. They chatted and smiled mechanically, waiting for the first decent moment to leave.

She relaxed a little once they were in the car. "How's your new place coming?"

"It's perfect for me. There's a lot left to be done, though. The bathroom isn't papered yet, and the rugs have to be nailed down. And I haven't hung any paintings yet."

"I'd like to see it, anyway. Let's go up."

Philip had wanted to keep Doe away until he had finished decorating, but when she persisted he gave in. It was obvious that she wanted—needed—to be alone with him. He hoped it was not to talk about Johnny.

Doe's hands were wide, long-fingered, and tanned, the nails unpolished and close-trimmed. She shook hands like a man; her right was strong from tennis, and she could drive a golf ball like a pro. Boyish and long-limbed, she walked with easy, loose strides, feet pointing straight ahead,

177

using the whole sole from heel to toes. Yet somehow there was nothing masculine about her.

After exclaiming over the terrace onto which each room opened, poking into every corner, and inspecting every closet, she collapsed on the living room couch.

". . . Perfect for you, you're right," she said. "Plenty of room, but not—*big*. And I love the French windows."

Philip was ridiculously pleased at her enthusiasm. "You're the only one I really wanted to see it," he said.

For a while they were quiet, involved in their separate thoughts. Then Philip asked, "Do you think Jeffson will ever make it?"

"As an actor?"

"Yes."

She spoke absent-mindedly: "I dunno. But I'm not worrying about *that* boy. He'll get by."

"How do you mean?"

She did not answer.

"Doe, what do you mean, he'll get by?"

She blinked. "Sorry, Philip, I wasn't listening."

"What were you thinking about?"

"They're not happy thoughts . . . Look, Philip, I'd rather not explain but . . . can I stay tonight?"

"Well, of *course*, Doe."

"Don't ask questions."

"I won't."

"I can sleep on the couch."

"Of course you won't. You'll sleep in the bed, and I'll sleep here."

"All right. Now, how about some music?"

Philip fiddled with the radio until he got some Gleason. "Funny Valentine." Junky, but it suited the mood.

Doe was obviously not going to talk. It occurred to him

that although they saw a great deal of each other, he knew very little about her private life. Of course he'd heard all about her family, had read about her in the columns for years. Just a few months ago there'd been items in them about her romance with Tony Martán, a Brazilian playboy people said had fucked his way through three continents. It seemed unlikely, unbelievable. Doe seemed the last girl to be involved with such a man.

Philip had only seen photos, but Martán had the kind of good looks that went perfectly with his crazy reputation as a wild man. Still, even if she found him attractive, surely Doe was too detached, too sure of herself, to be involved with someone so—lurid.

Tonight was the first time Philip had been allowed a look at the other Doe. He was intrigued, curious; he did not want her to say, "Christ, Philippo, I must be off my rocker. Let's finish the coffee and I'll be trundling home." That would be the old Doe. He did not want this new one to slip away.

She showed no change of mood as they sat listening to the music. At 1 A.M. the announcer gave a news summary and Doe stirred. "Mind if we turn in?" she said.

He made up the couch while she undressed in the bedroom. She reappeared wearing a pair of his pajamas, the legs and sleeves rolled up.

"Thanks, Philippo. For the couch, and for not asking questions."

"Okay, Doe. I hope—"

"What?"

"Nothing. Sleep well."

He closed the bedroom door. The living room was bright with moonlight because there were no curtains. He switched off the lamp near the couch and lay down atop the blanket.

He had entered her life, if only for a peek. Now they were new to each other. Who could have hurt her, unless it was the Brazilian?

Martán, tall and dark. Long hair. That massive chest . . . Did Martán have strong arms, huge thighs, hair on his back? Did his hands hurt Doe? Did he drive in, and did Doe shout or moan or whisper? What did she say when Martán spread her. Did she fight, did she love him back, did she want to get it from him? Did she want Martán now, tonight, next door in bed this very second?

The bedroom door opened. Doe came to the couch in two long strides. She put herself in Philip's arms and he held her, automatically, until he sensed that with her he was holding—Martán, the smell of him, the feel of him. Philip grew big thinking of the massive, dark-skinned man. Doe's hand closed around his bigness, and Philip shut his eyes. There was no Doe—only Martán who was Doe. Martán's skin. Martán's mouth and tongue moving downward, all the way down. Doe groaned, and it was Martán who made her groan as Philip shuddered.

When it was over, he was sobbing and she was holding him close the way she might a small boy. She rocked him. "Everything is all right, darling, it's all right now . . ."

When he had finally calmed down, she took his face in both her hands and looked into his eyes, still filled with tears.

"Philip. Did you like what I did to you?"

"Yes."

"Will you let me love you again?"

"Yes."

"Soon?"

He simply nodded.

He fell asleep in her arms. She moved his head to the pillow, went into the bedroom, and wrote him a note on the pad next to his bed, dressed, and left the apartment without waking him.

The note said: "Thank you, my darling."

No other man had ever been hers, alone. Now, Philip was hers. She had begun him, and after tonight she would always own Philip, beautiful Philip. For once in her life she was strong and sure about a relationship with a man.

She had never loved one who knew her value. Cheap flirts had taken men away from her. Lovers had come to her from other legs and arms and mouths, she a way station, a stopoff, a casual link in the chain of their cocksmanship. They never needed her brains or friendship or strength; so often there was only bed and fucking and their pride in their own pubic athletics. "I'll make you come again, Doe . . . Let me eat you, Doe . . . Did you like it? Has anyone fucked you better?" That was all over now.

She would give *all* of herself to Philip.

The bell woke him. Thinking it was the alarm clock, Philip rushed to the bedroom to shut it off. The clock was silent, and the bed was empty. He found Doe's note, read it, and immediately felt guilty. She had brought him Martán; he had cheated her.

His back ached from sleeping on the narrow couch. He needed coffee, a shower. The bell rang again, and he started. He was not used to the sounds of the new apartment. It must have been the doorbell which had waked him. He wrapped a towel around his waist and went to answer it.

The scruffy delivery man outside handed him a telegram. Philip signed for it, realized he had no change, and rushed into the bedroom to get the man a quarter. He noticed for the first time that it was 6 A.M., an hour before he usually awoke. When he had handed the man his tip and closed the door, he opened the telegram.

His mother had died.

He was expected to attend the funeral in Florida.

He looked at the paper in his hands. Nothing. He should have felt something, he knew that. But there was *nothing*. His name was spelled "Roth."

She had died during the night, while Doe Perrin was blowing her son.

He stood in the middle of the living room. The towel had slipped from his waist; he was naked, like a little boy. He began to tremble.

It was important for him to think. No, if he started thinking he would start to feel something, guilt, anything. He would call Doe—no!

He dialed Howard's number.

"What is it, Philip?"

"Did I wake you?"

"Yeah. What's the matter?"

"Howard, could you come over?"

"What's *wrong*?"

"Nothing. Which is what's wrong. Look, I don't want to talk over the phone, I have to see you."

"I'll be right over."

When Howard arrived Philip was half-dressed, his hands still trembling. Howard took one look at him and poured him a glass of scotch.

"You look like you need it."

Philip automatically took a huge swallow, choked as the liquor hit his stomach, and slumped on the couch. Howard noticed the sheets. None of his business.

"Howard, there's something you've got to do for me." He handed over the telegram.

"God, Philip, I'm sorry . . ."

"I've got to go to Florida for the funeral. Explain to Leon."

"Of course."

"And look . . . call Doe Perrin. Tell her about this, I don't want to talk to her. Tell her I'll call her when I get to Florida. She'll understand."

"Okay. Shall I help you pack?"

"Thanks, I'll manage."

"Then let me make reservations for you."

"All right. It's near Sebring."

"Is that where the sports-car races are?"

"Yes."

Howard went to the phone. Obviously, there was nothing he could say that would help.


The country was flat and the heat made the road ahead shimmer. The taxi, an overused veteran of stop-and-go Miami traffic, creaked and groaned on the open road. As they neared Avon Park, the orange blossoms announced themselves by their scent. From then on, the road led through the groves.

The taxi driver's neck was creased and purple-red, as if he were a farmer and not a hackie. He pulled into a gas station and asked directions in a sing-song whine, even the mono-syllables of which were pronounced with the interlaced vowels of the Florida cracker.

Philip tried to find a comfortable position, but the taxi's back seat was spring-lumped on both sides. He tried once more to remember his mother's face, the way she had looked the last time he saw her before he enlisted. It was no use; all he could see was the sunburned, old-looking woman in the last snapshots from Glory Groves, her gray hair carefully crimped into place just like the other women in the same photos. Obviously they all went to the same beauty parlor.

At last they came to a sign and turned off the main highway. Minutes later they stopped in front of the house. Philip recognized it from the snapshots, but then he had mistaken several other houses on the same street for his parents'.

Was she—it—still in the house? Or had they moved her to a funeral parlor? He felt an overpowering, almost nauseous reluctance to get out.

The driver opened the door, and Philip took three steps to the aluminum screen door. Slowly he entered the dark inside. His father was watching television. The sound was turned low, probably so the neighbors would not be able to hear.

For a moment Henry Ross did not recognize his son. Then he switched off the TV and stood up. He was shorter than Philip remembered him, and fatter, and quite bald.

"Hello, Dad. I—I'm so sorry."

Henry Ross nodded. Then he said, "Sit down, Philip. Where's your luggage?"

"I only brought this small bag. I'll have to leave right after—"

"Fine. If you'd like some juice, it's in the icebox. Fresh-squeezed."

The kitchen was off the living room. Everything was pearlized pink—refrigerator, washing machine, dishwasher. There was a note pad on the wall with a shopping list in his mother's neat, labored Germanic script: bread, toilet paper, Kleenex, Lux. He found a bottle of orange juice in the refrigerator and poured it into a decorated dime-store glass.

In the living room, his father was in front of the TV again, although he had not turned it back on.

"There were some notices in the papers, Philip." He pulled some clippings from his shirt pocket.

Anna Ross, the wife of Warrant Officer (SG) Henry Ross, U.S.A. (Ret.) passed away suddenly this morning. Mrs. Ross, born in Germany, became a naturalized citizen in 1923. She was on the Board of Glory Groves Charities and her cookery brightened many bazaars and picnics. She is survived by her husband and an only son, Philip, who is active in the garment industry in New York City. Her many friends will mourn her passing. Funeral services at the First Lutheran Church of the Groves at 3:00 P.M., Thursday, February 11th.

"You want one, son? I've got quite a few." His father pulled copies of the same article from an end-table drawer. Philip did not want one, but he took it anyway.

There was a knock on the door.

"Henry?" A woman's voice.

"Come in. Philip is here."

A small, quick-moving woman came through the door with an air of expectancy. Henry Ross did not get up. Pointing at Philip, he said, "This is my son, Philip." Then he shifted his finger to the woman. "That's Emily. She's been helping out ever since it happened."

"I do what I can," she said in a tinny voice. "Whenever we're not too busy, at the diner."

"Emily works at Ridgeley's. That's the diner on the main highway—you probably saw it." Philip did not remember noticing a diner.

The three of them fell silent, each unable or unwilling to speak. Philip finally spoke to her:

"Thanks for helping Dad."

"Okay. It's okay," she nodded and smiled.

She was about forty, and quite pretty. "Emily" was embroidered on the left front pocket of her waitress uniform. Her hands were well kept, the nails were painted red. Despite her thick-soled white shoes, she had slim ankles and good legs. Her reddish hair was styled in a thick beehive, carefully pinned into place.

"Anyway, you okay then, Henry?" she said.

The older man nodded. Emily held out her hand to Philip. "Nice t've met you, Phil."

She waved at them and left the house. When they heard her drive away, Henry Ross said, "She's a friend. She lives over in Sebring, but she works in Ridgeley's."

Whatever chance or need there had been for them to talk had been stunted by Emily's visit. Father and son, reunited after years, had nothing to say to each other.

A grave had been hastily gouged out by a bulldozer, which still stood in the groves nearby. The smell of orange blossoms was overwhelming. The pastor, a tall man with a Minnesota voice, read standard phrases from a slip of paper in his open prayer book. It was over quickly, and Philip never once looked at the coffin, even while it was being lowered by two workmen.

Neighbors from Glory Groves shook Philip's hand and murmured condolences.

Afterward, they all sat around the living room, the only sound that of the men opening cans of beer and sipping at them with little smacking noises, careful to be as quiet as they could. As the afternoon moved on, a panic grabbed Philip, sitting wordlessly between two heavy-set, elderly men. He could never stay the night.

Finally he stood up and said, "Dad, you know I have to get back . . ."

Henry Ross seemed unconcerned. He shook Philip's hand without getting up and said, "All right, son, stay well." His face showed nothing, not disappointment nor pain nor even friendliness.

"Godday'm!" said the taxi driver.

On the road to Miami ahead of them there was nothing, so Philip looked through the rear window. They were being tailgated by a big white station wagon towing a race car on a trailer. The station wagon tried to pass, but couldn't manage it quickly enough with the taxi's speed.

The taxi driver pulled over as far as he could, and the station wagon began to pass. When it was alongside them, a girl in the back seat leaned out of the window and shouted something, waving. It was Dolores Corhan, and her husband was in the back with her. The station wagon passed them and pulled over.

"Hey, they're friends of mine," Philip told the driver. "Stop the car."

They rolled to a halt behind the trailer, and Philip got out.

"Small world." It was Dan Corhan, smiling. "You on your way to Sebring?"

"No, I was visiting someone near here. I'm on my way back to Miami to catch a plane."

"Why don't you hang around for the races Sunday? We've got a suite at Avon Lodge. Stay with us."

"Thanks, Dan, but I really should get back."

"Oh, come on," Dolores said. "It's Friday. There can't be anything doing over the weekend!"

Anything to forget that funeral and the wake and his father. The hell with it, thought Philip. He paid off the cab driver, who seemed happy to be rid of his uncommunicative passenger. Then he put his bag into the back of the station wagon, on top of a stack of racing tires. He was introduced to the driver, Carlos Langmann, a Mexican amateur racer.

Dolores pointed her thumb back to the trailer: "That's a three-liter Mondial Ferrari, the car Carlos will be racing. Just flown in from Italy." She had certainly picked up the language.

The Mexican shrugged his shoulders. "I'm going to try to drive that monster, I was not doing so hot, today."

"We were at the track, it's open for practice," said Dolores. "We were timing Carlos." She touched the two stopwatches on leather thongs around her neck. She was wearing chino pants and a short-sleeved knit shirt. There was a man's straw hat on her head, but despite the wide brim, the tip of her nose was burned red.

"Tomorrow you'll come to the track with us."

"Maybe tomorrow I can turn in a few better lap times for you," said Langmann.

They turned off the highway into a wide palm-flanked driveway which curved toward a large Spanish-style house. When they pulled up to the pink stucco porch, an attendant in a white uniform came out to meet them.

"I'll park the rig, Señor Langmann."

They walked into the lobby, dark and cool. A reception desk at the end was the first indication that this was a hotel. There had been no signs on the highway.

Upstairs, in a sunny room adjoining Dolores and Dan's, Philip looked out his window at the surprisingly large grounds. Next to the main house were a deserted swimming pool and a caddy house, which led to a beautiful golf course.

On a gravel-covered parking lot, surrounded by manicured hedges, was an assortment of the world's finest sports racing cars: Ferraris and Maseratis, Aston-Martins, Allards, Jaguars. Looking down on their large racing numbers, Philip thought that they resembled thoroughbreds in the stalls before paddock time.

A rabbit shot across the lawn and ducked into the hedges. Everything was very still.

The quiet was broken by a knock from the Corhans' bedroom. "Philip . . . take a shower and relax," called Dan. "We'll meet you in the bar."

Philip, still in his funeral-dark suit, asked if he could borrow some clothes. Corhan pointed toward the closet. "Help yourself. Something will fit." He was wearing slim white ducks, a yellow V-neck pullover, and lightweight suede loafers over bare feet.

Philip found a pair of red pants and some blue canvas espadrilles. He showered and put them on, adding a clean white shirt of his own which he left open at the throat, rolling the sleeves to the elbow. Not bad for an improvisation. He was a little pale, but tomorrow would take care of that.

The bar was noisy. Philip, walking in, heard conversations in Italian, French, Spanish, and some very pukka English.

The Corhans were sitting at the bar with Langmann and two other Mexicans. Philip also noticed a slim American girl, obviously "society." She had all the signs: a strong-jawed face and clamp-jawed speech. The center of attention seemed to be a fair-haired Englishman introduced to Philip as Bill Tenley. Philip sat down next to him.

"Of course," Tenley said, "you didn't see me having this drink, did you?"

Philip was puzzled. "Why?"

"Not supposed to booze, you know. I'm racing Sunday."

"The best," put in Carlos Langmann. "In case you didn't know. The *jefe*, the world's champion. And not just behind the wheel."

"Cut it out, Carlos," said Tenley.

"You done your scouting yet?" Langmann looked at the women around the room.

Tenley seemed more willing to talk about his sexual prowess than his racing reputation. "Yeah, it's all lined up. Stars and understudies."

"Don't know how you do it."

"With my cock."

Langmann laughed. "You know what I mean, chico."

"Yeah, well, I just like to fuck. What's wrong with that?"

He stood up, and Philip was surprised to see that Tenley was short, though compactly built, wide-shouldered like a featherweight boxer. He grinned and Philip could see that his front teeth were false. But it was a handsome grin and a handsome face. A deep scar ran from the end of his right eyebrow across his right cheek and upper lip, whitish against his tanned skin. His hair was flecked with gray, although he looked in his mid-thirties. He waved once and left the room, dodging tables and greeters. He was obviously the most famous man in the room—and certainly the most attractive. Philip was sorry to see him go.

Langmann shook his head. "You know," he said to Philip, "that man really is *loco*. He is the top professional of them all, probably of all time. Of course I"—he shrugged—"I am only an amateur. I buy my own cars, like a fool. And I shouldn't be racing anyway, I should be home in Mexico taking care of the family business. But, *diós*, you only live once."

"Is Tenley always so ants-in-the-pants?"

"Hot in the pants, my friend. Always. And you know, five months ago we all thought he was dead. Had a bad shunt, as we say. A lousy accident."

"Is that where he got the scar on his face?"

"That was the least of it. A broken cheekbone, jaw, all his teeth knocked out . . . Now he has to *warn* a woman before he kisses her."

"Because of the teeth?"

"*Sí*. You noticed? And when he drives he never wears them, so if he crashes he doesn't choke on them. This morning his mechanic had to rush to him after practice so Tenley would not sound like a grandmother when they interviewed him on television."

Philip laughed. "Why does a man go on with this thing when he's nearly been killed?" he asked.

"Oh," Langmann shook his head, "they write a lot of junk about the death wish and all that, but how else could Bill have become one of the big men in Europe and South America? He was born poor, his father was a factory worker, and everywhere in the world except in the States racing drivers make out better than movie stars. Everyone fusses, and besides, Tenley is very tight with the money, so he stashes away *mucho* in Switzerland. He makes a lot, you know."

"He should," said Philip. "All that risk . . . Have you ever crashed?"

"*Hombre!* Of course. You can't help it. But here I am, and it won't happen Sunday."

Langmann waved at a tall man who had just entered the dimly lit bar. The American socialite, who had said nothing since Tenley left, came to life as the man threaded his way through the tables.

"Johnny!" she called out, and the man turned toward the bar.

It was *Johnny*.


Three A.M., and Philip had been drunk since midnight. What he could see of the room in the darkness seemed to be shifting sideways, particularly the ceiling.

He clutched Johnny's bare shoulder and tried to say, "Christ—I'm drunk!" but he had trouble forming the words and gave up. He wanted to stand, but Johnny pushed him back onto the bed. Johnny was even drunker than Philip, but he was stronger, and when Philip tried to strain against his hand, Johnny slapped him. It did not hurt. Then Johnny's hands clamped his face and his mouth was on his.

For a moment the booze made Philip feel sick, but then the stronger feeling took hold and they made love, terrible love, with hands, fists, hard elbows. It was more like a drunken fight, and each caress bruised and slashed and hammered.

Whenever they raced, at Monaco or Le Mans or Sebring, Johnny was there. He traveled the same nomadic circuit as the drivers. He had once tried sports-car racing in Hawaii, but he had not enjoyed it. He preferred to trim an aircraft or a sailboat and then let the craft perform instead of working every goddamn second the way a horseman, skier, or race driver did. He was not competitive in the usual sense of the word. He liked to win in the long pull, the way you did at sailing.

He was happy he had found Philip again, and pleased at the changes in him. Philip was someone, now, or close to it. There was sophistication there, and toughness, not just the snot-puss ambition of a kid willing to be kept. Pity they'd both been boozed up last night, but there would be other nights. He felt old, tired. Partly because of last night, but also because literally following the races was beginning to seem silly. He no longer felt that little twinge of envy when he compared himself to the drivers. He was starting to feel sorry for them.

Johnny and Philip were on the balcony of the Auto Racing Club, in the middle of the pits overlooking the track. The start of the race was twenty minutes away.

Outside was the maelstrom of mechanics, journalists, drivers, and hangers-on. Photographers, everywhere. The club, expensive and exclusive, was an oasis in the midst of turmoil. Its members could watch the cars screech by while they got loaded on martinis with overgroomed young society women who had flown in from Palm Beach or Rome or Paris. This week, Sebring was the thing to do, the place to be.

Down below on the oil-streaked concrete the cars were being warmed up. Knowing hands worked on the engines, tuning them to the limit, amid great noise and clouds of exhaust fumes.

The drivers stood nearby, helmets slung over their arms, goggles around their necks. Soon, they would stand on their mark across the track from their cars. At the drop of the starter's flag, they would run to their cars, jump into the cockpits, and launch themselves onto the track with howling engines and smoldering rear tires. They would race for twelve hours over the twists and turns and along the wide straightaways of the Sebring track, switching with their relief drivers every four hours. They might crash in flames or end up under their overturned cars, unhurt, completely conscious, praying that flag men would lift the car off them before dripping gasoline hit the red-hot exhaust manifolds.

Johnny toasted Philip, who was leaning over the railing, looking down into the infield. Philip looked fresh, as though the hard night had never happened. Johnny shook his head. The years!

Tenley and Langmann were standing behind the club on the grass. Both were wearing poplin coveralls and driving gloves. Tenley was pulling on his helmet, Langmann polishing his goggles.

"Look, it's no good trying to beat everybody to the start," said Tenley. "You've got twelve hours. What matters is who finishes, not who gets away first."

"But you, Bill, you always get away first," Langmann said, and moved away.

Tenley laughed. "I have to," he called after him. "That's what I get paid for!"

It was true. Tenley's backers expected him to lead each race from beginning to end, and he always tried to give them their money's worth. They expected him to win because he was the best, and they paid him enormous sums. He did not doubt his ability to deliver, and they had never questioned it. The fans took bets on him, he was their god. But after the last crash . . . Well, they would see, the automobile executives back in Europe and the journalists and the racing fans. They would—wait.

Tenley's scar hurt, as if to remind him that he had not raced since then, and his stomach hurt where Lila had bitten him last night. He knew he should have been sleeping instead of fucking, but tail is tail, and Lila was particularly lively tail, and he'd banged her until she couldn't take any more. He grinned, thinking of her up there on the club terrace, playing the little Connecticut debutante—she must have a helluva sore pussy. Her ritzy Greenwich parents would be surprised to know that when they brought her to Sebring, their darling daughter was rolled and chewed by an expert, by Old Iron Prick Bill Tenley, all-time great driver and cocksman . . .

He tried to remember her last name, but he couldn't. In the sack, he had called her "Cunty." He'd better watch it, or he'd call her that in public. After the race . . . Would there be any "after the race"? Or was this it, the end, last night the last piece of tail he'd ever have, the last time he'd come? Not to think that way. Always got away with it before. Even this last time when the doctors spent weeks clucking their tongues and poking his aching body. They had given him up, all except that little Scottish nurse who came by at night to blow him, when the hospital was quiet and his pain was so bad he couldn't sleep. Her busy little mouth had been a damn good anesthetic . . .

He watched Langmann pull at the diagonal zipper of his coveralls and tuck in the scarf.

Fuck those rich boys, he thought. They drive big expensive cars but don't know their asses from their . . . Still, he'd have to race in Mexico come May, and Langmann had a big house in Acapulco and plenty of pussy on the string. Worth being nice to the rich boys. Anyway, a few years ago it had been *all* rich boys, all the drivers Italian contes and German barons and English "sirs" and he, Tenley, feeling like the hall porter whenever he was with them. But now he was *número uno*, and they were all ass-kissing him, and he could tell them all to bugger off.

He waved at Langmann and called to him: *"Merde!"* Then he zipped up his coveralls and walked toward his pit.


Philip was bored and hung over and grimy. The start was a real heart stopper, and during the first forty laps it had been exciting to watch the cars howling past the stands singly or in packs. He tried to keep track of Langmann's yellow number 32 and Tenley's blue number 1, but he lost count after a while. He had no idea who was in what position except for Tenley, who was leading—as everybody obviously expected. The crowd at the club had begun to drink. Except for an occasional look at the track, they had forgotten the race. Their interest would return at the first driver change, about two hours later. Meanwhile, they could talk Palm Beach and Europe or the latest Swiss banking laws. Or try to score.

Johnny was with a blonde, apparently an old friend. He'd introduced Philip, but the girl wanted to talk fashion. He wasn't in the mood, so he'd switched her off. He waved at a waiter for another drink and nearly hit a suntanned brunette who stood behind him, looking through binoculars at the back stretch of the track.

"Sorry," he said.

"That's okay." She sounded nervous and tense. Her smile was forced.

"Pretty exciting, isn't it?" said Philip, although he did not feel that way. Small talk.

"Glad you think so. I think it stinks."

"Then why're you here?" It was really none of his business.

"Someone I know is driving. I always try to watch him when I'm near where he's racing."

"Boyfriend?"

"Ex-husband. Bill Tenley. You've probably heard—everybody here has. I suppose they think I'm crazy, or still nuts about him or something." She shook her head. "Sorry. Didn't mean to make this a confessional. I guess race tracks bring out neuroses. By the way, my name's Pamela French."

Philip was fascinated. "Philip Ross. Look, I had no idea. Were you married long?"

"No, just a few months. It was some years ago."

"I met Bill last night. Seems like an awfully nice guy."

"That he is. Nice. Nuts. Poor Bill . . ."

"Poor Bill? He seems on top of the world!"

"I suppose he is, what's left of him." Philip lit a cigarette for her. "When I first came to London from Australia, Bill was just starting out and we sort of teamed up. We polished our upper-clawss accents together. We read up on the society people who invited us to dinner. It was all pretty rough on Bill at first. He's awfully proud, you know. Hated being patronized. Then we married, and that was no bloody good. Everything went bad between us. So we divorced. But"—she smiled and waved the field glasses—"I'm still his friend."

"I didn't meet you last night. Are you at Avon Lodge?"

"No. He has no idea that I'm in Sebring. I flew over with some friends from Palm Beach." She pointed at a twin-engine plane parked on an empty runway at the edge of the field. "That's their plane. My friends are down in the Porsche pits. And I'm here." She shrugged. "Doing whatever it is I'm doing."

Philip noticed the enormous square-cut ruby in a sporty setting on her right hand, the expensive silk shirt and skirt. Obviously Pamela French had done all right for herself.

"There he is," she said. He looked through her binoculars and saw Tenley's car come into view, flying down the back straightaway, then entering the long horseshoe turn around the pits. When it came past the club, Tenley looked up. He seemed to spot Philip and Pamela and gave a half-wave.

"There," said Philip. "Now he knows you're here."

"The hell he does!" she laughed. "I ducked behind you, and Bill only waves at broads. Bound to be a little piece of ass up here he's interested in." She did not sound bitter, just matter-of-fact.

Pamela was a beautiful girl, but Philip felt he understood Tenley's preference for going it alone. He remembered the way he had wanted to be free of Johnny and the penthouse . . .

Now Philip became absorbed in the race, enjoying this curious feeling of kinship with the man in the yellow crash helmet whose face whizzed past every three minutes at over a hundred and fifty miles an hour.

It was all right, after all. Perfect, in fact. His timing was perfect, his lap times were low, he was getting through the slower traffic on the track with ease, and he was not tired. He was in first place and he would bring the car into the pits with a lead of four minutes. There was nothing like handing over a big lead to your relief driver. Also, he had babied the car. Oil pressure, water temperature, suspension, and handling were perfect. And he had saved the brakes; that would pay off later when other drivers would be riding on bare brakeshoes and guts.

He approached the sweeping bend after the home straight going nearly flat out in high gear, seven thousand rpm, nearly one hundred and fifty miles an hour. His arms were straight out to the steering wheel and he was leaning back like a man in an armchair, completely relaxed. Two hundred feet from the curve, he lifted his foot from the gas pedal ever so slightly. Then he gave the tiniest jiggle to the steering wheel, and the car started sliding, very slightly, with all four wheels, nose pointing toward the inside of the curve. He fed more gas and began to drift through the turn in a long smooth arc, like a skier doing a turn.

It was beautiful, and the fans loved it. The Tenley technique, all liquid and smooth. Through the whole turn he moved the wheel by fractions while he held the drift. Then he was through into the backstretch, straightening his car at the very outside of the track, inches from the grass. He had barely lost speed since the previous straightaway, although other drivers lost as much as ten mph in this curve.

Christ, it felt good. Good as fucking. Better!

During each lap, he smiled or waved at three girls around the track. First there was little hot pants from last night, waving each time he passed the club. Then there was a little blond piece at the hairpin who always grinned. And a tall sun-tanned broad sitting on the roof of a station wagon near the final horseshoe curve. She just stared. No smiles. But he knew what she wanted, and later he'd do something about it . . .

Perfect.


Philip checked his watch. Eleven minutes until Tenley's first pit stop, three or four more laps. Chances were, Pamela explained, that Tenley would go only three. He was over a lap ahead of the second-place car—no need to squeeze out another extra few seconds the way only Tenley could when the pressure was on.

He came around once, and then again; the sign in front of his pit said: TENLEY IN. He raised his hand as he passed. He had understood.

The next three minutes were tense. Pamela and Philip stared to their left at the distant place where Tenley's car would appear on the back straightaway, flat out toward the final horseshoe turn, and then home into the pits. Ninety seconds passed, and then Langmann's car came into view. He seemed slow compared to Tenley. But then, everybody did . . . Two minutes, and still no Tenley. Ten seconds later they saw him. His car seemed to fly, literally. Then came the ripping noise of his engine.

They could hear him shift gears as he bore down on the turn. Pamela grabbed Philip's arm. Something was wrong. The car was not slowing down enough. It began to weave from side to side. Philip found himself hypnotized by the tiny man in the toy car a half-mile away. The car spun around completely, then slid onto the scrub grass beyond the track, raising a thick cloud of dust. It disappeared from sight until it flipped high into the air, belly up. Philip watched—horrified, mesmerized—as it bounced back to the ground and slid along on its back. It came to rest upside down, wheels spinning. For an instant all was quiet. Then a flash, a rumble, and the fire. It burned bright orange. A fat, oily cloud of smoke lifted from the wreck and began to float toward the stands like a giant genie freed from its bottle.

Pamela had dropped the binoculars and was running toward the stairs. Philip, frozen in place, stared at the pyre. Men were running toward it and then around it, as helpless against the destruction as were their fire extinguishers. An ambulance raced across the infield, a fire engine moved down the back straightaway.

When the smoke reached the clubhouse terrace, Philip sat down on a folding chair and put his head down. He was staring straight at Pamela's binoculars on the floor. Then he felt a hand on his back. It was Johnny.

"I'll take you back to the hotel, Philip."

"No."

Philip hitched a ride back to Avon Lodge with a young couple he'd seen in the bar the night before. Dull-looking, slightly overweight young marrieds, with twin madras bermudas and twin-peaked golf caps. They had come to Sebring to play golf. Never knew about the races until they got to the hotel. Now they wanted to get back to the golf course.

"Sebring is one of the great courses," the man said.

His wife nodded proudly. "They played the Masters here a few years ago." Like her husband, she spoke with a flat twang. Milwaukee, Philip guessed.

Now they were talking about the crash. "Those fellows must get paid a lot to take chances like that—a crash like that, they must all be nuts!"

Her husband nodded, and she went on. "And all those racing people in the hotel. They just took over the bar last night. We could hardly get a drink."

Her husband grinned. The wind barely ruffled his crew cut. "You just didn't speak French or Italian, honey. Or maybe if you had a nice English accent?" He did a bad Cockney imitation: "Oy'd loyk to 'ave a mortinay." They both laughed, and he touched his knee to her plump knee. They enjoyed each other's little jokes.

"You're not with the racing crowd, are you?" she asked Philip.

"Yes," he said.

"Oh!"

The hotel was still and empty in the hot sun. The parking lot made Philip think of a deserted lion's cage. The ani-

mals were over on the track ten miles away. The snarl of
their engines couldn't carry all the way to the hotel.

He went to his room and called room service for a
Bacardi and soda. Then he stripped off his dusty clothes and
turned on the shower.

A little Cuban waiter brought Philip's drink. He put it
down on the table. "Have you heard, sir?"

"What?"

"About Señor Tenley?"

"Yes."

"He is dead?"

"Yes."

The Cuban looked stricken. He left quietly, shaking his
head.

Philip took the drink and sat down on the bed.

*You didn't see me having this drink, did you?*

He set it down on the night table and lay down, his
forearms crossed against his eyes.

Slowly, terribly, he began to cry.


The great droning DC-7 passed Cape Hatteras after the
long overwater haul from Miami. Johnny, who had been
dozing, was awakened by the land-caused buffeting that came
up from below. He looked out. They were cruising at about
eighteen thousand feet, he guessed, over a thin broken overcast. From the angle of the plane, there must be a strong
crosswind from the west. They would be a bit late arriving
in New York.

The race drivers on the plane would visit New York,
stop off for lunch at the Chanteclair on Forty-ninth Street,
and then disappear to Europe for the next race. They were
joking and laughing, apparently unwilling to be touched by
Tenley's death.

"You know," one of them had told Johnny, "next week Tenley and I had a suite reserved in St. Moritz. We were going skiing. Now who am I going to get to share the cost?" Tenley had committed a gaffe by getting himself killed, sticking a buddy with the cost of an expensive suite.

Johnny, knowing the fear that lay behind such reactions, did not find the comment heartless.

He glanced at Philip, asleep in the next seat, his blond hair sun-bleached, his face tanned, his long-lashed eyes closed. Philip was beautiful, and Johnny was in love with him all over again.


"Philip?"

"Yes?"

"It's Doe. How are you, darling? When did you get home? I tried to call." *All* weekend. Over and over again.

"Yes, well, I just walked in."

"Are you all right? I've been worried sick since Howard told me what happened. It was so awful . . . I'm so terribly sorry!"

It took a moment for Philip to realize what she meant. Then he said, "I'm fine, Doe, thanks. It wasn't too pleasant. I'll tell you about it tomorrow."

"Why not now, darling? I'll come over. Have you had anything to eat?"

"Yes, thanks, I ate on the plane. Look, Doe, I'm bushed. Don't be mad, but I want to turn in, okay?"

"Of course. Get a good night's sleep. I understand." But she did not, at all. He sounded cold and distant.

Although she felt the lack of sleep the next morning, her spirits rose. Philip, poor boy, must have been too exhausted or miserable to see even her. She resisted the temptation to call him at work. He'd probably call her, anyway, and if not she could always try him later, when she got home.

She began calling at seven, then every half-hour through despite the self-ministrations of a hot bath and a large brandy. the evening and into the night. At 2 A.M. she was still awake, She even tried making love to herself—that had brought drowsiness or at least relaxation more than once over the endless weekend—but it was no use. The necessary accompanying fantasies of Philip and her together simply would not come, and her lovingly detailed memories of their one night together, already overused, had lost their power to arouse.

Tris Perrin had three great loves: his tiny, gentle wife; his home, which sprawled over a hundred acres on the north shore of Long Island Sound; and his eldest daughter, Doe. There were two other daughters. He loved them both, but— as people—he could take them or leave them. Tris Perrin was an objective man. Yet it was difficult to be detached about Doe's anguish. He had brought up three daughters and was used to their ups and downs. But Doe—he knew, the minute she called—was suffering very real pain. Still, he had always guaranteed his children's privacy, and he would not now invade Doe's with an offer to help.

From his study on the second floor he watched her little red Alfa coming up the poplar-lined driveway from the gatehouse. He walked quickly down the wide staircase to the main hall and outside. The Alfa pulled onto the cobblestones which had endangered Perrin horses since the house was built, and shuddered to a halt. Doe did not get out. She stayed behind the wheel, looking up at her father with a forced smile.

" 'Lo, baby," he said. "No work today?"

"I took some time off."

"Good. Glad you came out."

She looked tired. Had she been crying? She still kept clothes and make-up in her room upstairs and never brought baggage. He opened the car door and held out his hand to pull her up. For a moment they stood facing each other.

"Look, Pop, I'm not going to be much company, all right?"

"Okay, baby."

"I'll go upstairs now, and don't wait dinner for me. I'll get some stuff from the kitchen and eat in my room."

"Whatever you like."

"Is it all right, Dad?"

"Yes, baby, it's all right."

He hugged her close and tight, the way he had ever since she was a child, and kissed her on the top of the head. Then she went upstairs. He drove her car into the garage and headed back to his study.

Good thing Meg was over in Oyster Bay attending one of her charity things—she would cluck and fuss and worry. And eventually she would go to Doe's bedroom, driven by curiosity and compassion. He had better explain to Meg, to his wonderful silly Meg, that Doe wanted to be alone and that there was nothing she needed, and if she did, she'd ask for it. Better: he would take Meg to the movies over in Glen Cove. They hadn't been in months.

For a moment he wished that he were not always so calm and judicious. The thought of his daughter upstairs, torn up by something he knew nothing about, made him miserable.

When Meg got home he explained, and they drove to Glen Cove. They had a hamburger at a coffee shop and then went to a movie. Meg seemed to enjoy it—it was a Western with lots of psychological stuff, and her hobby of the moment was psychology. He barely watched the damn thing until the end when there was a shootout. Sic transit psychology.

They got back to the house at about eleven-thirty. The light was out in Doe's room.

In the morning, very early, he heard her Alfa driving off. There was a note on the breakfast table. "Everything okay now, got things sorted out. Love both of you, many kisses . . . Your dutiful daughter Doe, dammit!"

She wrote much as she had at Brearley, all round and upright with circled *i* dots. He was glad she had straightened out whatever had upset her. If possible, he loved her more than ever.

Driving back to New York, Doe checked to make sure she was under the speed limit. The cops on Northern State could be rough, and her Alfa seemed to attract them.

It had been a long, tough night, and now she was sleepy. But she had come to terms with this thing and with herself. Philip hadn't *meant* to hurt her, she knew that now. He simply could not help himself. After all, the whole thing had been her idea. She must be fair to him and to herself. She had no—*right* to love him. Or to think that he could love her. Now, it was up to her to find a way back to their friendship. That mattered to her, very much.

What she needed in the meantime was work. Lots of work, and the best goddamn job she knew how to do.

ORDINARILY, Howard welcomed letters from home. Most of his friends tolerated their folks; he genuinely liked his. But this letter committing him to looking up Kathy Newman was too *much*.

He remembered Kathy, of course—the Newmans had lived two houses away from the Sands on Rockley Drive in L.A., before the war. Kathy's parents were younger than his, but they'd played bridge together, and his dad and Mr. Newman, who both worked at Columbia Pictures, had driven into town together every morning, alternating cars. Neither family was religious, except at Rosh Hashanah and Yom Kippur, but both had belonged to Temple Beth El.

Howard had liked Sid Newman—he seemed so much younger than his own father—but the only time he'd paid attention to the little girl was when she irritated him. Like that time he'd come home on his final leave before going East to ship out to the ETO. Lieutenant Howard Sands, USAAF, very sharp in his Class A blouse, his busted pilot's cap, shiny new wings.

"Eileen Silver's brother is a captain," she'd said. "Are you a captain?"

She was like that. Skinny, too, even for a little girl.

Now his mother had written that Kathy Newman was coming East to study drama and try for Broadway. Arriving Friday—*Friday*, for Christ's sake—and expecting him to call her. Staying with a girl friend, Village address, and here was the telephone number. *Such* a nice girl, Sid and Nedda happy to see her go because of a wrong—*you know what I mean*—romance. Jesus!

Kathy had to be twenty or twenty-one by now. If she'd taken after Nedda Newman, she wouldn't be thin any more, but dumpy. "Studying drama" somehow suggested thick glasses and thicker ankles—Howard had learned that there were few Audrey Hepburns among young actress hopefuls.

He got to her apartment on Friday after one of those embarrassed and embarrassing phone calls that was as hard to end as it had been to begin. She had sounded nice enough, slightly Beverly Hills–Jewish–intelligent, and that confirmed his thick-ankle theory. When they sounded this intelligent on the phone, it was usually kinky-hair myopia time. Or maybe allergic to convertibles (very sensitive skin), or to skiing (I get a rash from snow).

Of *course* she and her goddamn roommate (Cecily Levy, yet!) had to live on the fifth floor and of course it was a walkup. By the fourth floor he was ready to turn back. The stairs smelled of stale garlic and dirty scrub water! He finally got to the apartment. "Levy" was painted artily on a pink card. He rang, and the girl who opened the door was everything he had anticipated: glasses and kinky hair *and* thick ankles. Except she was Cecily Levy and Kathy, who came from the other room a minute later, was a less bony image of Audrey Hepburn.

Within a week, they were enormously, extravagantly, unbelievably in love. Three months later, they went home to Los Angeles to tell their parents to start planning a wedding. The Newmans and the Sands were, predictably, ecstatic.

Howard's father was now in TV production at Desilu, and Sid Newman had opened his own accounting office. Both families had moved to Brentwood; instead of pooling cars, they now exchanged dips in each other's swimming pools. They also switched to Temple Israel and shared complaints about the steep cost of high holy days tickets.

The wedding would be at the Newmans', the reception at the Sands'. When they got back to New York, Leon and Sandra gave a large party for the engaged couple. Everyone adored Kathy, and by the end of the party Philip had brought out a sketch pad and was working out the wedding gown details with her. "You're tall and slim, lovely neck, perfect figure for an Empire gown. Long sleeves, certainly, and maybe a matelot neckline . . ."

The wedding on the Newmans' lawn in Brentwood was attended by nearly four hundred relatives and friends of both families from all over California. After the reception, Kathy and Howard flew to Nassau—a wedding present—where they swam, ate, and made love.

Tom Brett, Howard's old roommate, met them at La Guardia when they returned, made the necessary cracks about their suntans and presumed state of exhaustion, then handed them a hotel key. "It's a room at the Ambassador," he said. "A present from Leon Fassman until you find an apartment."

The room seemed large until they had lived in it a few days; they quickly moved into a three-room apartment on East Fifty-fourth Street, long before any but the bare necessities had arrived. The building was air-conditioned ("self-service elevators, too!"), and the floors in the apartment were parquet. They enjoyed the newness, and uncomplainingly ate on a bridge table, used paper plates, sat on packing crates, hung bedsheets over their windows, slept on two cots pushed together.

When most of the furniture had finally arrived, they gave a housewarming, which was noisy and awash with liquor. Models, photographers, actors, garment salesmen, ad men, designers, magazine people. At one point, Tom Brett mopped his brow and said, "Good Christ, P. J. Clarke's must be *empty* tonight!"

The Sands were now official.


Ellen Wilson pulled a small stand-up mirror from a desk drawer, checked her make-up, and combed her hair. She was a vice-president now—her promotion had come through in January—but she was still Paul Bender's, and an executive staff meeting was, whatever else it was, an hour during which she would look her best.

For a time, her attractiveness as much as her youth had made her new position difficult. It was hard for other Torrey's staff members—over many of whose heads she had been promoted—to accept the fact that a woman so young and pretty could be effective as a senior executive. But when the first showdown came—a buyer who had overbought an item was reluctant to take a shellacking—she had managed to make her authority felt without causing a company flare-up.

The fact was, nothing in her life made her so happy as this exhausting, exhilarating job. Nothing, that is, except Paul.

She checked her watch, put the mirror back in the drawer, and left for the tenth-floor conference room. Entering, she nodded at Len Wilkerson, the general merchandise manager.

The chairs around the vast table were soon filled. In addition to Wilkerson there were the advertising people, the three divisional merchandise managers—including Ellen, who ran all Women's Apparel, and her eight buyers—and Paul Bender.

It all happened in minutes. They had barely begun when Paul Bender stood up and excused himself. He left his place at the head of the table and walked into his office, which adjoined the conference room, closing the door behind him. Everyone was puzzled. What could have caused him to leave in the middle of a conference?

Ellen suddenly knew, and was terrified. She said, "I'll see what's keeping him," and followed Paul into his office. She closed the door, shutting out their faces.

He was lying on the big red leather couch at the back of the room, gasping for air. His shirt collar was open. His face flushed with effort, and he was groaning. When she rushed to him, he tried shaking his head to reassure her; his face now sickly pale, drained of color. She started for the door to get help but he gasped, "No. Come here . . ."

It happened while she was hurrying back to his side. He died. He just stopped. Everything stopped. His eyes remained open, but they stopped seeing and his hands stopped reaching and his chest stopped breathing.

In desperation, Ellen pushed at his chest, tried to breathe into his mouth, but there was nothing. She was holding a dead man.

Slowly, she stood up and walked across Paul's office to the door of the conference room. She turned the knob on the door and opened it. All the men at the table were silent instantly, looking up at her. She beckoned to Len Wilkerson, large and fatherly. He followed her into Paul's office. When Len saw Paul's face, he picked up the phone and told the operator to rush a doctor to the tenth floor, although it was clearly too late.

With every last ounce of self-control, Ellen went back to the others. "I think we'd better adjourn," she said.

"Why?"

"What's wrong?"

The answer was in her face. And so, like most people not anxious to look closely at death, they shuffled quickly out of the room, shaking their heads and mumbling.

Ellen closed the door behind the last one and sat down in her own seat at the conference table. She could hear voices in Paul's office; thank God Len had taken over. She spread her fingers in front of her and bore down hard on the table top, then harder, as if she could force her pain into the table.

Ellen checked the figures on the typewritten sheet. She could have guessed its contents almost to the dollar. Her division was in good shape. Inventories were well balanced, sales were good. She had nearly completed her buying plans, and the season ahead looked promising.

Soon she would be able to resign with a clear conscience.

The intercom buzzer rang and her secretary said, "Mr. Tomlinson calling again." He had left a message earlier, but she'd wanted a breather before calling him back.

"All right." She heard the outside line open and then Tomlinson's rather fatherly voice. Unlike most executives, he preferred to dial his own calls.

"Ellen. Will you have some time for me this afternoon?"

"Of course."

"All right, then. Why don't you come over here to my office at three?"

"I'll be there, Mr. Tomlinson."

She had been planning to write him a letter. Now she could tell him face to face.

Promptly at three, she entered Cal Tomlinson's office in the Amalgamated Building on Thirty-ninth Street. He gave her a warm handshake and gestured to two armchairs which flanked the fireplace. They sat down and he leaned forward, elbows on knees, a corpulent man in his late fifties who ran twenty-two large stores with the enthusiasm of a high school principal.

He began: "I'd like to outline an idea, Ellen . . ."

Ellen was really not very curious. They were probably trying to get her over to the Amalgamated central buying office. They were having trouble servicing the fashion departments in their stores and needed a central fashion director. But that was not for her, not now. All she wanted was to get as far away as possible from New York, from merchandising, from a Torrey's without Paul.

Tomlinson continued: "We had a meeting of the board yesterday. We wanted to review a recommendation Paul made a few months ago. You see, well, now that he's gone, that recommendation has suddenly become very timely."

His eyes twinkled. An executive Santa Claus, she thought.

"Ellen. We were voting on your appointment as the new president of Torrey's."

She hadn't heard right. *President*, at thirty-one? She shook her head. "You can't be serious."

"Look, Ellen, we considered this very long and seriously. Shortly after Amalgamated bought Torrey's, Paul strongly urged us to appoint you as his successor once he retired. And now this awful business has simply advanced the timetable."

Ellen lifted her chin. "Mr. Tomlinson," she said, "don't think I'm being ungrateful, but at this point, particularly at this point, it sounds so unlikely. And how do you know I can handle the job? I'm not at all sure I could."

"Paul Bender was an excellent merchant," said Tomlinson, "and his instincts about the business and the people in it were even better. I must admit when he first told us about you, well, that was over a year ago and we thought he was off base. Why you? Don't misunderstand, you're one of the brightest people in the business. But to run a store?"

"I am sure there were some guesses as to *why me*," she said.

He stood up, struggling a little to extricate himself from

the deep chair. "Yes, there were," he said, and suddenly his voice was like metal. "Certain board members had heard rumors, and—one checked."

He smiled to cover his embarrassment. "Anyway. We've known for a long time that the rumors were true, that there was more than a business relationship between you and Paul . . ."

Nothing could hurt her now. Nothing. Not even hearing it here, in this office, like a detective's report in a divorce case. She was neither embarrassed nor shocked nor hurt.

He waited for a reaction, but when she said nothing, he went on: "Paul was too smart and too devoted to Torrey's to recommend anything but sense, whatever his personal feelings. The more we learned about you, the more we agreed with Paul's judgment. We are sure you can handle the job. And, we'll be here to back you up and help you—should you need us."

Well, they really mean it, she thought. She needed time. "May I take a few days to think it over?"

"A sensible idea," said Tomlinson. "We know how hard all this has hit you, and we don't want to rush you. Why don't you relax somewhere, anywhere? Take a trip. We've arranged for a bonus payment with some semivalid reason to charge to Amalgamated. Would a month be enough?"

"Of course."

"Then we'll wait to hear from you."

She shook his hand and turned to go.

"Oh, and Ellen."

"Yes?"

"Don't be too concerned about how other people in the business will take to a young woman as a department store president. Once we found out what you could do, we got used to the idea faster than you would think."

Faster than *I* will, she thought as she left the room.

Tomlinson was right. Within a few months the pretty young woman in her fashionable clothes became an accepted member of New York's senior executive community. Torrey's changed gently with Ellen's touch, and soon, when people thought of Torrey's, they thought of Ellen Wilson. *Now!* devoted the front of one whole issue to her, flattering her extravagantly while sticking pins into the craggy gentlemen who ran the other Fifth Avenue stores. Ellen's photo was on the cover the day she took over Torrey's, and *Now!* patted itself on the back for having discovered her.

"Ellen Wilson . . . *We* said she was *tomorrow!*"

Rolls-Royce, vintage 1930, stood in front of the Leeds mansion in Bel Air, that peculiar residential area just beyond Beverly Hills which is a harbor for those who want privacy among their fellow prominences. The Rolls had been rescued from a rundown second-hand car dealer in London. One day it was awaiting the junk heap; the next it became the property of a wealthy man in faraway California.

Had the Rolls been human, it would have wept with gratitude. Instead it was drained and crated and shipped to a Cahuenga Boulevard specialist who restored classic cars for wealthy collectors. The torn leather upholstery was replaced with new hides, the body was sanded and repainted with ten coats of high-gloss lacquer. The metal trim was replated, the tires were replaced with imports, and the engine was rebuilt piece by piece. The two-thousand-dollar car now cost eleven thousand dollars, and Barry Leeds, the new owner, felt it was worth every penny.

Barry, an attorney, had earned his fortune in Los Angeles real estate. He had a pretty wife, three children, aged five to sixteen, and a large home. Also a beach house in Malibu Colony, a steady table at Romanoff's, and a membership at exclusively Jewish, exclusively rich Hillcrest Country Club. He was in his late forties, chunky though not stout—thanks to daily massages and workouts; tennis at Hillcrest, at the

Beverly Hills Hotel, or in Palm Springs, where he rented a house in winter.

Barry's partner, Jim Storp, handled the movie end of their practice. They did the legal work for two huge talent agencies, and also represented many producers, directors, and actors. Jim was a bachelor, a rather famous bachelor at that, never married, although he was handsome and youthful at fifty, with attractively graying hair. He had escorted some of Hollywood's most prominent actresses since the late 1930's and was photographed as often as most stars. He was Hollywood's all-time favorite spare man; hostesses booked him months in advance.

Barry's wife, Louise, following a short-lived affair with Jim, became his best friend. She watched with detached amusement while Jim tackled new actresses from Europe or Broadway. Usually he got more press coverage than sex.

The old Rolls was only one of the Leeds' cars. There was a Caddy convertible for Louise, a Thunderbird two-seater for teenage Barbara, and an XK120 Jag, which was Barry's daily transportation to his office on Sunset Strip. The curvy road between Beverly Hills and Bel Air became his private racetrack, greatly enjoyed. On rainy days he was more cautious, because Sunset Boulevard quickly turned to glass. When the weather was really foul, he gave in and borrowed Louise's Caddy. It was dry and comfortable, and the windshield wipers and brakes worked, which was not always the case with the Jag. The Rolls was driven only on Sundays or to parties.

Louise and Barry were, admittedly, social climbers. Of course, at their level of wealth and prominence, climbing was a relatively subtle procedure, and the outsider might well have asked, "Why climb, and where?"

Their target was a small crowd of Hollywood aristocrats known as the Clique. The Clique "made" restaurants, gave "the" parties, owned the columnists, ran the charities, everything. The Clique was female-dominated. Wives. Ambitious. Southampton and Palm Beach wives who wanted movie-style publicity and conned their husbands into buying movie-style Bel Air houses. Producers' wives who wanted Southampton and Palm Beach. Directors' wives who had flunked as actresses. Stars' wives, happy to be stars' wives until they found out they were just actors' wives.

Barry and Louise were not in their league—not yet, not quite. But there were ways of getting there, and they pursued their ambitions openly and happily, the way others tried to win at golf or bridge. Their main instrument was charity, and the main charity was St. Thomas Hospital. The Clique ran St. Thomas, and, given a fair appearance, a good reputation, and a great deal of money, one could get within striking distance. The Leeds had finally landed on the exclusive Events Committee. Louise had even been invited to several Clique homes and had, in turn, entertained the ladies at her house.

Jim Storp helped. He dealt with some of the St. Thomas people on business, and Barry had been asked to three men's committee luncheons at the Beverly Hills Hotel.

The Leeds were actually nearing the final rungs of the ladder when a great opportunity fell into Louise's lap. She was asked to organize a fashion party at Farber's Beverly Hills branch. Farber's Department Store was introducing its new Armand Boutique with a personal appearance by Philip Ross, the New York designer. The affair would be an after-store-hours invitational cocktail showing, twenty dollars a ticket, proceeds to St. Thomas, of course.

Farber's and all its Los Angeles branches belonged to the Amalgamated group. Their Beverly Hills store drew business from the plum-rich three B's: Bel Air, Brentwood, Beverly Hills. A conservative store, Farber's had always catered to old-line and nonmovie Angelenos. In Beverly Hills, this stuffy image had damaged their fashion business. One shopped at Farber's for children's clothing, or housewares, or maids' uniforms. But for a chic dress? Saks or Magnin's, never Farber's.

In New York, Amalgamated asked Ellen Wilson's advice. Not surprisingly, she suggested an Armand Boutique similar to Torrey's and recommended a personal appearance by Philip. Farber's at first rejected the idea, then reconsidered. After all, if the thing flopped, the blame would fall on Amalgamated and Ellen Wilson.

Eileen Bean, a bright fashion coordinator at Farber's who had apprenticed in the PR department at Paramount, had no intention of letting an Armand Boutique flop. She immediately suggested the St. Thomas benefit showing.

The Clique was pleased. It was *their* sort of event. The Ladies of St. Thomas held an inner sanctum meeting and chose Louise Leeds to organize things. After all, she always wore the latest clothes, and she knew her way around the Beverly Hills fashion shops and fashion in general. Besides, it would take a lot of work.

Louise wrote Philip and received a charming reply on gray stationery with his large red monogram at the top. Mr. Ross was looking forward to his first California visit. Mr. Howard Sands, the national sales manager, would handle all the details with Farber's.

Eileen Bean did a long-distance telephone interview with Philip. Drawing on his telephone replies, the *Now!* story, and —most heavily—her imagination, she wrote a crisp release filled with "statements" by Philip. ("I like a woman with a sense of fashion *adventure*." "There are no middle-aged women these days!" "Clothes must amuse, not shock.") Photos of Philip and of the Armand collection went into the press kit along with "The Story of St. Thomas."

Eileen's PR job was, in fact, highly professional. Stories about the upcoming showing appeared in L.A. social and movie columns weeks before the event, bringing a flood of requests for tickets. Any woman not actually planning to attend the showing was at least talking about it.

Eric Marshall's West Coast editors had a fine time. They filed story after story about the pre-opening gyrations, and *Now!* ran a weekly report on the progress of the invitation list. They even reported that several Clique wives had flown to New York to scoop the others by wearing new Philip Ross designs to the opening.

As the Farber party became the *cause célèbre* of the season, Leon was torn between joy and fury. Armand-Klein's name never got mentioned in the press clippings, only Philip's.

Howard had to calm him daily. Philip was, after all, "part of Armand-Klein." Also, Farber's order was substantial, and Armand-Klein had never been strong in California.

"Besides, I should think you'd be glad for the chance to cut in on those expensive West Coast dress houses."

Leon smiled. "You're right about that, at least. Bastards have ruled the Hollywood roost long enough!"


Philip climbed down the boarding stairs of his plane, still gaping inwardly over what he'd seen out the window during the last hour. After the towering Rockies, they had passed over the last craggy lower mountains, and there it was: the Pacific. Then came the long glide over low houses, huge freeways, and hundreds of turquoise swimming pools into Los Angeles International Airport. It was every bit as exciting as his first trip to Europe.

He was met just inside the gate by an attractive woman who said, "Mr. Ross? I'm Louise Leeds. Welcome to Los

Angeles!" She was wearing a pink Armand suit from the new collection. Her loose hair was sun-streaked.

"Do you mind if we take some pictures?" A photographer. A phony handshake from Philip, as if he and Mrs. Leeds were just greeting each other. Then, a long, chauffeured ride to the Beverly Hills Hotel. Large ground-floor suite with patio, gardenias, bougainvillaea. Outside, the thud of tennis balls. Liquor from the hotel, caviar from the Leeds, and a lavish, incongruous flower arrangement from Farber's.

Louise Leeds left Philip to relax and unpack. The car would call for him at six-thirty for a "little cocktail party and dinner at our house."

It was only 4 P.M. Philip unpacked, then walked through the shop-lined lobby and out to the pool. The tennis and sun-bathing crowd were packing up for the day, but the gazebo-like bar was still open. He ordered a drink and sat down near the pool. There were forty or fifty people in swimsuits stretched on rows of reclining chairs in front of the cabanas. Philip, still in his city suit, felt like a man in black tie at a turkish bath.

Looking around, he recognized a suntanned woman in tennis shorts with a racquet under her arm: Katharine Hepburn. *Katharine Hepburn!* Minutes later, the loudspeaker paged "Mr. Henry Fonda, please." He was in Hollywood, all right. And he loved the whole gardenia-sweet, sun-drenched, palm-swaying idea.

The phone rang promptly at six-thirty.

"Your car is here, Mr. Ross."

Operators at the Beverly Hills knew how to make guests feel special. They were addressed by name from the moment they checked in. At the driveway, under the pink canopy, the doorman showed "Mr. Ross" to the long black limousine which had brought Philip from the airport. Not bad. They pulled away, followed by the glances of other guests who were waiting for their cars. Philip could almost hear their curiosity. He leaned back, half-embarrassed, to tuck himself out of sight.

They serpentined along Sunset Boulevard past large pastel homes, manicured and palm-covered lawns, and flowered hedges. Other cars zoomed past them—he counted two Bentleys, one Rolls, and a flock of Thunderbirds and Jaguars. A poster: "Maps to Movie Stars' Homes," then a large gate with an overhead sign that said "Bel Air." Now the streets became narrow and winding, flanked by high trimmed hedges. Here and there he could see magnificent homes surprisingly close to the road. Finally, they drove through a driveway onto a wide flagstone yard in front of a rambling Mexican villa. Guests' cars were parked to one side, and an ancient Rolls peeked from the huge garage next to the house.

The doorbell set off a dog's furious barking, until a stern British voice said, "Stop it, Thor!"

The butler who greeted Philip held the dog, a huge Great Dane, in check. More attentive to the dog than to the man, Philip gingerly made his way past them into the pink-floored living room, where Louise Leeds detached herself from a group of guests. She kissed him on the cheek. California informality. "Welcome, Philip!" More informality. She had changed into another Armand outfit, a new chiffon from the latest collection at Torrey's. The woman had to absolutely *commute* to New York.

She introduced Philip to Barry Leeds, Jim Storp, Eileen Bean, and Craig Robinson, the senior vice-president of Farber's. Eileen Bean was small and chubby, but attractive. Robinson looked like a country lawyer in his Sunday best, not quite comfortable in this atmosphere. Storp and Leeds seemed the sort Philip had expected to meet.

Jim Storp presented Philip to several couples who were St. Thomas committee members and to the director of the hospital, a man with curly gray hair who looked like an actor playing a hospital director. Next, Jim introduced him to Loretta Young.

From then on, Philip was in a fog. Dozens of famous stars arrived. It seemed that everyone he had ever seen on the screen was suddenly there, speaking to him, wishing him luck and promising to be at the opening. Philip suddenly realized that he was—a movie fan.

Finally a familiar voice: Jeffson. He rushed up to Philip after kissing Louise Leeds. "Hi, Philip, how're the Corhans and old Johnny?" He had heard. There must have been gossip after Sebring.

During dinner, served on the patio under palm trees strategically lit by spots, Philip found out that all of them were movie fans. Including the stars, who treated each other as if they believed everything that was written about them. And to cap the evening, they were all shown a film in the living room, which converted into a screening room.

It was a preview starring two of the guests, produced by another, and directed by yet another. Bursts of applause during the titles as each guest's name appeared; then, during the rest of the film, buzzing conversation and snide remarks. At first Philip was embarrassed for those who had made the film, but they seemed unruffled. Apparently this was a movie-business game, the rules known to everybody there except Philip (and possibly Craig Robinson).

Once the film was over, guests began to leave. Jeffson explained that early-morning movie-making schedules meant early hours.

He offered to drive Philip back to the hotel, and Philip said goodnight to his hostess. Another kiss.

"Still not quite paid for," said Jeffson as he started the Bentley's engine. "That first movie was a stinker."

Philip was not sleepy. Excitement? Something. "How about a drink at the hotel?"

"Fine with me," said Jeffson. "No shooting tomorrow, I've just wrapped up number three. Probably just as bad as the first two."

There was nothing Philip could possibly say to that, so he kept quiet.

"Who cares if the film flops?" Jeffson said when they were seated in the Polo Bar. "I got good money, sold my place in Malibu. Paid off the mortgage, put the rest down on a real hocus-pocus movie-star home and now I'll see what happens. Everyone's feeding me caviar because I'm so pretty and I dance like a dream, and, of course, I know Palm Beach and Southampton. That society stuff goes big out here. After tonight, I'd say you will too."

"Come off it. Not with that crowd."

"Lord yes, sonny! There you were all Fifth Avenue and handsome as a picture and sponsored by St. Thomas—what more could anyone ask? By tomorrow you'll be the catch of the movie colony. Wait and see."

They had another drink in the half-empty bar. Jeffson was incredible! He seemed to relish his insecurity and the thin ice on which he apparently skated. To Philip, there was something appealing about his nonchalance.

"Acting?" Jeffson said. "Who gives a damn? No one in movies really knows how to act, except maybe a few Broadway people and the English. Everything is really up to the director. Once you know your way around the camera, you can become an Academy Award winner if you have the right director. One of these days I'll go back East and learn how to act—on the stage—for real. Until then I'll futz around here or wherever they send me; maybe I'll get a break and land in a money maker. All you need is one big-grossing picture, then they think *you* made the money and decide you're box office.

"Producers and directors are funny guys. Lazy, really. They think of one guy for each part. Right now when they think of a society comedy guy they yell for Cary Grant. If they can't get him, they ask for the nearest thing to Cary Grant. Maybe next time they'll think of me, who knows?"

Louise Leeds had won her first major victory. It was she who had decided whom to invite to the dinner party, although she had made some concessions about fringe cases—people who might invite the Leeds in the future and had not snubbed them in the past. Also among the guests were a few producers and directors who might never invite them but were too prestigious to exclude. But anyone who had snubbed them was definitely out, St. Thomas or no St. Thomas.

There were ruffled feelings the next morning when the trade papers and the Los Angeles society writers reported who had been at the Leeds' party. Eileen Bean had released the guest list the day before. The columnists understood: they would be "invited" to shop at Farber's one day. The party was given a big play.

*Now!* also ran the story, along with photographs of the guests. No one but Louise Leeds had noticed the girl with the Minox who looked like a guest. The *Now!* article revealed who had designed each dress worn at the dinner; Philip got the lion's share of the credits.

Cobina, Louella, Hedda, and Sheilah all covered the party, each mentioning Philip. The stories were read by millions, including Sandra Fassman's maid.

"That Mr. Ross, he sure is getting big time. Did you read about him in Louella Parsons, Mrs. Fassman?"

Sandra had. She assumed Leon had, too. And worried about it.

Jeffson called Philip at ten the next morning.

"What'd I tell you?" he said. "I'm beginning to feel like a pimp. Already had three calls asking me to ask you to people's homes."

"Thanks, but I've got to get the show together. They've got me tied up in rehearsals for two days."

"Good luck, then. Wait'll you see the models!"

"How do you mean?"

"Just wait," said Jeffson. "After all, it *is* a charity show." He hung up, chuckling.

The models, as it turned out, were society women and movie stars. No paid professionals. The society women were shapeless and the actresses were all prima donnas. Fittings were hell, but Philip, drawing on his Farrow experience, was the soul of diplomacy. The ladies were bewitched, even the stars. Susan Simmonds, who had just won an Academy Award, even asked Philip to design the wardrobe for her next film.

Philip called Jeffson.

"Christ, Philip, her temper is more famous than *she* is. I've heard she thinks all Hollywood designers are butchers, forces her producers to buy Paris wardrobes and then give full screen credits to the couturiers. You're not Hollywood, but you're not French, either."

"Look, she's been called the best-dressed actress of her generation—I've seen her in V*ogue, Bazaar, Ambience.* And she likes me."

"Suit yourself, but you'll probably run into one of her mountainous rages."

Philip, having solicited Jeffson's reaction, decided not to

pay any attention to it. He liked that bit about giving credit to the couturiers. He would talk to Leon and Howard as soon as he got back.

The show went like clockwork. Philip ran the presentation exactly like a Farrow opening, silently blessing every moment he had suffered at James Farrow's. Everyone in the standing-room-only audience was impressed.

The show got even more attention from the press than the Leeds' party had. St. Thomas had made a mint. Farber's was overjoyed—even Craig Robinson had to admit there was "something to this fashion game." From the day of the opening on, Farber's Armand Boutique began to sell dresses faster than it could keep them in stock.

Philip could not wait to see Leon and Howard.

The plane began the long climb east toward the San Bernardino range. The no-smoking sign went off. The hostess, completing her seating plan, asked Philip for his name.

"Philip Ross."

"Are you—the designer?"

"Well, yes."

"I've been reading about you in the papers."

"Oh?"

"Loved the styles I saw in the photos!"

"Well, thanks, you're nice to say that."

"Glad to have you aboard, Mr. Ross!" She smiled pertly and moved away, making a mental note to talk with him later in the flight. Maybe she could get some clothes.

Philip smiled and tilted his seat back. First time that had happened, and he liked the feeling. No more "I'm Philip Ross, I design clothes." Instead: "That's Philip Ross, the designer." It would be marvelous if he never, ever again had to explain anything about himself to anybody. He had always hated it. Particularly the lies he had made up like the one about his father being an officer. If people he met already knew all about him, that was perfect. It might all be publicity bullshit, but he'd never disillusion them.

Bless you, dear airline hostess, for making me feel good. Bless your store-dummy smile and your stupid shoes and your lacquered hairdo and your tight little ass! And the way you walk down the aisle, half burlesque, half secretary . . . Your blouse has pulled up, I can see the skin, and you're wearing a Frederick's bra that makes your tits point in. I bet you have corns and I bet you blow your boyfriends and are a lousy lay anyway, but bless you.

Between Monday and Wednesday, calls came in to Armand-Klein from stores all over the country. They had seen the stories in Now! and they were impressed. This was a different case from Torrey's. A New York store could sell all sorts of high-style stuff, but Farber's was pretty conservative. If an Armand Boutique could click with them, why not in Cleveland and Chicago and Omaha? All the retailers who called naturally wanted Philip Ross to make a personal appearance at their store.

Howard was enthusiastic. They would triple their Armand business within a year. Torrey's would still be the biggest customer, but the other stores could be forced to buy in depth. No big order, no Philip Ross.

He had to convince Leon.

Sandra Fassman felt the same way Howard did, but she also understood Leon's feelings perfectly. She knew that he was wary of anything that distracted from Armand-Klein's expensive lines. A small, avant-garde division was fine, provided it was the icing on top of the cake. To Leon, quite naturally, the cake was Armand-Klein.

Besides, he was vain. Much too vain to enjoy taking back seat to some kid he'd hired. He had been touchy ever since that original *Now!* story.

Sandra picked the time to talk to him carefully. He was mellowest after dinner.

"You know, Leon," she said, "it's amazing how the fashion game is changing."

He waited for her to continue, but she opened the evening paper. Finally he asked, "How do you mean?"

"Seems to me it's getting to be more like the movie business. Designers are becoming like actors with personal appearances, stories in the columns. Like Philip. And the big manufacturers like you, well, you're producers. Sam Goldwyns or Louis B. Mayers."

"And just what does *that* mean?"

"You hire the designers, they go out and perform." She smiled. "It wouldn't surprise me if pretty soon they print 'Leon Fassman presents Philip Ross and his new fall collection.'"

Leon gave her a sideways look. "Sam," he said, "would you mind very much cutting out the crap? I know you think I'm crazy because Philip is getting more publicity than Armand-Klein, but don't think I'm a *shnook*. I'm perfectly aware that it's good business, so long as Philip doesn't get too big for his britches. So never mind sugaring the pill, okay?"

He was annoyed, so she knew she had registered. She hadn't meant to underestimate him. She had learned never to do that.

Howard got one of his periodic surprises. There he was, all set to sell Leon on more Armand Boutiques, when the old bastard called him in to ask him about the same thing.

"So what do you think we ought to do?" Leon said.

"I think we ought to open at least ten more boutiques."
He braced himself for the storm.

"Right," said Leon, "and I want you to get on it right
away. We'll be Metro-Goldwyn-Mayer behind Philip, call
the tune with the stores, and have Philip perform. If the
stores are good children and buy plenty and promise to ad-
vertise plenty."

"I think they will," said Howard lamely.

"Why don't you lay out a program for each Armand
Boutique. Everything. Size of order, type of ad, opening
party and all, so we can give the stores a complete package.
Right?"

"Oh, right," said Howard.

He'd given Howard the go-ahead, but Leon knew he
would remain uncomfortable about the boutiques. He tried
to relate his own far-seeing instincts during the years when
he was starting out to what was happening in fashion now.
After all, he'd hated not just the small-time, the tawdry, the
cheap, but the backward. He had been one of the first to
understand that old-fashioned salesmanship and outdated
Seventh Avenue thinking had to go. He'd replaced old men
with young, had been the first to consider a top New York
designer name when the rest of the business was still stuck
on Paris.

Today's designers simply were not nice little ladies like
Mrs. Meltzer to whom one handed a bolt of cloth so they
could "make up a group" of dresses. Philip was a new breed,
and Leon had to admit that the Armand collections looked
refreshingly different from the Paris stuff. Of course, not all
the Armand things were actually designed by Philip. Everybody had a hand in them. Still, Philip supplied ideas, and
his publicity was certainly responsible for the dramatic success of the line.

Then why, he wondered, did the whole thing still bother him so much? Why was he suspicious—even of Howard, who was like a kid brother to him?

He knew Sandra thought part of the reason was vanity. She had a point, but personal publicity was not the question. He had turned down publicity agencies who'd wanted to glorify him, determined not to be made a fool of like some of his competitors, who allowed themselves to be promoted as "designers" because it sounded good, much better than "garment manufacturers." Their PR agents churned out tons of stuff, but of course nobody in the business believed it. They could not draw a line or sew a seam.

No question, that was not his sort of vanity. But the idea that anyone might think Armand-Klein depended on Philip Ross for its success tormented him. He, Leon, *was* Armand-Klein, and had been for years.

For the moment, he'd try not to dwell on that. But one thing he promised himself: if Philip failed to perform, he'd not only lose Leon's backing, he'd lose his job.

The thought made him feel better.

# BOOK 4

P

HILIP stifled a yawn. After all, they *were* on the air. "No," he said. "No, Miss Turner, I really don't think skirts will ever get long again as they were during, say, the Dior New Look days. The mood just isn't right. My guess is that women will wear very *short* skirts before long."

Elva Turner was the star of *Girl Gab*, Toledo's most popular daytime TV show. It sold more detergents and cake mix than any other TV show in town. Elva was barely listening to Philip. She treated guests as a necessary evil—they were there to boost her rating or to pay off a sponsor. She interviewed them with mechanical charm, beginning with the questions lifted from their prefab biographies. Then she led them through a series of innocuous responses. She was not about to have any controversy on *her* show. *Girl Gab* was a housewife's show which guarded its moral *p*'s and *q*'s.

She steered the conversation away from the potentially explosive subject of skirt lengths.

Elva herself, a bleached blonde in her late forties, stuck to the rules of the Rita Hayworth era: tightly belted dresses with swirling skirts, very high spiked heels, deep-red lipstick. She took hours each morning to produce her camera face without help from the make-up man. She could smile without letup from 11 A.M., when the show went on the air, until 1 P.M., when they wrapped it up. It was a virtuoso performance of filling air time, trading banalities with her guests:

movie stars plugging their films, authors pushing their books, politicians on the stump, designers visiting stores. They all had to "do" *Girl Gab*. It was a selling show.

The ladies of Toledo adored her, sent her avalanches of mail, sat in the audience, and applauded or laughed on cue. The men at the station were not so devoted to Elva. Off the air, she was demanding and foul-mouthed. She was also plagued by flatulence, which made for some tense moments.

An off-camera assistant held up five fingers: fifty seconds to go. Philip was glad. He made sure that Storm-Angstrom, the Armand store in Toledo, got its plug. Then Elva smiled him off the show, to the enthusiastic applause of forty chubby pairs of hands in the audience.

The PR girl from Storm's led Philip to a car, ready to hustle them to a press luncheon at the Statler. Philip was seated between the two rival fashion reporters in town, neither of whom asked questions. Each wanting an exclusive, they had set up private interviews for later that afternoon, one at Philip's suite, one at the store. Storm's PR girl would chaperon both sessions and have models there so the papers could take photographs.

The whole routine had become a grind, which Philip performed twenty times each year. He had made the identical rounds six months earlier to introduce his spring line. He was tired and, what was worse, bored. He dreaded the up-coming evening with the store's executives, who entertained visiting fashion celebrities by laying on dinners at the city's best restaurant. Semi-French, semi-Italian fare, served with Ohio enthusiasm in place of finesse. He would brush aside self-conscious apologies about the restaurant and praise everything. With luck, he'd be back in the hotel by midnight and gone from Toledo on the first morning flight. Letters of thanks to the reporters and Elva Turner once he was back in New York. In time, they would mail him clippings of the

Toledo interviews: "Famous Designer Introduces Line," or "Philip Ross Has Designs on You," along with crude photos of himself and the models.

Crap!

Sometimes the local socialites, usually businessmen's wives and their debutante daughters, gave parties at the local country club or in their homes. As potential customers, they were worth his act: lots of smiles, discreet name dropping, flowers sent afterward with a nice little note thanking them for "the beguiling evening."

Occasionally, if a local reporter seemed amusing, he bought the morning papers at the airport on his way out and read the interview. Usually he did not bother. The kick of reading about himself had worn off, and anyway they usually wrote what he fed them. He wished they could say something of their own, even if it was bitchy. But no. He said: "I love blue," and they wrote: "Mr. Ross loves blue."

It seemed a hollow triumph when the dailies printed glowing stories about his visits. The stores' heavy advertising inclined local papers to be "cooperative" anyway.

Three more cities to go. Six more days of TV and radio and PR girls and store executives and rich-bitch local society. Christ!

Eric Marshall was jittery. His relationship with his father was too formal for surprise visits, and here he was on his way to the old man's house in Maine without having called ahead. He didn't even know himself why he had changed his plans, finished his business in Boston, and driven north instead of going back to New York. There was still time to call from a gas station, but he'd decided not to. After all, it *was* his father's house. That should entitle him to some privileges.

The shore road wound through rocky bluffs until the

237

house came into view, chopped out of the cliffs overlooking the Atlantic. Hundreds of feet below were rockbound coves with small patches of beach where the ambassador liked to swim in the mornings and just before dinner. The old man was proud of the way he'd kept in shape.

Mrs. Cluett, his housekeeper, cooked the sort of plain New England food he loved. He had very few visitors, since he was working on memoirs to be published after his death. Every so often the news magazines phoned for comments about international events, but Eric knew he rarely gave interviews. No doubt there was still the occasional call from the White House—although they had parted in disagreement, the two men still had a grudging friendship based on respect.

Eric turned into the narrow private road to the house. It was late afternoon, he would have to stay the night. Mrs. Cluett, who met him at the front door, wasted no time on greetings. "Your father is taking his swim," she informed him. "They will be up soon. Are you staying for dinner?"

"Yes." *They?* Apparently he was not the only guest.

Mrs. Cluett went back to her kitchen, and Eric carried his luggage up to the guest room. Obviously, it was in use. A man, he judged, and one who liked his comforts. A full grooming kit was laid out on the dresser, matching wooden-backed brushes, combs, shoehorn. A thin silk Japanese-style short robe was lying over the arm of a chair, and a terry velour robe hung on the bathroom door. On the desk, in a pigskin folding frame, was a photo of an elderly woman. Probably the man's wife.

Eric took his suitcase back downstairs. That was the only spare room; he would have to stay in a motel over in Camden. He could not help feeling somewhat relieved.

He sat down in a high-backed Windsor chair in front of a living-room window, from which he could see only the ocean. The high cumulus clouds over the Atlantic had turned rose-gold in the late sun, and the shadows of the cliffs reached far out to sea. The water had settled some since afternoon, when he'd seen whitecaps from the road and spindrift being blown off the waves.

The house had originally been a sea captain's. Eric could understand how a man might long to look at the ocean even though he had spent his whole life on it. This must have been the captain's favorite window.

Corinne had visited here once, had loved the view and the sea itself. That was the weekend she had said: "The three of us, you, the magazine and I, we live together, eat together, sleep together. . . ."

The familiar pain. There had been no one since her—no woman, no bed, no spilling of himself. She had been everyone, and there would never be anyone like her. For the thousandth time he felt like weeping for her, for himself, for both of them.

"Eric."

His father's voice. No gladness in it. A summons.

The ambassador's guest stood behind him, a young man, rather slight, in a knit swim suit. His blond hair looked incongruous, bleached, against his dark skin.

The ambassador made an elegant gesture: "This is Lance Wallace." Then, to the young man: "My son, Eric."

Wallace stepped forward with a wide smile and held out his hand, which was ice-cold from the water. His chest and legs, deeply tanned, were covered with gooseflesh.

"Of course I've heard of you," he said. "Who hasn't? That *mad* magazine of yours! How d'you do?"

A queen! A screaming queer!

His father's deep voice: "Lance is staying the summer. We met in Spain last year. His mother is a dear friend of mine."

239

That was an unusual lot of explanation from his father, who seldom explained anything. Staying the *summer?* Oh God, no! Poor sad bastard of a father. All those years of perfection—all pissed away!

Eric got out, fast. He drove to Camden, then on to Boston, where he turned in the rented car. He bought a fifth of gin at the airport and took it onto the 1 A.M. plane to New York. Sitting alone in the back of the empty DC-6 he began to drink, never really stopping until four in the morning when he fell asleep in a stupor, sprawled across his bed.

The next morning he was in the office on time, touchy but in control. The first thing he did was to call Doe Perrin for lunch.

Philip arrived in Palm Beach at nightfall on a Friday, having dozed his way through a bumpy flight from New York. He checked into the Colony.

"Welcome back," said the desk clerk. You're damn right, thought Philip. This was his third Palm Beach weekend this winter, sandwiched between work on the collection and those personal-appearance trips. He went South to recuperate, to forget the slushy industrial cities he had visited, the late nights of catching up in the sample room, the weary face he could see in his bathroom mirror each morning. He even came to get away from Johnny.

The clerk handed him his mail. Invitations. Christ, he was tired.

He followed the bellman to his room, gave him a dollar, and told him to hang up his clothes bags. The room was stifling; he opened the window to the smell of hibiscus, which came in with the cool air. Shuffling through the envelopes, he suddenly recognized the handwriting on one of them. He had seen it before, he knew, long ago.

He unfolded the stiff little sheet:

28 Palm Grove

Dear Philip—

Heard you'd be down! Can you join
us for dinner Saturday night? Do call . . .
the hotel knows our number.

Fondly,
Emily Debenham

Philip stared at the note. What was it she had said that
day at her house when he'd tried to get her back for Farrow?
"Would you give Mr. Farrow this note from me?" Same
handwriting, same creamy beige paper. So, now he was no
longer a messenger boy.

He called room service for a drink.

When he'd been Farrow's assistant, none of the clients
had cared if he was alive or dead except for that nympho
daughter of the Debenhams . . . Farrow, that silly fart, *he'd*
known all about these people. He'd given them nothing but
his designs and his contempt. Philip could almost understand
Farrow, now.

Not that he wouldn't *accept* Emily Debenham's goddamn invitation. Of course he would. After all, wasn't this
what it was all about?

His drink arrived.

Farrow! It seemed so long ago. For the first time in years,
Philip wondered what had happened to him.

James Farrow had committed himself to Ferndale Sana-
torium after one of his worst sieges, when he had gone without sleep for over a week and lost fourteen pounds. His
doctor had made the arrangements. Ferndale was expensive,
but there had been just enough money left to afford it. Medical insurance helped to carry part of the cost.

Ferndale was located fifty miles out of New York on a
well-fenced and guarded estate. The surrounding hills were

241

of such beauty that they seemed to mock the fate of the patients they imprisoned.

Farrow, diagnosed as a manic depressive, was now sixty-one. His body, which had shrunk slightly, was bent with constant abdominal pains. Headaches plagued him, as did kidney trouble and constipation. The doctors had tried to avoid an operation, but the frequency of his kidney attacks had increased, and it looked as if surgery was imperative. Moreover, his periods of depression had lengthened alarmingly.

Farrow seldom said anything. He spent most days in his room, his back to the barred window, staring at the whitewashed wall above his bed. Whenever he was well enough, and when the male nurses allowed it, he shuffled to the dining hall for his meals. He was usually dressed in pajamas and a robe—it was difficult for him to wear normal clothes, as he had little control over his bodily functions. He was quite bald, and his hands shook badly. When he was alone, he sketched his room, the view from the window, the male nurses or the physicians. Occasionally he read from the book of prayer, the siddur, which he had requested soon after he arrived.

Only Farrow's doctor could have told anyone where he was. No one had visited him since he had been admitted to Ferndale, and there was no mail.

The lifeguard's back was lean and tanned, with long muscled ridges tapering from the massive shoulders down to his swim trunks. He sat on the diving board, relaxed, watching the shallow end, where two little boys were splashing around. Their nannies were nearby, not much for him to do.

He put his hands in back of his buttocks and did a few liftups to exercise his stomach muscles. He usually did about twenty each hour. The hotel liked him to look handsome, and he had his own reasons . . . He was flat broke. Lost all his tip money in a crap game down at the yacht basin last night, four charter skippers had cleaned him out. He'd have to find some broad, some rich old broad who wanted to get banged. He looked around: nothing. Only pretty stuff, young stuff. They'd want to get laid all right, but they'd never pay.

He noticed a blond guy giving him the eye. Usually he avoided queers; it was messy business and anyway he didn't get his kicks that way. At least with a dame, even an *old* dame, it was still pussy and he could close his eyes and pretend. But with the queers it was always strictly business. He twisted his body so his waist showed extra small and his shoulders looked enormous. No doubt about it, the queer was all googoo eyes.

He stood up, breathed deeply, raised his arms, and stretched. Then he bent down to massage his thighs. That ought to make the guy heat up. He uncoiled, walked to the man's beach chair and leaned over, brushing against his arm.

"Can I get you anything, sir?"

"Yes. A rum and Coke, please."

He brought the drink, and while he was setting it up he licked his lips as if they were dry. "Will that be all, sir?"

"No," said the guy. "Can you drive me tonight? I rented a car, but I hate to drive."

"Sure. What time?"

"Seven-thirty, the doorman will show you my car. I'm going to dinner on Palm Grove. Do you know where that is?"

"Yessir." The Debenham house? That was the biggest estate on the Grove.

"Right. My name is Ross."

"Yessir, Mr. Ross. Seven-thirty."

No problem. He'd make some dough tonight, that was for goddamn sure. These queers were always ready. He would have preferred pussy, but then, beggars couldn't choose. He went back to the diving board and did some more liftups.

For the first time since he had arrived in Palm Beach, Philip felt relaxed. It was 2 A.M.; he had showered and gone to bed. He felt drained, drowsy, all the tension gone.

These pickups were a new thing. Quite new. Almost therapeutic, he was convinced. There had been one boy in Los Angeles on his last trip, a parking lot attendant on the Strip. Then another in Chicago. He hardly remembered their names, it was done and over with each time. Nothing *to* remember. No feelings, no heart, just sex; like masturbating, only better. He used it sparingly, discreetly.

It worked; that was what mattered. He had the appetite. He satisfied it with beautiful bodies, not like a glutton but like a gourmet.

He turned out the light. He could sleep now.


Voting was about to begin for the annual fashion business award. Forty ladies of the award jury, mostly fashion editors, were perched on folding chairs in a hotel meeting room. The room was split, almost visibly, into two camps: the old guard and the new, the bright young women who worked on the younger magazines. They had all seen the names up on the board. Although ten designers had been nominated, certain ones were definite favorites.

The floor was open for speeches in favor of each choice, but only three editors had announced their desire to talk. First, a sportswear editor from *Girl* magazine suggested a rising young female designer, a disciple of Rudi Gernreich. Then Susan Ahern extolled the virtues of her favorite designer, Sid Stirling, a distinguished gentleman in his early sixties who had produced some of Seventh Avenue's most tasteful collections throughout the years. He was the sentimental favorite. The speech was Susan Ahern's *beau geste*.

Finally, it was Doe's turn to speak. "I appreciate the suggestion by our colleague on *Girl*," she said. "Her choice, Sally Simonson, is without question enormously talented. After only three years, she's made fantastic strides. Sally will no doubt be worthy of the award very soon."

Now things would get ticklish. She continued: "Mrs. Ahern's proposal is equally appealing, but I wonder if we aren't perhaps being swayed by feelings of affection? We all adore Mr. Stirling, there's no doubt about that. But . . . if I had to make an ice-cold *clinical* judgment, if I had to think of taste and quality and creativity and durability, I'd have to pick *Philip Ross*. I hope you agree." She sat down.

The voting began. The younger fashion editors were willing to vote for Philip, who was also young, thereby getting in their licks against the dowager editors. Besides, they were damned if they'd play into the hands of *Girl*, which had monopolized Sally Simonson for three years.

Susan Ahern, sensing at once that the younger votes were in the majority, decided to back Doe. Ross was an *Ambience* pet, after all. Too bad about Stirling. She had tried.

Philip won the award.

It was announced a week later to the nation's press.

While Philip finished dressing, Johnny, who had come to the apartment to take Philip to the award ceremonies, waited in the living room. His prewar, London-made dinner suit fit him impeccably, which pleased him. All those years, and his figure had barely changed.

"Come *on*, Philip," he called into the bedroom. "You're going to be late for your own goddamn award!"

Philip knotted his black bow tie slowly and deliberately, and when it was still not quite right, retied it. Johnny could yell all he pleased.

Lord, he hated to admit it, but Johnny's intrusions into

his life, though infrequent now, were less welcome than ever. Johnny was a dear, but he could also be a leech. Like tonight: Philip would have preferred to go alone. He would have liked some time by himself to taste this award thing before the ceremonies. He had imagined himself walking there, and then standing across the street to watch the limousines pull up. Then strolling up to the guards without a ticket—"I'm Philip Ross"—and walking into the place, the only one of the five hundred there who could get in without a ticket. Or maybe they would give him an argument at the door. Even better. He would wait for someone to identify him. (Officer, this is *Mr. Ross*. He *won* the award.)

But no, Johnny had decided to hover around, had told Leon and Howard and everybody to leave him alone before the ceremony—even Doe. Everybody except him, Johnny, old reliable. *Old* lover.

There was no getting around it, the fun had gone out of Johnny. He was watching other people these days, instead of doing things himself. The other part, the feeling they had for each other, that was different, too. Easier and easier for him not even to feel, except for an occasional night like that first one at Sebring, when he was loaded.

Philip tucked a red kerchief into the chest pocket of his dinner jacket, checked his shirt studs, and walked out into the living room.

"Hi," he said. "How're things?"

"All right, award winner. Let's get going."

"Take it easy, Johnny. They can't do much without me, can they?"

"No, but— Oh, I suppose you're right. The car is waiting downstairs. Want me to fix you a drink?"

"No, thanks . . . New tailor, Johnny?" *Naturally* he had to be wearing one of those old Savile Row *shmattes*.

Johnny chuckled, a little uneasily. "Come on, Philip, do allow me my little snobberies like old British suits."

He flashed a charming smile, but Philip was not about to let him off the hook. "Look, if you're going to be a snob, be a *today* snob, not a yesterday snob."

He took a light coat from the closet, and they left.

There were probably four hundred people in the ballroom. The award had been presented, and Philip was seated at the center table. Nice of Leon to throw this supper dance for him, but nice for Armand-Klein, too. The other designers, all supereffusive with their congratulations, were probably choking.

All the parasites were there, the fashion writers, coordinators, textile salesmen, photographers, art directors, ad men, PR and display people—all the ones who sold fashion or used fashion but never *made* fashion. They had come to be seen, and they wanted to be seen around the winner. Including, of course, the socialites, most of them dressed in Philip Ross. The Corhans—they'd hinted ever so discreetly the week before, and Philip had had invitations sent to them— and Julia Debenham and her chums, the Young Goddesses, some of the magazines had started calling them.

Next year, they'd be mad about some other designer. But he had no intention of losing his place in the top rank. He had waited too long for this to let it slip away—he would design new things, marvelous things, and Leon would be scared shitless. Howard, though, would understand. He could count on Howard.

Kathy and Howard were at Philip's table. Kathy looked smashing in Philip's corn-yellow chiffon dress, just one thin rhinestone strap, halter top flowing into a full skirt, very Empire. Doe was wearing steel-gray, one of his crepes;

Johnny was fake-flirting all over her. Nothing sillier than an old queen playing straight.

Of course, Johnny was only forty, and he was still a handsome man. But the good body was softer, more slack now, and his face seemed to have more skin than it needed. Sometimes he seemed to Philip like a bad imitation of the young Air Force captain he'd met at the Stork.

Doe was talking: "I hope you're not as tired as I am, Philip. Worked since six this morning on the presentation. Did you like it?" Philip's collection had been shown as part of the ceremony.

"Darling, I don't have to *tell* you—it was perfect. I'm really grateful to you." He hugged her. "For everything," he whispered into her ear. He knew the whole routine on the voting, of course. He'd had flowers sent to Doe's apartment every day for a month after he'd won the award.

"I really *am* pooped," Doe said. "Johnny, would you take me home?" Johnny nodded, and they left.

That set Philip to wondering when he would be able to get out. Leon was bringing over some people again, a stupid-looking couple he did not recognize. They turned out to be movie people from the Coast. The woman, overflowing an old Adrian dress, was an incurable gusher.

"Susan Simmonds is *crazy*, just mad about those clothes you've been designing for her. She raves to absolutely *every-one* about her custom-made Philip Rosses, half of Hollywood is ready to choke her because we can only get the ready-made things. Leon, you just *have* to let Philip do some special things for me . . ."

Philip shuddered. She must weigh in at one seventy-five.

"*What* things for Susan Simmonds?" asked Leon.

Sandra, sensing trouble, laughed and shut off the subject. "That's Leon for you, doesn't even remember what movie stars they dress."

248

Philip was relieved. He'd never gotten around to telling Leon he was making private clothes for Simmonds—no sense in raising a stink. Her special styles had been sent to California as "magazine samples." Howard knew all about it, of course. Anyway, Simmonds should have kept her big mouth shut. Of course, he did want people to know he was doing her clothes . . .

The hell with it, he was not about to try to figure it out. He'd won the award, Leon should be in seventh heaven. It might help pull Armand-Klein out of mothballs. The straight collections looked tacky, dull . . . Thank God he had nothing to do with them.

The fact was, he was sick of being bossed by Leon, of having to feel guilty about things like the Simmonds specials. Soon, he'd have to do something about it.

From his seat at a nearby table, Eric Marshall watched the socialites walk past him and wave hello to the star of the evening. Ross was probably snubbing them; fine, they had it coming. *Now!* would use them, flatter some, slap others, set them to competing. They'd be good for a laugh, and Eric had editors who could keep the whole pot boiling. Bright Brooklyn kids who hated the ex-debs. It would be a pleasure.

As for Ross, the awards were pretty heady stuff. Could it be that puberty time was over? If it was, there'd be real trouble.

Eric leaned back in his chair and relaxed.

Philip finally got away at one-thirty. He never even said goodnight to Leon, although he did blow a kiss at Sandra, who was not as bad as her husband.

When he got home, he was too souped up to sleep. He took two Seconals and finally drowsed off.

At 3 A.M. the phone rang. Johnny. Drunk and cheerful and obnoxious. Philip was drug-logy and drug-honest.

"Go away, Johnny, just go away. It's three A.M."

"Look, I'm sorry, I just wanted to talk—"

"And I *don't* want to talk. *Johnny, you're a bore!*"

Johnny no longer sounded drunk. "Sorry, old man," he said and hung up.

Philip lay back down. There was one tiny moment of guilt, but then he forgot it and fell asleep.

Johnny stared at the bottle of Johnny Walker. Same name, same idea, just like it said in the ads: *Still going strong.* Not so strong now, maybe? Slower, much slower, getting his ears pinned back. The ungrateful little prick.

He was not drunk, really. These days he could *sound* drunk on a couple of shots, but he was not drunk. It was time to think sober, to sort things out here and now, at 3 A.M. in front of the bottle.

He forced his perceptions toward the truth. He had picked up Philip long ago, then pensioned him off to Farrow when he got bored with him. Ignored him for years before wanting him back, and now things were not the same. And why should they be? Philip had become famous and tough and grown-up.

Johnny smiled. You did hang around, he told himself. You did play Uncle-Johnny's-protégé-made-good. Be fair.

He felt better. Now he *would* get drunk.

And anyway, he said to himself, you always knew that you were a *ridiculous* man!

Among the letters of congratulation was one from Philip's father, who had read about the award in the Florida papers. Nice, Philip thought. Not that the old man had the first notion about what the award was *for.*

Couldn't say he cared much for the rest of the letter:

> . . . Also, Philip, I'm getting married again. You
> remember her, Emily. You met her down here after
> your mother passed away. I don't want to live alone
> any more and she'll make me a good wife that's sure.
> Anyway, son, I wish you all best again and congratu-
> lations and if you could write Emily for luck it would
> be nice. I showed her the newspaper story and picture
> too and she was proud like me. It's Miss Emily
> Dorette, 18 Cedar Road, Sebring.
> > Your Father.

Philip crumpled the letter. Write that *waitress?* The hell
he would. They were probably screwing around while his
mother was still alive.


Philip's dresses for Susan Simmonds had blown up into
a major crisis. The day after the award, Leon stalked into
the design room with Howard in tow and started question-
ing Philip. Bang!

"For Chrissakes!" Philip yelled, so that he could be
heard even back in the cutting room. "How can you be so
*stupid* about publicity? You're such a goddamn hog about the
blessed Armand-Klein name. I could have told you she
wanted me to do her clothes! We could have *all* told you!"
Thereby implicating Howard.

Leon controlled himself. He wanted to hear more, and
Philip obliged:

"I won this award for the firm because Doe Perrin helped
me—after you forced me to beg for every sample I do for
her! I drag my ass all over the country to sell our stuff, make
this firm into the hottest house on Seventh Avenue, and
then you give me a lot of flap about a few dresses for a *movie*

*actress*, yet! Don't you *know* that every other firm on Seventh Avenue would kiss her butt in Macy's window for the chance to do her clothes?"

There was a long pause. Howard watched, hypnotized. Then Leon spoke at last: "Look, Philip. You're saying a lot of things you'll regret; why don't you *listen* a minute. I resent not being told that my sample room is being used as a private couture salon. This is *not* the House of Farrow. We're a big wholesale firm, we don't waste our time on custom dressmaking. I don't care if it's for Marlene Dietrich or Lana Turner, *unless I know about it and approve it*. I'm still the guy who's running this place, which you've apparently forgotten. Now, why don't you go somewhere and cool off and try to remember that you wouldn't have won any award if I hadn't given you the chance to work here!"

He turned and left the sample room. The operators and Cindy had witnessed the whole scene. Howard felt torn between rushing after Leon and staying to soothe Philip. Somehow, it seemed easier to stay.


Philip calmed down quickly. There was something sobering about the amount of money he was going to need, and soon. He was through wasting his energy and talent as another man's employee.

Emily Debenham? That would be a laugh. But after the Farrow mess she might put too many strings on the dough. Johnny? Out of the question, he'd be all over him again. Philip was out of that bind, once and for all.

Who else? Doe Perrin was too close. He needed Doe as an editor, not an investor. Ellen Wilson and Amalgamated? Perhaps. They'd want to protect their Philip Ross business. On the other hand, what would Amalgamated say if he wanted to sell to other stores? Anyway, he was not sure Ellen would be willing to slap Leon in the face like that. She'd buy anything he designed, she'd have to. But finance him? He doubted it.

The Corhans? Maybe . . .

He searched his memory for other names and faces he had filed away under "Rich."

Then it came to him. The *Leeds*.

They were rich, young, bright, ambitious as hell, and Louise Leeds understood fashion. Philip always visited them when he was in California, and along with Susan Simmonds' dresses, several outfits a year went out to Louise.

He phoned Barry Leeds in Los Angeles.

"Philip!" said Barry. "Great to hear from you. You're not coming out, are you? Because Louise and I are on our way to New York, we were just going to wire you. And also—well, I don't have to say it in a telegram now, but *congratulations*. The *Times* fashion page had all about your award—hey, guy, you really did it, didn't you?"

"Thanks, Barry, thanks so much . . . As a matter of fact I'm glad you're coming East. I've got something important to discuss with both of you."

"Sounds mysterious. What's it all about?"

"Fact is, I'd rather not speak about it on the phone."

"Okay," said Barry, "we'll be there next Sunday, at the St. Regis. Why don't you plan to have dinner with us about eight."

"Perfect. And give my love to Louise and the kids."

"I'll do that. *Ciao*, see you then."

Philip dialed Howard immediately.


The living room of the Sands apartment was thick with smoke. Kathy pushed open the windows. Philip and Howard had been at it for over an hour.

So far she had managed to keep her temper, fussing around the room, emptying ashtrays, fixing Philip a fresh drink. Finally she went to the kitchen to get more ice. She rammed the top onto the ice bucket, then quickly checked to see if she had broken the glass inside. It was okay.

She had every right to be furious. Philip had come along with an absolute godsend, he even had backers, and Howard? Questions, questions!

Where would they find the right showroom? How would they get the stuff manufactured? How would the stores take it? Would Fassman sue them? Like an old woman, goddamn it. Now she *would* open her mouth.

She took a deep breath, then carried the ice bucket into the living room.

"Howard, so far I've shut up. But I don't get you. Philip hands us a chance to go into business and you act like no one ever opened his own firm before. What in hell is *wrong* with you?"

Her sudden vehemence surprised him. It was all very well for Philip to rush in full of big plans, and maybe these Leeds people had all the money in the world, but there was no harm being cautious. Philip was a good designer, but what could he know about business?

Kathy had never told him she wanted him to go independent anyway. He brought home enough dough, they were comfortable, so why the big push?

What's more, he *liked* Philip's plan.

"Look, Kath," he said gently, "I know others have gone into business, but then lots of them have failed, too. I'm not *against* the plan—"

"Then tell me why you're acting like a scared kid?"

Howard laughed nervously and looked at Philip, who was staring at the floor. Then back to Kathy: "You know, I had no idea you wanted something like this. Anyway, we can talk later. Let's not involve Philip."

"Philip *is* involved! It's *his* idea, and *I* like it!"

"It'll work, Howard," Philip said. "I know it will."

Howard sighed. All he was doing was figuring the odds, something he had learned from Leon.

"Look," he said. "It's not that I don't *like* the idea . . . I'll look into the factory possibilities, I should have an answer in a few days. And maybe we can get a sublease on a showroom in our building."

"Meantime," he said, "we have to keep this thing quiet. If Leon catches on, we're dead. He'd freeze us out and the stores would go along. So, Philip, you'd better be palsy with him. Make peace, buddy!"

Philip knew he was right. But the prospect of playing good little boy was not pleasant.

One day each week, Howard lunched with Randy Kirsh, Armand-Klein's young production manager. Randy was a genius. Armand-Klein's quality was the envy of Seventh Avenue, its rate of canceled or returned merchandise microscopic.

The luncheons gave Howard and Randy a chance to exchange notes, valuable because their work drew them into opposite corners of the firm. Howard was totally outside, selling and promoting, involved with stores. Randy, who dealt with factories, was totally inside.

With his receding hairline and ever-thickening glasses, Randy looked more like a scholar than a production manager. His appearance was deceiving, as any textile mill could attest. Randy was tough. Even the unions respected him.

The two men always lunched at the Artists and Writers restaurant. Ancient, oak-beamed, and beer-sodden, it was the near-exclusive territory of *Times* and *Trib* newspapermen, at the northern edge of the garment district.

Randy, who had permanent possession of a small corner table and a crotchety, wheezing waiter, added daily to his girth with orders of corned beef, flanken, kidney pie, and draft beer.

For Howard it was a welcome relief from restaurants like the Colony or Voisin. With buyers, he lunched uptown. Other days he grabbed a fast sandwich at his desk—unless he was meeting Randy, who was more methodical. Randy could always be found at "his" restaurant between one and two.

Howard usually enjoyed their lunches, but he was not looking forward to this one. As usual, they opened with a discussion about the menu. As usual, Howard followed Randy's advice, and Randy tended to order the specials. Today it was smelts, so they had smelts. The elderly waiter approved.

Then they spoke of the new collection.

"Those bias numbers are a bitch," said Randy. "Hard to sew, and it's tough to standardize fit. Can't you get Philip to stay away from them?"

"Well, I'll try."

"Bias seams *stretch* so badly," explained Randy, peering at Howard over his horn-rimmed glasses. "The hems are uneven after the dresses are pressed."

Howard commiserated, although he knew full well that if Philip felt like designing bias dresses, no one was going to talk him out of it. "Tell me something," he said to Randy. "I know we make all our stuff in our own workroom. But couldn't we use outside contractors for difficult styles like bias dresses?"

"We could, but we don't. It's against our policy."

"But there *are* good contractors for our price range?"

"You bet," said Randy. "And right here in the city."

"You're kidding, I thought they were all out of town."

"The lower-priced ones are. In the luxury field there are several just a few blocks from Fifth Avenue."

"Come on, this I have to see."

"All right, smartass, I'll send you to see one of the best, just a few houses from where you usually eat your expense-account luncheons. His name is Tony Lavorno. He's not big, but his shop could sew nearly half a million dollars' worth of merchandise if they were going full blast year-round. They can work about forty seamstresses and a dozen tailors."

"That's incredible," said Howard. "They must be busy as hell."

"Sometimes, yes," said Randy. "Before Christmas, of course, and in the early fall. Then, everybody wants them. All the stores with custom departments give them work, and most of the expensive houses, except us, whenever they get stuck and need extra sewing. At other times?" Randy shrugged. "They're starving, like in midsummer."

They moved on to other subjects. At the end of the lunch, Randy wrote a name and address on a slip of paper and handed it to Howard. "Here," he said, "look him up. It'll open your eyes." Howard shrugged and laughed again. "Well, maybe," he said. "If I have time."

The slip said:

ANTONIO LAVORNO
39b E. 53 St.
PL 6-3837

He had what he wanted. He felt lousy.


"Mr. Lavorno?" Howard looked with disbelief at the tiny man who came to the elevator to greet him. Antonio Lavorno was in his early sixties and could have doubled for Toscanini.

257

He had a high sing-song Calabrian voice, and flashed a prim smile under his neat gray mustache.

"Yes. I'm Lavorno. You mus' be Mr. Sands?"

"Right."

"Come in," Lavorno said, pointing to the noisy workroom, which resembled Armand-Klein's except that it was smaller. Through the windows Howard could see East Fifty-third Street below with its fancy shops and restaurants. It seemed incongruous, a factory in the middle of all this.

They made their way past rows of machines and cutting tables. Howard spotted several Fifth Avenue store labels on the sample dresses which hung on pipe racks, probably custom work. When they reached Lavorno's tiny office at the back of the loft, Howard said, "I came because Randy Kirsh told me about your shop. He thinks very highly of you."

Lavorno made a courtly little bow. "That's enough for me," he said. "He's a good man." He handed out and accepted compliments gracefully, like the maestro he was.

"Now," Howard continued. "There's something I want to speak to you about, but it must be kept in complete confidence. We hardly know each other, but I feel you are a gentleman of the old school, and if I ask you to—"

Lavorno raised his hands to stop him. The gesture said: "It is understood. You have my word." He looked straight into Howard's eyes.

"You want to give me some work for Armand-Klein?"

Howard shook his head; Lavorno did not seem surprised.

"Not quite," said Howard. "I'd like to know if your shop would ever be for sale."

The question was delivered quite calmly. Howard wanted to shock, fearing that Lavorno might be a slow negotiator. Pussyfooting could involve him in weeks of palaver. He continued: "Of course, only if you stayed to run the shop, Mr. Lavorno."

Lavorno took a second to digest this. Then he said: "Why do you young men always rush? What's the hurry, tell me?" As if he had not heard that Armand-Klein was not involved, he continued: "If Armand-Klein wants to give me work, why not try me first? Then, if we are both happy, we can talk about buying and selling."

Howard swallowed and plunged. "Mr. Lavorno, I'm not here to speak for Armand-Klein, I'm doing a favor for a friend. Even Mr. Kirsh doesn't know about this—and I'm really taking a chance, talking to you . . . Possibly you won't consider selling, and possibly my friend won't go ahead with his plans. But I thought we might talk, anyway."

Tony Lavorno was no fool. He had heard of Sands, of course. One of the smartest salesmen in the business. The Italian garment business community was a close family, and Tony Lavorno was a king among them. He had the inside story of every expensive firm on Seventh Avenue. If Sands wanted to talk, it was because he wanted to go into his own business. He knew there had been a big fuss between Ross and Fassman, that was why he had not checked with Kirsh after Sands had called. He had guessed enough; now he wanted the whole story.

Nice young fellow, this Sands. Looked intelligent, clean, just like he had heard. Seemed like a good boy, and bright. Ross and Sands. Would they quit Fassman? If so, they needed his shop, of course.

He liked the idea for many reasons. First, Ross was very good, very hot. He knew from the foreladies at Armand-Klein how the stuff was selling. And he had seen all the publicity. Sands was good, too. And he, Antonio Lavorno, when it came to production, he was the best.

Ever since he had arrived as a little kid tailor from Calabria fifty years before, he had done well. The right connections, many favors, much hard work. And he had saved his money, he would never have to worry. There was one thing missing: he wanted to *own* something in the fashion game, not just a shop. He had had enough of sewing labels he was not part of into clothes *he* had made.

Some men took their chances when they were very young and had nothing to lose. He could afford to take his chances now that he was old and secure. He was no longer risking the kids' education. He had waited for just such an opportunity.

Sands would never guess how he had hoped for something exactly like this, and, *Santa Maria*, he was not about to tell him.

They went to Mario's, a small Italian eating place down the block, the kind one barely noticed because it was tucked between "name" restaurants.

"For twenty-five, thirty years I've eaten here every working day," said the little Italian, and Howard was reminded of Randy. From the greeting Lavorno received, one would have thought that he paid only rare visits and that each one was a privilege for the establishment.

"*Bon giorno, Signor Lavorno,*" said the owner respectfully. They were led to Lavorno's corner table. There was a ceremonious passing out of menus, although he probably could have rattled off the bill of fare from memory.

"When I have guests," Lavorno said, "they pass the menu." He chose veal piccata and a salad. No wine, no pasta, not even antipasto. Lavorno was a disciplined man. Being fat, to him, was unpardonable. Howard, surprised at the little man's light meal, ordered lasagne.

As the other tables filled, more and more elderly Italians waved greetings to Lavorno, who called off their names. Apparently they were all production managers or factory owners, had all known each other for decades.

"Look, Howard," said Lavorno. "I can call you that?"

Howard nodded.

"I'm not for sale. Let's get that straight." Sitting down, he seemed much taller than when he stood.

"But," he continued, "there might be a way of working this out with—your friend." His forehead creased quizzically; there was a certain rakishness about him. "His initials wouldn't be P.R.?" he asked.

"Well," Howard said, caught off guard, "I really can't say, but you may make any guess you wish, Mr. Lavorno."

"Tony," said Lavorno and shrugged. "Now, let me guess. A designer, initials P.R., who is very good, has a lot of, shall we say, disagreements with his boss. So he decides he wants to go into business on his own. He says to his good friend who is the sales manager, he says, Howard—pardon me, I don't know the sales manager's name—he says, Let's go into this together, I found someone to back me. Now we need a factory, says the sales manager, the finest factory in the business, and so they come to Lavorno, of course. *Basta!*"

Howard stared at the man. He had never realized just how efficient the industry grapevine could be. "Okay," he said. "So what would Lavorno say? So far all he's said is that he's not for sale."

"Right," said the little man. "But"—he put his finger next to his nose—"maybe Lavorno wants to be a partner too. Maybe Lavorno wants to invest in this new firm."

"Would you?"

"Look," said Lavorno. "There is nothing in the whole world that could make me sell my shop, because at my age, I am sixty-three, I work each day from seven till seven and I *enjoy* it. I certainly won't work *for* anyone and still enjoy it. But I could be interested in something I had a part of."

Beautiful. Howard put his cards on the table. They tentatively agreed that if the new firm came into being, they would form a partnership, Lavorno investing the factory as his share. If they needed additional contractors, Lavorno would find them. He would be in complete charge of production.

What a break!

One more luncheon to go, thought Howard, and I'll have tied up my end of it. One more person to see after Randy and Lavorno. The path to their new firm led through mountains of food. Meantime, it was up to Philip to take care of the moneybags.

The Leeds, of course, loved the idea. When Philip mentioned seventy-five thousand dollars, plus the possibility of another fifty, they didn't bat an eye.

Barry and Louise had scaled the mountain in Los Angeles. They were now members of the Clique in good standing. Time to take on New York by way of Philip Ross, *Vogue*, *Town & Country*, *Ambience*, cocktail parties, press openings, and all the society women who wore Philip's designs. And, of course, there was *Women's Wear* and *Now!* Also, the chance to cash in.

It was really the height of something or other, an opportunity to make money while climbing.

Barry asked questions about the proposed corporation, but Philip said Howard would discuss all that with him. It was Howard, he explained, who had set up the budget and estimated the amount of money. He described Howard to them. Bright, clearheaded, attractive.

"Why not ask him over?" said Barry.

"Well, I'll see if they're home." Philip called Howard's number from the suite's bedroom: the Sands were home.

Howard arrived a half-hour later, and shook hands with

262

the Leeds. He recognized the type—he could read Bel Air Jewish at a glance. After all, he had been born on the edge of that world. Still, the Leeds seemed like nice people who didn't take themselves too seriously. Philip was lucky he hadn't scored with real phonies.

Howard explained the setup, calmly, knowledgeably. The man who ran the finest contract factory in the city wanted to be a partner. Also, he was pretty sure they could swing all the Armand Boutiques into the new firm, which would give them at least a half-million dollars' worth of business to start out. They could quickly expand from there into double that amount. The boutique thing seemed to work. Of course, now they would be called Philip Ross Boutiques.

Barry was impressed. This boy seemed to know his way around. He would be good for Philip, who might get carried away the way creative people sometimes did. Sands would keep things tidy. That factory man sounded fine, too. He would ask a few discreet questions about this whole setup— his New York lawyer friends, like Stew Sherman, who handled a lot of garment firms. Meanwhile, he wanted them to get going. They could work out the legalities in two weeks when he came back to New York.

Howard was elated, but he was not going to show it.

"Let's not forget one thing," he said.

Louise looked worried. Howard continued: "The factory man, Lavorno, he wants stock."

Barry smiled. "He can have stock. He's going to be an important part of this."

"Mrs. Leeds," said Howard, "tomorrow, why don't I show you his workroom? It's near here. I know how you like good clothes, this will be a real experience for you."

"I'd love it," she said.

Howard was a smart boy. Now Barry was sure of it.

Howard's third lunch was with his former roommate. Tom Brett, who had quit the agency to open his own shop a few years ago, had prospered.

He was one of the new breed of advertising men who sold products with a low-key, witty, sometimes even snide approach. Where the large agencies muscled the public, the new ones winked and sold them with tongue planted firmly in cheek. The technique was shrugged off in many board rooms. It might entertain the public, but (small guffaw), "no one remembers the product!"

Tom's campaigns were the talk of the advertising business. His newest client was Ellbaum's, a large discount department store eager to upgrade its image after moving from Fourteenth Street to middle Fifth Avenue. Ellbaum's owners were ambitious and smart, but they had not found their image moving up along with the store.

Tom sold them on a semivulgarity which became enormously effective. Ellbaum's began a series of "*She* Was Here" ads, full pages in the *Times* and the *Tribune:*

> "*She Was Here* . . . !
> "Who?
> "The *Duchess,* that's Who!"

The duchess, by implication, was of course the Duchess of Trent, who was visiting New York. And, it was true, the duchess had been to Ellbaum's, shopping for table linens. There was also "The Red-haired Actress," a great movie star; "The Brand-new Divorcee," a tobacco billionairess; and other prominent women who supposedly loved bargain hunting at Ellbaum's now that it was within walking distance of their usual Fifth Avenue shops.

Guessing the identity of the Mystery Woman in the Ellbaum ads became the New York game of the season, and

"*She* Was Here!" found its way into TV comedy routines. Famous women came to shop at Ellbaum's, and ambitious ones hoped that they would be one of the Mystery Women. Often, Tom's agency prearranged it. After *Time* magazine's advertising section wrote a piece about the campaign, Tom's firm was deluged with hopeful new clients, many of whom were turned away.

As busy as he was, Tom always welcomed the chance to see Howard. He ordered coffee while Howard asked for a martini.

"What's the matter?" Howard asked. "Have you changed, dear boozy boy?"

"You mean the coffee?" Tom grinned. "Howie, it doesn't make sense for me to drink. Particularly martinis. The ad business is enough of a cliché, all by itself. Besides, teetotaling makes me an eccentric. Puts clients on their guard. Treat me like Torquemada."

"Your image?"

"That's a cliché, more Madison Avenue bullshit. Remember when I used to curse all the ads?"

"Do I remember? You'd sail the Sunday magazines past my head and spit after them."

"Enough," said Tom. "Now why don't you tell me what this lunch is all about. The rag business fallen in love with me?"

"Come on, they *hate* you. You're making Ellbaum's into a big deal."

"What's wrong with that?"

"They sell *copies* of originals. Cheap copies."

"Yeah, I know . . . Fuck 'em," he said, quietly and with conviction. They ordered lunch.

Then Howard told Tom about the plan and asked if he would help them put across their message.

"You realize," he said, "we can't spend much dough the

first couple of years. We'll have to shovel it all into running the firm."

"I realize," said Tom. "But I'll do it."

"For old times' sake?"

"Stuff that, Howie! I'd loan you dough, I'd feed you or bail you out of jail. But I wouldn't work for you for old times' sake."

"Then why?"

"Because of what you said before about how Seventh Avenue feels about Ellbaum's. I knew it, of course. But with your setup, I'll get a chance to operate on Seventh Avenue itself, and with the best stores in the country.

"I'll tell you what I'll do. Until you can afford to spend for real we'll heavy it up on publicity, which costs staff time but not much out of pocket, and on space advertising we'll kick back two-thirds of our commissions so you can add that to your measly budget. We'll get you six figures' worth of exposure for peanuts. And probably lose money in the process, but don't worry, when you get rich, we'll start stealing."

"Thanks," said Howard. "Where do we start?"

"Well," said Tom. "We start with"—he burst into laughter—"with the Philip Ross *image*."

Howard's next and final move was trickier. They had to make sure of Ellen Wilson and Torrey's. Visiting the store on the pretext of a meeting with the advertising vice-president, Howard stopped with Ellen's secretary and asked to see her boss "for a minute." He apologized for dropping in, and asked Ellen for a meeting later in the week. They had been friends since Ellen was a buyer; he was counting on this friendship when he told her that the meeting would be personal and confidential.

Ellen, as it turned out, was way ahead of him. By the time Howard left, she had not only figured out what he

266

wanted but had made her decision. Torrey's future was with young ideas. If Howard and Philip had the production end figured out along with the designing, she'd go along.

She listened patiently to the two of them when they met for lunch. When she heard that Lavorno would be making the goods, she relaxed. Like everyone in the high-priced retail business, she knew Mr. Tony. He would turn out Philip's designs to perfection.

Howard and Philip were all set.

Eric Marshall got the first clue through a publicity woman, who told a *Now!* reporter she had eavesdropped at Howard Sands' table during lunch. Eric knew about the Ross blowup with Fassman after the award, but had decided not to use it because it might harm Ross, and Ross was "on." Eric did not want to shake him. Not yet.

*Now!* policy as to who was "on" and who was "off" was determined by a C (for Confidential) note circulated from Eric's office after the weekly editorial board meetings. It reached reporters' desks within ten minutes. Sometimes the "on" and "off" ratings changed so rapidly that it was hard for the entire staff to keep pace, and favorable mention slid into a story after someone had been declared "off." C-notes were not confined to designers or socialites. They also covered stores, magazines, newspapers, politicians, authors, hotels, or plays.

Philip's rating had been rising ever since the original La Ronde story. These days, whenever *Now!* did a photographic roundup of designers, Philip's picture was placed in a prominent position. A C-note sent out to the art department had taken care of that. And certain reporters, anxious to please Eric, made it their policy to write about Philip with near-reverence.

Eric knew exactly what lay behind these accolades, but

had decided to do nothing about either the articles or the writers for the time being. Despite the award, Philip had not become obstreperous the way Villard had in Paris.

The C-note on Villard had gone out long ago. Villard was "off." *Now!* hardly ever mentioned him, and if it did it was with derision. It reported only his failures or detrimental rumors. Villard had signed his own warrant by writing a letter to Eric asking *Now!* to spotlight those designs which were his own favorites rather than the *costumes quelconques* that *Now!* saw fit to acclaim.

Eric had never bothered to answer Villard's letter. So far as *Now!* was concerned, Villard was through. Villard knew it, and some American buyers knew it. Certain stores preferred the couturiers *Now!* liked because their customers were faithful readers. Villard's sales during the next Paris openings slipped. For a while he felt the pinch, but he was a top designer and eventually his American customers returned. If the whole thing had happened a year earlier, when Villard was still a newcomer, it might have marked the end of his *maison*.

Susan Ahern continued to photograph Villard's designs despite his slide from grace, but the great fashion magazines were no longer the sole arbiters. Their power was being usurped by the daily press, television, wire services, the weekly national news magazines, and *Now!* It took *Ambience*, *Vogue*, and *Bazaar* four months to produce an issue. They were defenseless against other, faster-moving, media.

Eric Marshall sensed that the rumor about Ross and Sands was true. The big question was, where was Ross getting the money? One of his writers who covered society news suggested the Corhans, who were friends of Doe Perrin's. Eric was about to tell her to check with Doe, but he decided against it. Usually the Young Goddesses spilled their guts as soon as they heard that *Now!* was calling, but Doe was no society-dame pushover.

Next, he checked with his bureau chiefs. He drew blanks from Chicago, Dallas, and Boston. Then a girl in the Los Angeles office came up with the Leeds.

"As a matter of fact, they were in New York last week."

Eric asked her why the Leeds might want to invest in Ross, and got the whole story of their climb into the Clique after their first big break, the Farber's opening.

It looked good, but Eric knew that if the story was true more news would break soon. Sometimes *Now!* hurried along events by running small items which "quoted rumors." These were usually followed by angry denials or by solid evidence.

This time, Eric wanted to hold off the rumor approach and wait a few more days.

The clincher came from an unlikely source—*Now!*'s factory expert, a contributing editor who did stories about production, labor unions, manufacturing techniques. Eric rarely bothered to read them, since he had no interest in this important area of the fashion business.

The editor said that Sands had lunched with Lavorno, then patiently explained who Lavorno was and why it was important.

"Armand-Klein," he said, "would never use him, they only use their own workrooms, so Sands must be planning something private. It's all over the Italian workrooms, but *they* think Armand-Klein is *buying* Lavorno."

"Think Fassman's got wind of it?"

"I doubt it," said the editor, himself an Italian. "It's a very closed *familia*, and Fassman's production man is Jewish."

Ross and Sands, and now Lavorno! He had better talk to Doe.

"Look," Doe said, "I got into hot water the last time we 'talked.' Philip is a friend of mine, and you might as well realize I won't say anything that might hurt him. With you, that means not saying *anything*."

Eric was amazed. Loyalty was not a quality he encountered often in this business. But then, Doe was one of the few people in the business capable of surprising him.

"What I don't understand," she went on, "is why you *want* to print things that can do so much harm?"

"The point isn't to make trouble. We just want to be first, bring news to our readers."

"Bunk!" she said.

He was pleased, somehow. "All right," he said. "You have the right to your opinions. Now you tell *me* what harm will be done if we say Philip Ross is opening his own business and who is backing it."

"Look, Eric"—he always took pleasure in her use of his first name—"I know exactly why you want to run this story. You want to raise a stink, and you couldn't care less about Philip or what happens to him *or* about your readers."

She was right, of course. Eric had always resented anyone who presumed to lecture him about the morality of the magazine, yet he did not mind it coming from her. And, nothing she said would stop him from running the story.

It broke in *Now!*'s next edition, in a separate box, headlined as a fait accompli: "PHILIP ROSS TO GO IT ALONE!" Then came a résumé of every rumor, every wisp of evidence, every supposed statement from an "inside source." The story drew no conclusions except to say that this was "yet another step in youth's battle against the petrifying influence of old-line Seventh Avenue." Even this was attributed to "a major store buyer who refused to be identified."

It was perfect *Now*style.

Leon was in Chicago, where he had gone to hire two new salesmen. The last man interviewed had just left the suite. Leon fished four cubes out of the water in the ice bucket that had been standing uncovered since noon, then filled the glass with club soda. It was still mid-afternoon, and in Leon's lexicon alcohol was immoral at that time of day.

And so he slipped off his shoes, put his tired feet up on the ottoman and lethargically picked up his copy of Now!

The front-page box slapped him in the face: "PHILIP ROSS TO GO IT ALONE!"

He read it the first time as if it were in a foreign language. The second time he read it more slowly, as if translating. He moved his shoulders, which had suddenly developed a great, familiar ache.

Slowly, in his stocking feet, he walked to the telephone and gave the New York name and number to the operator. His mind must have been wandering because it seemed only a second before Howard was on the line.

"Howard, is it true?"

There was absolute silence.

"Howard, I'm too old for you to lie to me."

"I'm sorry, Leon. Yes, it's true."

"Tell Philip to pick up the extension. And you stay on, hear?"

He could hear the voices in the background, then Philip was on the extension.

"Philip?"

"Yes, Leon."

"Is it true?"

Howard started to speak. "Shut up!" Leon cut him off sharply. "I'm talking to Philip."

"Leon," said Philip, "I would have preferred a chance to sit down and explain it all face to—"

"Face," said Leon, surprising himself with the way he kept his voice in check. "Face I know about. I'd like to see yours right now. Are you ashamed?"

"Leon, please, let's talk this—"

"Please, a question is a question. Are you ashamed?"

"It was a great opportunity, I couldn't pass it up."

"An opportunity," said Leon, his voice rising, "is something that picks you up in the street. I think this opportunity you went looking for in every alley in Seventh Avenue, following the smell of money, am I right?"

"Leon," said Philip, "I want this to be amicable."

"I taught you."

"Yes, you did."

"I gave you chances."

"Yes."

"And you knife me like a mugger in the back, me who was, you hear me, a friend to both of you! No, don't you get off, Howard. In the Army, they shoot deserters, you'd be shot for doing this, hear? And you"—Leon could feel the sweat soaking his shirt, his voice and blood rising, but never mind it didn't matter any more—"you, Philip, I brought you along, and you—"

Philip cut in. "Leon, you have no right to attack us this way. You're not my father. This is just a business. And business is business . . . How many times have I heard you say that?"

Leon was screaming now, as if his voice had to carry the force of his message from Chicago to New York on its own energy: "*I want you both out of the premises, my premises, right now, today, this afternoon, you hear?*"

There was silence at the New York end but they had not hung up.

"Philip, you've heard me use the expression to be a *mensch*, a real man. Philip, you're not a *mensch*, you're a cunt!" With which Leon smashed the receiver down and kept it down with both his hands as if he were smothering both of them.

In New York, Philip and Howard glanced at each other over the dead buzzing phones in their hands.

They were free.

# BOOK
# 5

THE pancake make-up was cold and wet. The make-up man had not the faintest idea who Philip was, nor did he care. There were ten guests on *Nightshow* each evening; except for a few big-time movie names, he recognized none of them. He always wondered why a network show like *Nightshow* bothered with people who had written books or built bridges or designed women's clothes . . . At least this guy had a good face. Could have been an actor. Nice tan, too.

The make-up man had long ago given up being careful about his work. The big-time actors treated him like he was a butcher, and the others didn't know good make-up from shinola. So he slapped it on and got it over with. "Okay," he said, pulling the napkin from Philip's throat. "That's it."

A girl from the *Nightshow* staff led Philip into a small room where the other guests were waiting their turn to go on the air. The show had been on for an hour, and Philip was the next guest but one on the schedule. He had missed rehearsal earlier in the afternoon because he was on his way in from Chicago, but Patricia, the girl who handled publicity at Philip-Ross Inc., had set up the fashion show and rehearsed the models.

Philip read over the line-up, barely able to see in the dim light. The clothes were so familiar anyway that he could have done without the description. After all, he had set up each costume, from hair style to shoes, for his press opening earlier that month.

Patricia had picked the "joke" outfits, of course, the ones he had designed for shock. No use showing great designs on a nighttime TV entertainment show. You chose the extravagant, the silly, the sexy styles, the tit-and-navel stuff, as Farrow had called it. (Out comes an ostrich-feather pantsuit with a wide-open midriff, almost down to the pubic hair. Higher up, the bottom of the bust peeks out. "What do you call this, Mr. Ross?" asks the host. "My shopping center suit!" Laugh . . . "Do you mean to say that my wife could wear this to the shopping center?" Smile. "Well, no. But your wife would be a shopping center if she wore it." Laugh, laugh. "Tell me, Mr. Ross, how much is this little number?" "Oh"—pause, seemingly to search the memory—"about five hundred dollars." Audience ooohs. Host does double-take, "Five hundred dollars?" "Yes." Calm, now. "You see, we had marked it six hundred, but it seemed a bit high . . ." Laugh, laugh, laugh.)

He knew how it would go. He had done ten, no, eleven of these network shows during the last year. He knew the flood of mail that followed each appearance, and how it set off all the rest of the PR machinery. Philip Ross was becoming a name, a household word, far beyond Seventh Avenue.

Looking around at the others in the room, he recognized the new singer who was such a smash at the Persian Room. She had already done one number and now she was wiping her armpits with Kleenex. No wonder. It was hot out there under the lights, and her crepe dress was beginning to stain. Someone poked him in the ribs. Don Jefferson. He'd known Don would be on the show, but he hadn't seen him in the make-up room.

"I'm gonna *sing*," said Don, laughing.

"Didn't know you could."

"Can't act, either." Don's teeth shone white in the half-light. "Anyway, everyone else sings. And *I'm* prettier." He laughed again. Philip liked him more each time.

"I *heard* that you were entertaining at some White House bash and that you were damned good."

"It seemed to work out," Jeffson said. "The Kennedys are such good Joes . . . and there are so many *pretty people* around Washington now. Even pretty girls. In *Washington!*"

"I know what you mean," said Philip. "The Kennedys have given Seventh Avenue a big shot in the arm. We don't have to ass-kiss Paris as much any more . . ."

Later, when he was on the air and all the gags had been milked from the six costumes he had shown, the host, Don Darrow, turned serious. He asked:

"Now tell me, Philip. Famous designers like you, who really are so well known in this country, how do you feel about all the hullabaloo over the Paris designers?" He wrinkled his brows and shifted into sincere-and-warm gear. "Surely people like you and Norell and Trigère (quick aside to the camera: "There, Lora, I know their names") are much more important to American women."

Philip paused for a moment. Then he said, "I must say I think you're right, Don. Frankly, there's very little reason to go to Paris now. I'd say the couturiers there have pretty much had it. American fashion can make it entirely on its own."

The spontaneous applause from the audience made it clear that Philip had been a smash.

Cindy switched off the set. That arrogant, loud-mouthed "American fashion can go it on its own." Of course it could. But not the way Philip Ross worked. The bastard had spent years going over there to copy, and now he was playing Balenciaga! She poured herself a scotch and threw herself on the couch. It was just too much! She could *not* get away from him.

First the story on her in *Women's Wear*: ". . . the genius young girl Veep in charge of design at Armand-Klein who learned her craft from the great Philip Ross . . ." And that idiot woman doing a Detroit *Free Press* story who called to ask her questions about Ross: ("We know you must be *devoted* to him.") Devoted her ass! But she couldn't very well say that, so she'd rattled off some lukewarm things like how she would always be grateful to Philip. Then the "Tops of Seventh Avenue" spread in this morning's *Now!* where Philip's photo took up a third of the page and hers was a postage stamp at the bottom in the last row.

There had been twelve, count 'em, *twelve* Ross credits in the last "Fashions of the Times." And to top it all off, Fassman had made her redo some of Philip's old bodies—four-year-old stuff!

The phone rang—some guy asking her for a date that weekend.

He got short shrift.

The sparrows were making a great racket, the way city birds do on a gray morning. Eric rolled over on his back and put his hands behind his head. There were dark clouds outside, and he sensed the brooding mood of early, dubious spring when a man wishes he could go back to sleep until it is sunny again.

Doe's side of the bed was empty. " 'Morning!" he called into the next room, half expecting to find her gone off to work, leaving him juice and coffee.

" 'Morning." She came into the room carrying a breakfast tray. In her jeans and loose shirt, hair tied back with a ribbon, she looked sixteen. Then it came to him. Saturday! Today was Saturday.

He drank his coffee, ate some toast, and read the *Times* and the *Trib*. She watched him, he thought, as if she had never before seen a man eat breakfast in bed. He loved her. And he had made up his mind.

"What's the plan?" she asked.

"Let's loaf."

"Where?"

"Here. I'll get magazines, and you've got your lousy novel. We'll order in pizzas for lunch, watch the ball game if it isn't rained out. A fine *bon bourgeois* Saturday in Manhattan. What do you think of them apples?"

"I like them."

"Then tonight we'll go to an artsy-fartsy movie on Third Avenue . . ."

"Yes. Let's be *culturels*."

"If the line's not too long."

"Right. If it is, we'll go for hamburgers."

"And screw the movies."

"And screw the movies!" she agreed.

He shaved and showered, put on clean chinos, a faded shirt, and a golf jacket. He kept his Sunday loafing clothes at her place, and she was no longer embarrassed to send them to her laundry. Good God, he thought, for a girl who's been around . . .

Leon turned to the market quotations. Armand-Klein's stock was up again. He was still not used to the idea that he no longer owned Armand-Klein, that thousands of stockholders did. Or that after years of trying not to show a big taxable profit, he was now anxious to show a blockbuster before taxes.

It was one year since Armand-Klein had gone public, one hell of a year. After the Ross disaster he'd been fed up, ready to pack it in. Then along had come the downtown bankers, who persuaded him to float an issue of Armand-Klein stock.

It was incredible. People all over the country had bought it. He didn't kid himself; they weren't buying Leon Fassman, they were buying potential dividends. And yet, in a way they *were* buying him. After all, *he* was responsible for their damned dividends, responsible to every one of them, all year, every year, not just the month before stockholders' meetings. That was the strangest experience of all: having to face complete strangers who could ask questions about every detail of the business.

After all those years when he was so proud of being accountable to no one . . .

Still, he was a very rich man.

Tom Brett had done a remarkable job for Philip-Ross. He had demanded only two things: a set budget and the right to spend it as he pleased. Philip and Howard had given him a reasonable budget for the first year and increased it the second. Nothing extravagant, but it had figured to be a disproportionate 10 percent of their first year's projected sales volume.

Two-thirds of the first year's ad and promotion budget had gone for public relations. Tom did not care about the magazine commissions he sacrificed; he was laying the groundwork for the following year's advertising. He gave press parties, three of them, at five thousand apiece. He got Philip on every network talk show. He paid two well-known writers to do stories about him, and the pieces—along with photographs Philip had posed two days for—were sold to two mass-circulating magazines.

Before long, textile-fiber companies were running national ads using Philip's name. The new firm was swamped with license requests from manufacturers of everything from children's wear to luggage.

Other Seventh Avenue designers sneered at Philip's "overexposure" and his constant, "vulgar" guest appearances on TV.

"They're peeing in their tight pants," said Tom. "Because we're building a national personality instead of some chi-chi cocktail-party hero. *They* think they're famous when the pansy decorators in Beverly Hills or a few rich bitches in Palm Beach recognize their names? We're getting Philip known in the smallest towns in the country."

He was right. On planes, in restaurants, even just standing on a street corner, Philip often found himself recognized by complete strangers. Press agents used his name to publicize nightclubs. Columnists he had never met wrote that he dined in restaurants he had never heard of.

Fashion magazines used more of his designs than ever. Now that he controlled his own sample room, he encouraged editors to ask for special styles. Tom Brett was with him on it all the way.

"Even if we spend a thousand dollars a month on special samples, it's worth it," he said.

Howard had decided to do without out-of-town salesmen for the first few years. All sales were booked at 551 Seventh Avenue in the Philip-Ross showroom. They had spent a lot for "premium" space. Seventh Avenue had its own snobbery; had they been only one building away, they might as well have been in Queens.

Certain buildings specialized in cheap sportswear; others had only coat and suit manufacturers. The "intimate apparel" manufacturers, as they delicately called themselves, were on Madison Avenue in the thirties; the children's-wear houses in one monster building on Thirty-fourth Street. The buyers insisted on buildings that specialized in their particular area of merchandising, and 551 Seventh was the Buckingham Palace of the luxury dress manufacturers.

The Philip-Ross reception room was decorated in stark black and white, accented with modern original prints, mostly color lithographs. But the focal point of the inner showroom was the Philip Ross collection, without a single thing to distract the buyers' attention.

Compared with the solid wood-trimmed décor of the older houses, the showroom seemed contemporary and successful, but not reassuring. At Philip-Ross fashion was presented rather than sold. The younger buyers were at home with this kind of unsentimental professionalism, but it chilled some of the older merchants. No matter. The designs were good, the clothes sold, and Philip's name was a huge drawing card.

Soon the name began to outweigh the designs, and even the standard, "safe" dresses began to sell in great volume. Many women shied away at first, thinking Philip Ross would be "too high-styled" for them. They would go to his boutiques "just to have a look," select a simple, standard dress, and proudly wear "their" Philip Ross. Dresses almost exactly like them were to be found in many other lines, but as Philip Ross dresses, they were special.

Howard was delighted by this development. Philip was irritated when he noticed the sales figures for the "dumb" dresses.

"I don't get you," said Howard. "I think it's great we're selling so many staples. That's where the real profit is, not in the tricky, high-styled stuff."

"That's just it," Philip said, shaking his head. "It's the wrong *kind* of selling for us. A lot of dull dames all over the boutiques will put off our *fashion* customers. And before you know it we'll be making clothes for the 'average woman,' whoever the hell she's supposed to be."

282

"Dammit, Philip, the staple stuff is easy to make and we don't have to break our balls getting it into the stores. Best of all, we don't have to sit around with crossed fingers hoping it will sell."

"And what about the women who expect me to do something different, new, something they'll get a kick out of wearing?"

Howard shrugged. "Go right ahead and design for them, nobody's stopping you. Meantime, we've got to make dough. It's only our second year. We're still babies—"

"—With a five-hundred-grand volume."

"—And a thirty thousand first-year loss."

"Come on, Howard, we spent more than fifty thousand just to open our doors, so if we only showed a thirty-thousand loss, we made money the first year."

"As a businessman, you've got the head of a flea. We still have to make back the thirty . . . Come on, be a good guy and give me some more of those dumb dresses."

Philip softened. "Okay," he said. "But next year no more crap. As soon as we're in the black, we concentrate on new ideas, not those dumb dresses you love so much."

"I don't love 'em," Howard said. "Customers do."

"Which customers? The kind that make you want to throw up?"

"What do you care, Philip?"

"I care."


Someone at *Now!* cared, too. Among the predictions for the forthcoming season there was an item which read: "Hopefully, Philip Ross, his great talent now unharnessed, will resist his recent tendency to play it safe . . ."

Philip phoned Eric Marshall. "Look, Eric, it's not really fair to needle me for playing it safe."

"Why?" Eric sounded pleasantly interested, willing to listen.

"Well, you know, we've just started the business a year and a half ago and we've got to get into the black. There's plenty of avant-garde stuff in the line for those who'll buy it."

"I suppose you're right, Philip."

"Just so you understand why I have to show some dumb stuff in the collections."

"I understand."

"Can we have lunch next week?"

"Afraid I've got a helluva schedule next week. Guess we'll have to leave it till later in the month."

"Okay," said Philip. "I'll check with you in a couple of weeks."

"Right, Philip. 'Bye."

Eric had sounded rushed. He must have people in his office.

There was another reason why Philip was disturbed by the *Now!* item. For some time, he had felt that the clothes he was designing were somehow—*wrong*. They were not suitable for tomorrow's woman. Her life would be busy and fast-moving, and her clothes would have to live with her, *move* with her.

There were designers, new ones, who were trying for a new look: shorter skirts, lower, more comfortable heels, dancer's tights to replace stockings, and pants for almost any occasion. Women's figures were changing, too. Some of the new designers said tomorrow's women, with their slimmer bodies, would not need girdles or uplift bras.

For the first time since he'd begun as an apprentice at Farrow, Philip *sensed* a new manner of clothes. His own adventurousness had always been limited—he had styled, shuffled, redecorated things on the basis of an old formula which he had never thought to question. There were dresses, and coats, and suits. One designed them the way one could cook stew—in a hundred different ways. Still, it would always be stew.

Now he wanted to wipe away the limits which had tied him to words like "dress" and "suit." At first the ideas came to him piecemeal. He sketched them on the backs of envelopes, menus, theater programs, and stuffed them into his pockets.

Before long, he was sketching in earnest, putting samples to work. The theme that emerged was not entirely his own, but the look *was* new: tunics, loose and very short, worn over tights. The tunics and tights complemented each other's colors and patterns or even matched. He added shoes with almost-flat heels, like children's shoes, which would allow a woman to walk with long, free strides.

The woman he envisioned looked rather like a schoolgirl, with short, loose hair and practically no make-up except for the eyes. Very slim, very young, very innocent. Admittedly, he was aiming at an ideal, but he knew no other way to make his point. Eventually, *everyone* would want to look young.

He met with Belettinis, a shoe firm, and they promised to make the "little-girl" shoes. The milliner, Somo, suggested schoolgirl boaters, worn on the back of the head. Philip loved the idea. Next he asked a ballet supply store to dye special tights in specific colors. The store was happy to cooperate with the great Philip Ross. Finally, he and the head of Torrey's beauty salon worked out a new haircut and subtler make-up for the models.

The fall collection was already in work when the new styles, a total of fifteen pieces, were added to the overloaded sample room. Philip was happy. For the first time, he was in the forefront of a trend.

At Philip-Ross there was a gentleman's agreement that once the outline of the collection had been discussed by the three partners, the sample room was off limits to Howard and Mr. Tony until Philip was ready to show them the finished new collection, usually ten days before the opening. The staple numbers, of course, were always predictable. Sometimes the new styles were a bit startling, but Howard and Mr. Tony were pros, and they usually understood them. But nothing had prepared them for the shock at the end of *this* preview.

The first fifty pieces were safe enough, all quite familiar, all in the Philip Ross manner. They were not new, but they were charmingly redesigned and very salable. The pieces buyers would place in depth after they had bought the newer things from the collection.

Then Philip walked out of the models' room. "Now, gentlemen," he announced, "I shall show you something completely new. It's called Little Mary."

Out came six girls with short hair, pale faces and huge, doll-like eyes who wore kids' clothes—little girls' clothes. Smocks and tights!

Howard and Mr. Tony looked at each other. Surely these were gags? Philip was playing a little joke! They would have laughed, but they did not want to seem rude. They smiled, and Howard said, "That's very cute. Now, how about the new dresses?"

"You're looking at them," said Philip. "This is my new look for the season. Little Mary."

"You're kidding," said Howard, though he suddenly knew Philip was perfectly serious. "Look, Philip, the staples were fine, but we must have some new *dresses*, some new ideas I can sell."

"You've seen the new ideas."

"Oh come on, now. We've seen some new, well, costumes. Why, they're more like—sportswear. You can't expect women to buy sportswear at Philip-Ross Boutiques, not at our prices. With our sewing costs these things will be just as expensive as real dresses—am I right, Tony?"

Mr. Tony took his time before speaking. Then he said, "Philip, I think I understand what you've tried to do. Don't think I have no feeling for what you showed us. They are— how shall I say it?—very modern clothes. They are *interesting*. But they are not the sort of thing we can make, because we would have to make them too expensive for what they are. Why would a woman pay two hundred dollars for a little smock?"

"You two don't understand," Philip protested. "These are not sports clothes. They're much finer, much more subtle. These will be worn in the streets very soon."

"In Cleveland? Or Seattle?" Howard said with heavy irony. "You must be nuts! You really expect grown-up women to wear those things?"

"You saw them on the models, *they're* grown women."

"Right," said Howard. "And if all women looked like our models we'd have no trouble. Have you forgotten the fat-assed dames you meet on your trips?"

"They're changing," said Philip.

"In a pig's eye!" Howard stalked out of the showroom.

Tony patted Philip's arm. "I'll calm him down," he said, "but, Philip, you must understand, you're making things very tough for him. And for me, too. You know I never interfere with your work, but I think you should prepare a few new-looking things we can sell, not just experiments."

It was the first time Howard and Philip had really

clashed. Luckily, Tony Lavorno was there to balance things. Philip boiled, but the next day, after an hour of Mr. Tony's cajolery, he sketched some additional dresses. They *looked* new, but to Philip they were the same old stuff, more rehash, not really different from the things he had designed all along.

Howard was delighted with them. He apologized to Philip for blowing off.

As usual, Philip invited *Now!* to a special advance showing of his collection, before the regular press opening. It was best to satisfy *Now!*'s demand for advance news. American designers who refused to allow previews of their collections were brushed off with secondary coverage.

Usually he showed to senior editors, but the two girl reporters who arrived from *Now!* were new to him. They seemed like nice kids, though they looked rather scruffy in a Greenwich Village way. They were lavish with their praise— particularly for the Little Mary look. The photographer who came with them took dozens of shots of Philip as he answered their questions. After taking voluminous notes, the girls left and a staff artist from *Now!* arrived to sketch several styles. *Now!* would run the story in the upcoming issue, which would appear the day of Philip's press showing. Perfect timing!

*Now!* was delivered to Philip's apartment on the morning *before* his opening.

On pages four and five were four sketches of Little Mary, superimposed over a large photo of himself. The sketches were marvelous. Then he began to read the text.

### ROSS REACHES!
After only two years on his own, Philip Ross, who has prospered by playing a safe game for safe ladies,

has gone experimental! Probably because he now re-
fuses to go to Paris—as he stated on nationwide TV—
he attempts to create his own silhouette. Successfully?
Who knows? Much of what he does seems to suffer in
the translation. Is it couture? Is it sportswear?

"Tomorrow's woman wants to have new, free
clothes," declares Ross. He is adamant about his new
shape. He calls it Little Mary. Is Little Mary too juvenile? Is New York the place to *originate* fashion, and
will the Fashionables pay attention?

Philip Ross has cast himself adrift from Paris. Has
he cast himself adrift from fashion? *Is Ross Reaching?*

Philip could not believe it. He reread the story. The sons
of bitches were trying to sink him! He slammed the magazine
on the table and picked up the phone to call Howard, but
hung up before dialing. Howard would gloat, so would Mr.
Tony. No! They would be scared shitless, because this was
the first time Philip had ever been downgraded by *Now!*

And that wasn't all. He could see Louise Leeds' face
when she picked up her copy at the St. Regis book shop. She
had flown in for the opening, and, of course, she expected a
glowing review. And how about the press people who were
coming to his show later that afternoon? They'd feel like
suburbanites who had bought advance tickets to a musical
that got panned. And the buyers? Oh, great!

Damn those two little tramps from *Now!* What in hell
could they know about fashion? They had smiled and smiled
and said it was just *marvelous*. Goddamn them!

Eric Marshall himself had assigned the two new kids to
cover the Ross collection. He was interested in their reaction, although he had already decided how *Now!* would
handle the story.

The girls had raved, of course. They loved everything

Ross had done, and described Little Mary in ecstatic clichés: "Great, free new look, fresh as spring . . . A new leaf in the fashion dictionary!" It must have been flattering to have the great Philip Ross explain his own ideas.

Too bad.

Because that was not the way the story would read. If the kids objected, they could quit, but he doubted they would. Working for *Now!* was big time. New staff members rarely quit the magazine. Three or four years later, maybe, but not when they'd just started.

After Philip's last phone call, Eric had considered sending out a C-note to play Ross down for a while, but he'd decided to wait until this collection. It would crunch harder to give a mediocre review before the all-important fall opening.

He *had* to do it, of course, Ross was getting too big-mouthed and too sure of himself. His anti-Paris statement on *Nightshow* had been the clincher. The Paris office of *Now!* had been swamped with complaints from the couturiers, whose American spies had reported the whole thing. The French knew that Ross was a big name in America and that he just might influence other Seventh Avenue people to stay away. If Paris ever lost its American buyers, it would lose interest in *Now!* and Eric could not afford that. He had spent too many years keeping Paris friendly and frightened.

Eric himself had written the earlier gossip piece about Ross "playing it safe." He had hoped it would warn Ross not to get too high and mighty. Obviously it hadn't penetrated, because Ross had phoned and whined about the item.

As always, he was thinking of the magazine. His personal feelings did not count. Of course, this would be the end of any semblance of friendship between him and Ross, if you could call it that. Who was kidding whom? Ross was a friend as long as *Now!* praised him to the skies.

Looking back, *Now!* had done a great deal for Ross. It was their original "young designer" story which had started him toward fame . . . So it was over, and Eric had lost another "friend" like the dozens who had preceded Ross. Damn them all, he was well rid of them. Puberty time was over, once again.

The whole stupid unending round of it! Seventh Avenue was sickening, and so was Paris. The couturiers were like sharks who smelled blood. They tackled anything in sight, including each other.

No doubt, he would be in for a furious phone call from Doe on this one. The thought lightened his mood.

The opening was over.

To Philip, who had stayed in the models' room during the entire show, the applause sounded phony, the backstage congratulations hypocritical. (Louise Leeds: "Of course, darling, it was all just marvelous! The new things, well, I don't *understand* them but they were awfully *interesting!*" Unlike her to gush like that.)

Howard tried to soothe Philip. Of course he didn't like the *Now!* story, but it *was* a two-page spread. Howard's job was to sell the normal dresses, and for all he cared, no one had to buy Little Mary.

Tom Brett asked Philip to join him for a drink at the Plaza after the show. He wasted no time on diplomacy.

"What did you do to screw yourself up with Marshall?"

"Look, it *was* a two-page spread."

"Come on, buddy, this is me, Brett, your image maker. Marshall has never reamed you before."

"Honestly, Tom, I don't know."

"Well, let me have a guess . . . You shot your mouth off about Paris, remember? Not smart, that."

"Why, for chrissakes?"

"If you don't know, chum, I can't tell you. But never mind, you're a big name now, and every time you're on network TV you get to more people in five minutes than you can reach through *Now!* in a year. *Now!* hurt your vanity because they made you look sick in front of your own industry, but don't overrate them . . .

"Look, Philip, in Hollywood they have *Insider*, a scandal sheet, prints things you wouldn't believe about love affairs and gambling debts and blow jobs. Everyone in the movie business reads it, but no one has ever lost a job because of it—if they're big. If you're box office they don't care if you screw lampposts; they'll hire you anyway, so long as you bring in the loot." He smiled. "Same with you. Long as your clothes sell out in the stores, you don't have anything to worry about. If this had happened two years ago, well, it might have been a different story. But you're pretty solid now, so don't get your insides in an uproar."

Tom sounded reassuring, but still, Philip wished it all hadn't happened.

When he mentioned the *Now!* story to Doe at their next lunch, she dismissed it.

"Why do you think I reserved Little Mary for *Ambience*? Because I thought it was bad? Or to do you a favor? I couldn't care less about *Now!* And neither should you."


Philip had written each word carefully by hand.

Dear Eric—

I must say I was amazed by the odd review of my new collection. I was sure both of your reporters liked Little Mary, and even the artist and photographer seemed enthusiastic. I have always considered you my friend, and am naturally surprised that you would allow an unfair story to be published without asking me to show you the collection personally. I hope you will give me a chance to do so!

Please call me so that we can set up a date.

As always,
Philip

The next edition of *Now!* carried a boxed item:

### ROSS RAPED

Philip Ross, unhappy about the press reception of his new silhouette, is complaining vociferously to anyone within sight or hearing . . . but the buyers turned thumbs down on his little-girl look. They say Ross should stick to the tasteful staples which are his trademark . . .

Philip received no call from Eric Marshall and no answer to his letter.

Howard felt pretty good about the way the season was going. No one had bought that crazy stuff of Philip's except a few retailers who wanted to tie in with the five-page spread in *Ambience*. They would take a pasting on Little Mary, of course, but they sold so much from the rest of the line it would more than balance out.

Philip's run-in with *Now!* was a pain, all right, but it would all straighten out. After all, Philip and Eric Marshall were asshole buddies.

The firm's figures were up, its profits good. They had made up another twenty thousand of the original loss. The following season would clear up the rest and from then on it was all gravy. The Leeds would be pleased, too. They were sort of a joke, the way they insisted on being seated next to celebrities like the governor's wife at each press show; but all in all they had been damned nice, and if that was how they got their kicks, fine. The Leeds spent a lot of time in

New York these days. Whenever they arrived at the St. Regis, the invitations began to flow in. Lately, Philip had taken them to every party in town. They were having a ball.

Of course, Kathy was convinced that Louise Leeds was snubbing her, and she'd taken to bitching whenever she read that the Leeds had been at some social thing with Philip. There was a woman for you. First she'd wanted him to go into business, then he took the plunge, and still she found things to complain about. "Don't let Barry run your business," she said. "He'll be just like Fassman if you let him."

As if Barry cared. He was much too busy to get involved, and as long as Louise could pose for *Town & Country* in Philip's designs and be on a lot of invitation lists, everything was fine with her.

Kathy was pregnant again, in her ninth month, and she was bitchy this time, very difficult, very demanding. Howard was getting the brunt of it, and what's more, he had hot pants. There was this new model of Philip's, a great, big, strapping girl. After all these years of working around models, it would be a shame to break down, but it all depended on how far Kathy would drive him and how long he could control his cock. Maybe things would get better after the baby was born, but he had his doubts . . .

Tom had outlined a new advertising campaign, a take-off on the automobile ads—like Cadillac announcing that the new models would be at the dealers a certain month. Except the ads showed groups of dresses and announced the *exact day* they would be in the Philip-Ross Boutiques. The copy implied that only a limited number of each dress would be cut, which was a crock. But it would send women stampeding into the boutiques.

To make it work, the whole thing had to be planned six months in advance, and the dresses had to be safe enough so that every store would buy enough stock for the ads. They'd back the stores with inventory, a risk that had to be taken, so they could cash in on reorders. The styles couldn't be too exciting, but they'd be photographed by Avedon, who could make a housedress look like a ball gown. With Philip's name on them, they'd be a smash.

Still, he and Mr. Tony would have their work cut out, selling Philip on the idea.

At seven-thirty every morning, Carlos, Philip's Mexican manservant, brought a breakfast tray into the bedroom. He also brought the *Times,* the *Tribune, Women's Wear,* and *Now!* As a matter of self-discipline Philip read the front pages of the *Times* and the *Trib* before turning to the fashion pages and *Now!* In the past he had suffered some rude shocks when he ignored this rule. It was unpleasant to see cheap copies of his designs or rave reviews of a competitor's opening before he had drunk his orange juice or coffee. Later, when he was wide awake and less vulnerable, he could take annoyances more calmly.

It was the week of the Paris openings, and there were hardly any fashion journalists in New York. Philip opened *Now!* This was the issue with the first smuggled Paris sketches and reports, the one that made the editors of other fashion publications grind their teeth. Pages three and four were devoted to Jacques Marchand and André Coleaux, the two young Paris designers who were *Now!*'s new darlings. *Now!* usually played them off against each other, but this time they got equal space and praise.

TOMORROW'S GREAT LOOK . . .

THE DOLL, tomorrow's shape, short, loose, worn over deliciously colored dancers' tights . . . THE DOLL . . . for tomorrow's doll-girls! Both of the new masters, *Marchand* and *Coleaux,* on the same superb wavelength . . . *They understand!*

295

Philip stared at the sketches, almost unable to believe his eyes. The silhouette was identical to Little Mary! Neither of the two Frenchmen could have copied him; he knew better than that. There had been too little time, and, anyway, designers often came up with similar ideas all over the world at about the same time. No, Marchand and Coleaux simply thought as he did.

He got dressed and headed for his office, as angry as he had ever been in his life.

No sooner had he arrived downtown than Howard walked into the design room, waving a copy of *Now!*

"You see the Doll story?"

"I did."

"Looks great, doesn't it?"

"Yes."

"Well, now, we can try this thing again, this Little Mary silhouette." Howard sounded very earnest. "Maybe it'll sell now, what do you think?"

"I think you're a son of a bitch!" said Philip.

"What the hell is the matter with *you?*"

"You don't know? *You don't know?*"

"No, I don't! I should think you'd be—"

"You—*prick!* A few weeks ago the dirty bastards called Little Mary too juvenile, said I was 'reaching'! Now they're kissing ass in Paris and praising the identical silhouette from those two French cocksuckers, and you can't figure out what's the *matter* with me?" Philip, his eyes slits, was screaming.

"Don't you *care?* Don't you care at all what they do to me? Doesn't it mean anything to you that they're making me eat shit? That they're telling all of Seventh Avenue Philip Ross *tried* to do something but the fucking French know how to do it *right?*"

Howard was stunned. He had no answer.

Philip tried to speak more calmly. There were things he

had to get said. "You always made big noises about believing in me, at Armand-Klein you were forever running off at the mouth about American designers. But you're like all the other pricks"—he'd almost said "kikes"—"on Seventh Avenue who won't recognize a new trend until it's been played back from Paris."

He stopped short, turned, and headed for home.

Mr. Tony understood. He called the apartment. "I know you must be upset, Howard said how mad you were. But please listen to me, Philip, you'll have to face it, that's the way things are. No one can create fashion in America, not as long as our magazines and manufacturers keep running over there. And anyway, within a month there'll be nothing left of the original Doll look, no matter if it's your look or the French couturiers. Every bit of junk in the market will be called Doll. Now! will probably sketch Doll brassieres and Doll panties, no matter what the manufacturers call them. You know how the whole thing goes, *capisce?*"

"Yeah, I guess you're right, Tony," said Philip. He was spent. He knew he could never fight it. But he would never let the Now! people into his place again; that much he could do.

He need not have bothered. A C-note had gone out from Eric Marshall's office as soon as he received Philip's letter. Ross was "off." Permanently.

Iт was a warm night. Winter was finally over. The doors
to Philip's terrace were open, and for once the night air
smelled fresh. Down below, on the river, a tug was pushing a
line of barges upstream.

Carlos had left after finishing the dishes and opening the
bed. Philip was exhausted. The advertising meeting had
lasted until nearly eight, and when he'd finally gotten home,
Carlos's cooking had tasted warmed over and greasy.

Tom had outlined the new ad campaign for fall. It was
everything Philip despised, everything he had been fighting
against. He had fought Farrow and Fassman for his freedom
and now here he was in his own business and *still* fighting.

At least he'd fought at the beginning of the meeting. No
on the staples, absolutely not. Not with the Ross name on
them. He could set new trends, if Howard and Tom only
had the guts to back him up.

But he was talking to a blank wall. Howard was too
hooked on money, and Tom was an advertising machine who
would sell toilet paper made of steel wool if he thought
enough people would buy it. And Mr. Tony was tired. Old.
Mr. Tony was the only real fashion man of the three, and
Philip knew Tony would have fought them if they'd asked
him to skimp on quality. But he was not going to interfere
in a marketing project. He had laid out his own territory
long ago: "I run the production, you run the rest."

Even if he got his way this time, Philip would have to give in eventually, maybe the next year, maybe two years later. He was trapped, all over again. There was too much against him. The stores wanted to buy only the commonplace, and his partners wanted to sell goods. That was all.

He poured himself a drink and then another drink until there was that who-gives-a-shit feeling. The *Journal-American* was on the coffee table next to the cocktail tray. He skimmed it until a headline and an old, familiar photo caught his eye:

JAMES FARROW, COUTURIER, DIES IN MENTAL HOME

The story was brief. Farrow, for several years an inmate at Ferndale, an institution for the mentally ill in upstate New York, had died in his sleep. The rest was stuff from the newspaper morgue: Farrow had dressed the most famous ladies of his day. He had been regarded as one of the country's greatest fashion names. A naturalized citizen, he had been born in England . . .

Philip poured himself another drink. He could hear Farrow's voice, could see those plump hands and the sketches, hundreds of sketches with ideas pouring all over that table in back of the salon . . .

Then, with three drinks in his stomach and Farrow's obituary in his hand, the truth touched Philip. Like a tap on the shoulder from behind.

Creative? He was not creative. He could sense, he could feel, he could adapt, but he could not invent. He had drifted into fashion because it was convenient and glamorous, and he had learned well. But it had happened without plan and without urgency. Something had driven him, but what? Not creative talent, not burning ambition.

He had another drink. It didn't matter much. It simply did not matter any more.

MIDNIGHT, and the tables at the Sands were just getting into their stride. Las Vegas was like that. Nothing much happened until late, except for some people who made it happen all the time and who could never get away from the tables at any hour, day or night. For them, the swimming pool, the tennis courts, and the fantastic golf course might as well have been in Miami, two thousand miles away.

Others would go to the pool for an hour, get a sunburn that advertised time spent away from gambling, as if "How much did you lose?" was not the first question their wives always asked. At least, that was the idea. But who was kidding whom? People went to Vegas to gamble. Even the big-name entertainers served only as a temporary break from placing chips on the felt.

The bar was only a few feet from the casino—nothing in Vegas was far from the tables. Tom and Howard were having a drink, Tom just in from Los Angeles and Howard on his way there from New York. Neither one had begun to gamble in earnest. Howard wasn't much of a gambler anyway. He'd blow a couple of hundred, that was all. But Tom was a wild man, and it was a credit to his earnings that he was never broke.

Tom waved his empty glass at a bare-legged cocktail waitress and refocused his eyes from the cheeks at the bottom of her shorts to Howard. "Why should you *give* a damn if your pansy partner sulks? You've doubled your billing this year, you're running twice as many ads. And if I know you, you stingy Jew bastard, that means you gotta be making a mint."

Howard was better off than Tom, but less than sober. The bar, the casino, everything around him seemed padded and unreal. For him it was 3 A.M., and he had put in a hard day's work in New York before getting on that plane.

"Guess you're right," he said to Tom. "The fact is, I oughta be glad Philip's hardly speaking to me. All he's doing these days anyway is rehashing old stuff. He hired some kid, some little queen, who's doing more designing than he is, but who gives a damn? Long as the stuff sells . . ."

He sipped at his drink and went on. "Son of a bitch has it made, anyway, everyone wants him. Kidswear, swimsuits, girdles, wigs, God knows what. Now they even want him to design *menswear*. And the bastard hardly does any work, would you believe it? Right now he's off to Acapulco. Tony and I are breaking our hump, and Ross makes with the garden spots!"

"I tell you, Howie," Tom said, suddenly serious, "my shop has grown, we've got *big* ones now, real big ones and I've got lots of smartass creative kids doing the thinking for *me*. Jesus, we've even got a marketing division with research and all that crap. No more Torquemada. It ain't necessary . . ." He pulled a wad of cash from his pocket and began to count it. "Gotta get going." He waved the money at the jam-packed crap tables, and stood up.

"Tell you what," he said. "Tomorrow, you get yourself a stone slab made and put on it 'Here lies Tom Brett, *brilliant* young advertising man, who invented the Ellbaum campaign and the Bremmer campaign and the Philip-Ross campaign, all for peanuts, and now he's got big, fat, industrial clients and politicians so he don't *have* to be brilliant no more.' But don't plan on it yet because I may not be dead that quick!"

302

He waved goodbye and disappeared into the crowd in the smoke-fogged casino.

The Leeds' new house in Acapulco was high up in the hills near the Las Brisas Hotel, overlooking the bay. For months workmen blasted, built, plastered, day and night, and the house was completed just in time for the season.

The Leeds moved in, stayed for three weeks, and gave three big parties. Then, having established themselves as desirable additions to the Acapulco scene, they returned to Bel Air. They loaned the house to Philip, including two Mexican maids and a cook, all of whom treated Philip's manservant, Carlos, with suspicion. After all, Carlos was an expatriate, a near-gringo, an assimilated *norteamericano*. In his turn, Carlos snubbed these local hicks. After all, he was a New Yorker.

Now, Carlos sorted Philip's belongings out into one of the guest rooms and checked over the arrangements for the cocktail party. Since he collected under the table from liquor dealers and caterers, he liked parties. In New York he had made his connections years before. It was even easier in Acapulco, because he spoke the language and could read their minds.

He could also usually predict how these parties of Señor Ross would go. At first everyone was very quiet and pretty, all the *maricones* very well behaved. Then, after an hour or two of drinking, things would get wild. Señor Ross himself was no problem. He was usually blind with drink, and all Carlos had to do was put him to bed and make sure no one had taken his cash. Carlos himself felt entitled to a reward for such services, of course, and so he always pocketed a little of the money he found in Señor Ross's trousers. The Leeds' Mexican servants, the *acapulqueños*, knew that Carlos was a crook. They marked it down to his *yanqui* training.

The party began at eight. The water below glittered with reflected lights from the hotels on the opposite side and from the yachts anchored near the navy yard. Overhead, black clouds wandered past the moon toward the hills that ringed the bay.

Cocktails were served on the open terrace, beyond which there was a sheer drop toward the cliffs hundreds of feet below. A troupe of three *mariachis* sang sad love songs as if they meant them.

Five fashion designers visiting Acapulco that season had arrived, three of them wearing white Mexican wedding shirts, tight trousers, and *huaraches*. Don Jeffson, who was a guest on one of the yachts, dropped in at about ten. He was even darker than ever. He embraced Philip, Mexican style.

"*Hola*, star," he said. "Here we are again, you with your success and me with my suntan." He introduced his date, the daughter of a Mexican billionaire, who apparently did not speak a word of English. Quiet and reserved, she looked rather frightened by some of the guests, who were beginning to feel their tequila.

"A relief after Julia Debenham," said Jeffson. "My balls were getting tired!"

Carlos Langmann, whom Philip had not seen since Sebring, arrived with a large and noisy group of Mexican friends, all obviously rich, the men in *guayaveras* and their wives in Puccis. Langmann had offered Philip his yacht, but Philip had decided to stay at the Leeds' house instead. He wanted privacy, and he preferred to have Carlos nearby in case he blacked out after an evening's drinking.

"These," said Langmann with a sweeping gesture toward the Mexicans, "are my friends!" He paused dramatically and turned to them. "*Damas y caballeros*, this is—Philip Ross!" he said, as if he were introducing a direct descendant of Montezuma.

He grabbed Philip by the arm. "You ought to sell a ton

of clothes to the *damas*," he said softly, jerking a thumb at the Pucci'd ladies. "Stinkin' rich, all of 'em, and their husbands would rather buy them clothes and jewels than give up chasing *cono*." If the ladies had overheard, they did not betray it. They were Mexican women of good family, and, like their Spanish sisters, they accepted the inevitability of their husbands' playing around.

"While we're on the subject—there are no *girls* here?"

"Well," said Philip, "I don't know too many people in Acapulco. So I invited a few friends." He pointed at the queens.

Langmann raised both hands and waggled them. "What's an Acapulco party without, how you say—*broads?* Leave it to me, where's your phone? There are dozens in town, ready for anything. Starlets, airline hostesses . . ." He found a phone and got busy.

One of the designers waved to Philip.

"Come over here! We've been wondering who *did* this place, it's *dreamy!* A bit much in places, but all in all, dreamy! Doesn't it belong to your *moneybags?*"

"The Leeds, yes."

"There." He turned to the other designers, who were clustered around a marble table. "It had to cost a *fortune*, half the stuff was made to order, I'd say. Wouldn't you, Philip?"

"I don't know."

"Don't give me that crap," said the queen, suddenly booze-angry. "Look at those goddamn couches! They were obviously made to go into the niches. And those corner seats, how else could they get them to fit exactly?"

"I suppose you're right."

"Of course I am," he said, no longer miffed. "By the way, who're the Mexicans?"

"They're with Carlos Langmann. He's an old friend of mine."

"Oh, stop it, Philip. You mean that *the* Carlos Langmann is an *old* friend of yours?"

Philip was getting a bit fed up. "It so happens he is. Ask him, he's over there."

"I'll *believe* you," he said. "But I had no idea Langmann swung both ways."

"You're a joy," said Philip.

"*Aren't* I?" He moved off, happy with himself.

Before long, other fags arrived, friends of the designers, who were joining them from parties all over Acapulco. Langmann's broads also materialized: Americans, Swedes, English, all flat-bellied and flat-assed. After sizing up the party, most of them beelined for the Mexicans. The rest played temporarily hard to get, joining the queens. It was not a bad technique, and soon Langmann's friends came over to tackle them, while the queens tittered. Within twenty minutes the fag corner was homogeneous again. They occupied one end of the terrace, the heterosexuals the other, as if there were two parties in progress.

"Señor Ross." One of the Mexican wives was speaking to Philip. "I think it is time for me to get some sleep." She was a stunning woman, about thirty-five, with enormous eyes and a ripe but carefully tended figure.

"Already?"

"Yes. I prefer early evenings." Her English was impeccable, with a tinge of British accent, probably acquired in a Swiss private school. Her face was a mask. She did not look back at her busy husband, but walked out without another glance. Her chauffeur emerged from the kitchen and followed her to the car. Within ten minutes, all the Mexican wives had left.

Jeffson had begun a wild flamenco, and the *mariachis* were sweating. His date, the only non-tramp left at the party, stood nervously at the edge of the crowd. She gestured to him and he broke off abruptly.

"Sorry, Philip," said Jeffson. "I'll be back later. No use upsetting *this* little applecart." He smiled apologies. The girl was rich. Very rich.

Philip understood. "You money-grabbing son of a bitch," he said. Then to the girl, who smiled sweetly: "*Señorita, mucho gusto . . . Buenas noches!*"

At two o'clock the *mariachis* gave up and someone put on some rock records, turned way up until they could feel the music in their gut. Langmann had sent to the yacht for more booze, although this hardly seemed necessary. Everyone was very drunk.

After preliminary discussion and some straightforward trading of money, the Mexicans had arrived at their formula: they had unzipped their trousers and lined up on a couch; the girls were blowing them. The queens, watching from the other side of the terrace, applauded each orgasm and cheered the participants.

"Make 'em go again . . . Suck him *dry*, sweetie."

Langmann was lounging on another couch, alongside the balustrade over the straight drop to the rocks below. Spread-eagled, he was being manipulated by a tiny, sweet-faced English brunette. He looked bored, and the girl knew it. She was frantic, checking his face now and then to see if she was getting to him.

Some of the fags began to dance, clutching at each other like marathon performers in old newsreels. One, a window dresser from Dallas, had stripped to the waist. He was doing fancy gymnastic back bends and walking on his hands. Suddenly he yelled, "I'll *help* you, baby!" pointing at the little English girl with Langmann.

Langmann turned his head. "The hell you will," he said calmly, but the fag had climbed onto the railing atop the balustrade and was making his precarious way toward the couple, balancing like a tightrope walker. It was a desperately dangerous thing to do. A hush fell over the party as the

Mexicans, their whores, the pansies, everyone stopped to watch this madman.

Langmann pushed the girl away. He stood up, his fly wide open, and yelled:

"You stupid bastard, get *down* from there!"

The queen kept inching along the railing. When he was dead center, he stopped, turned to his audience, and bowed. Some of them applauded and yelled *"Olé!"* as if he had just finished a pretty *faena* in the ring. He was about to bow once more when his foot slipped.

He reached out to catch himself; instead, his face hit the railing with a sickening thud and then he yelled a high, screeching woman's scream which continued after he disappeared. All eyes were turned to the spot on the white railing which showed a smear of blood—as if he could be brought back there by wishing it so. No one heard him hit the rocks, but eventually one of the Mexicans walked to the edge of the terrace and looked over. He turned around and shook his head. One of the designers held a handkerchief to his face, sobbing.

Everyone rushed to leave, wanting no part of the scene to come. They jammed the door, calling for their drivers. Within minutes the terrace was empty except for Philip and Langmann.

Philip was terribly drunk. He had barely seen the accident. Carlos had been hovering nearby, ready to take him to bed. Now he tried to sober him up, but it was no use.

Langmann took charge. He clicked his fingers at Carlos, who snapped to attention. *"Hombre,"* Langmann said in Spanish, "get the *señor* to bed at once." Carlos obeyed.

Then Langmann called the police and instructed the other servants to clean up the terrace. There were panties, spilled drinks, and empty bottles everywhere. By the time a police captain and three officers arrived, the house and terrace were presentable.

Langmann seemed completely sober.

"*Capitán*," he said, looking earnest and a bit grieved, "there has been a terrible accident."

The captain already knew. Some beach boys had found the body and called, minutes before Langmann. The boys had spoken of a noisy party up there at the *quinta* Leeds, but it did not look as though there had been such a party. Perhaps the boys were mistaken. Perhaps it was only the music. The new gringo music sounded wild. And Langmann was *un señor muy estimado* . . .

"Señor Langmann," the captain said. "We know the man fell. He is dead. He was found. How did it happen?"

"An accident," said Langmann, raising his eyebrows, shrugging, and using his hands to show his regret. "He was feeling unwell, dizzy. He leaned over. He fell."

The captain asked for the names of the other guests, but Langmann shrugged again. They were all strangers. In fact, he doubted if the host knew more than a few of them, so many had drifted in. "You know parties here . . ."

"Yes," said the captain, whose weekly salary would not have paid a day's hotel rent in Las Brisas. "I know . . . How about the host, Señor Ross?"

Langmann shook his head. "In shock. I had him put to bed." The captain took some notes and left with his men. There was nothing more he could do. Tomorrow, perhaps, he could get some witnesses. A report had to be written. *Punto y basta!*

Carlos had put Philip to bed, pocketing two hundred pesos from his pockets. He was ready for Langmann.

"Tomorrow morning," he was told, "Señor Ross will call me so I can tell him what to say to the police. Then I shall send my pilot to fly you back to the States. It would be better."

Carlos understood, especially since the instructions were accompanied by a thousand-peso note.

He bowed to Langmann. This man he understood. *Un caballero* of the old school.

They would surely fly to Palm Beach, because it was sunny there, and the señor loved the sun. He smiled at the thought of Palm Beach. There was a *chiquita* there, a little *cubana*. Perhaps Señor Ross would give him a week off . . . *Certainly* Señor Ross would give him a week off. With pay.

After only two days in Palm Beach, Philip was bored. He thought of Nassau, but the hotels would be jammed. He'd have to stay with Lady Hatfield, who filled her large house on Lyford Cay with international society faggots during the season. After Acapulco, the thought was unappealing. The Corhans also had a place in Nassau, but he'd have to give them a few days' notice, and anyway the Hatfield woman would be furious.

Late Saturday afternoon, he took the five-fifteen National nonstop back to New York.

He arrived at the apartment at eleven that night. Carlos was still on vacation, and of course there was nothing in the refrigerator.

Philip was hungry, but the after-theater places were impossible on Saturday nights. He remembered a hamburger joint down the street on Madison that stayed open till midnight. He did not even bother to unpack his bags. Everything would need pressing anyway, and Carlos could do it when he got back the next day.

There was a new elevator man he'd noticed coming up, a tall, dark-haired boy whose uniform stretched across his back. Obviously, it belonged to a smaller man.

" 'Evening," said Philip. "You're new. What's your name?"

"Frank, sir."

"I'm Mr. Ross. Are you the new night man?"

"Temporary. I'm on eight till midnight. One of your regular men is sick."

"You mean Jimmy?"

"Right, sir. He's on the mend, they tell me. Pneumonia."

"Sorry to hear that."

"Yessir."

Philip walked west toward Madison. It was cold. He was thinking of Jimmy, a shriveled little Irishman with a thick brogue. He had never really looked at him; all he ever did was hand the man his tip if he came home late. Poor little bastard, he'd have to get some cash to him through Carlos. He couldn't really remember Jimmy's face, only his hands, one on the handle of the elevator, the other on the sliding gate. Surprisingly large, solid hands, like a farmer's.

The hamburger place was crowded. Philip took one of the two empty stools at the far end of the counter and ordered a hamburger, rare. While he was waiting, he read the signs on the back wall.

FISHBURGER DE LUXE 70¢

BOWL, CHILI CON CARNE 90¢

SPECIAL TARTAR STEAK $1.95 (WITH EGG 30¢ EXTRA)

When his hamburger arrived, he ordered coffee. He began to eat, but after a few bites his appetite left him. He picked up a Sunday *News* someone had left on the empty seat beside him. He turned to the horoscope and was reading the forecast for Scorpio, his sign, when a voice startled him. "Hello, Mr. Ross."

It was the new elevator man, now dressed in a zipper jacket and chinos. "My relief came a few minutes after you left," he explained. "I usually grab a hamburger here. Good place."

Philip nodded. "It's the only one around here that stays

open late." There was a tattoo on Frank's wrist, an anchor. "Were you in the Navy?"

"Marines," said Frank. "Just got out. This is my first civvy job."

"Pretty rough hours," said Philip.

"It's not so bad. Except for some of the tenants."

"How do you mean?"

"Like last night"—he stopped to order a fishburger—"this guy comes in with a chick, seems to think his girl is making eyes at me. I can't even *see* her, I've got my back to her"—he shrugged—"so we get to the tenth floor, the guy wants to give me an argument. I tell him I never even looked at her, so he says, 'Don't let me catch you doing that again,' and pushes her out of the elevator because he sees I'm getting steamed. Guess I'm still a Marine." Frank grimaced. "I'm no good at taking horseshit, that's for sure." His fishburger arrived.

He was very handsome. A muscular neck, dark, flushed skin, and thick black brows. His long back was bent forward. He ate with his face close to the dish, like a laborer, as if someone might grab the food from him.

Why the hell not? thought Philip. What else was there to do except go home alone and drink himself to sleep?

"This is a hell of a way to spend Saturday night," he said. "When you've finished eating why don't you come up to my place for a nightcap?"

Frank kept chewing, then he wiped his mouth with his hand. "You sure it'll be okay?"

"Why not? Sure."

"Well," said Frank, "the twelve-to-eight man goes off at one. I mean, he puts the elevator on self-service and goes downstairs to check the burner. He locks the front door so you have to ring to get in, but I've got the key and we can go up without him seeing me."

"What difference does it make if he sees you?"

"Wouldn't look so good for the relief elevator man to go visiting with the tenants, would it?" said Frank.

"Guess you're right. Although it doesn't mean a damn to me."

At ten past one they walked back to the building. Frank unlocked the front door and they took the empty elevator up. Philip turned on a few lights in the living room.

"What'll you have?" he asked.

"Scotch."

Philip poured a double, straight, and another for himself. They sat down on opposite armchairs and drank.

"Down the hatch," said Philip.

"*Salut*," said Frank. "Like the guineas in my outfit used to say."

When they had finished the drinks, Philip refilled both glasses. "Do you know why I asked you here?" he asked.

Frank said nothing.

Philip went on: "You're very good-looking, you know." The words were familiar, as was the whole routine. Crude, but he liked getting to the point. He didn't need conversation, he just wanted to get laid. Usually the boys got the idea quick enough. Sometimes they told him to go to hell. Mostly, they did what he wanted, if they needed the dough.

"You must be broke," he said. "Just out of the service, and you can't be making much on this elevator job."

Frank kept still. He finished his drink, then walked over to the bar to pour himself another, without asking. When he turned around, Philip had left the room.

Frank shrugged and, drink in hand, meandered around the bookshelves, pretending to look at the titles.

"Any one of those interest you especially?"

Frank turned to face the voice and saw that Philip had changed into a black-and-yellow silk dressing gown, tied at the waist by a sash.

"Frank, I've got money," said Philip. "It would please me

if I could help you out until you get the kind of job you really want."

"Okay," said Frank. "I guess every pansy in the country wants to get blown by a Marine. Well, I'm not your boy. But what you said about having lots of dough, *that* interests me." He tossed off the liquor and poured another one, then walked over to Philip's armchair.

"How would you like the whole fucking building to know why you conned me up here? And maybe the police, too?"

"Come on," said Philip, suddenly frightened. "Nobody asked you for a goddamn thing! I was only trying to help."

"Yeah, sure, you're some helper, some *friend*. You don't even know me! Don't give me any crap, just let me see some of that dough you were talking about."

Philip knew what might happen if he did not answer, but when it did, he was unprepared.

Frank hit him and his fist felt like hard wood. Philip's hand went up to ward off another blow, but Frank was quick and the fist smashed into his head again.

When Philip touched his face, it felt wet. His left eye began to close on him and he could feel a vast numbness setting in as he slid to the floor.

Philip had no idea what time it was when he came to. His face stung where the rug touched an open cut. When he tried to push himself erect, his hand landed in a patch of dried blood.

He got to his knees. It was gray outside, no longer night. A wave of nausea seesawed in him. He staggered into the bathroom and threw up. A mess, all right. On his good robe, too. He let it slip off onto the bathroom floor. Wet towel. Vicious headache. Blood all over the towel, and the bathrobe, sticky, half-congealed. He touched his nose, and yelped. Broken?

He was badly hurt. He had to call someone. But who?

First, some sleep. Later . . . He stumbled to the bed and fell across it. No thinking. Out.

The first thing Carlos saw when he let himself into the apartment Sunday afternoon was the blood on the living-room floor. *Madre de diós!* In the bedroom he found Philip, face down. He shook him gently, turned him over, then called the police.

The two detectives, short men in wrinkled raincoats, had tired faces and bored voices. They examined the naked body with weary professionalism, then questioned Carlos, who gave them his flight number and the *chiquita's* address. They checked the apartment room by room, making notes. Finally they called their precinct.

The apartment would be sealed off for the time being.

"How about the señor?" Carlos asked the cop who had questioned him.

"We'll have it picked up now, so they can do an autopsy."

"What?"

"Find out how he got killed."

"He got *murdered*, didn't he?"

"We don't know that. Seems to have been hit in the face."

"But how could that kill him? He must have been okay, he tried to wash himself in the bathroom."

"We saw. Puke all over everything. Anyway, the fact that he woke up after he got hit don't mean anything."

"He's right," said the other cop. "I seen guys hit just once and come around, then later"—he snapped his fingers. "Inside bleedin', I guess it is." He tapped his head to show where. "Anyway, you better let us know where you can be reached, we'll probably have more questions." He took Carlos's phone number and address, then left.

Carlos followed them down in the elevator. He was

sorry, the job had suited him. Before the detectives arrived
he'd made a final search of his employer's pockets, but they
were empty. Whoever had killed him had cleaned him out.

Carlos crossed himself as he left the building.


The Sands rode back from the cemetery in grim silence.
The Frank E. Campbell chauffeur was disappointed. He
liked overhearing what people in back said about the stiff
they had just put away.

Howard stared out the window at the Queens scenery.
Most depressing in the world, he thought. Kathy sat at the
other end of the seat. They had taken Philip's death sepa-
rately, like two strangers, without discussion.

"Howard . . ." Kathy's first word since morning. "It was
a sad mess."

"Yes."

"So are we."

Silence. Then Kathy again, in a small voice, unlike her:
"Not much love left."

"No, you're wrong. But you're also a bitch."

They dipped into the tunnel, and the lights flashed by.
Like a huge men's room, Howard thought.

When they got back to the apartment, Howard sat down
on the couch without taking off his coat. He needed a drink
. . . Now what? Would the stores swallow Philip-Ross styles
without Philip? That was what they'd been getting. Ken,
Philip's assistant, had been the real designer for months, but
they'd all made damn sure the stores didn't find out.

He looked up at Kathy, standing there in her mink. "Am
I such a bitch?" she asked.

"Mostly."

"What comes next?"

Goddamn women and their one-track minds. He shrugged
and said nothing. If she wanted a divorce, she'd have to be
the one to bring it up. That could cost!

316

"Well, say *something*, even if it's wrong. Where do we go from here?"

"In business?"

"No, *us*." He didn't answer. "Then how about the business?"

Better not paint a rosy picture. That could cost, too. "We're in trouble," he said.

She gave him a long look and then smiled with one side of her face, the way he had seen her smile a thousand times when she was about to say something snide.

"I'm *sure* you'll figure it out, darling." She left the room.

Howard poured himself a drink, then called the office. "Tell Ken to call me as soon as he's back from the funeral."

"He's already here." The girl rang the design room.

"Ken? Howard . . . Yeah, it was depressing. Look, why don't you put me down for lunch tomorrow . . ."

A lot of work lay ahead of them.

Johnny eased over the wheel and reversed the engine just a touch. The big ketch kissed the dock softly, despite the wind, and came to rest.

The dock boy watched with admiration. This guy knew how to bring a boat alongside. He picked up the bowline and came aft so that Johnny could hand him the stern line. No hurry, no sweat. Sixty feet of boat, gusts to thirty knots, and the guy docked her single-handed the way other people brought in their dinghies.

When the boy had secured the spring lines, he glanced topside to where the owner's signal was snapping in the breeze. He'd have to look it up in Lloyd's, back in the dockmaster's office. The ketch flew Seawanhaka Corinthian out of Oyster Bay, a pretty snazzy club. He gave a disdainful look to all the fat Chris-Crafts and Trumpys along the dock. Whoreboats!

Johnny went below to get a sweater. The old bones felt chilled. Then he walked to the dockmaster's to sign in. Next?

317

Who knew? Maybe he'd stop over at the Racquet Club for a drink. Maybe some of the Florida yacht bums were there. He could stand a little dry land. The passage from Nassau had been choppy—he had no business single-handing at his age—or, rather, in his condition. Booze, booze, stay up all night, get laid, then out into the Atlantic. When would he ever learn?

He phoned Hertz, picked up the Miami paper, and sat down in the office to wait for the car.

Page two. Philip's picture. And a dreadful headline. He began to read. Then he put his face in his hands.

The dockmaster looked at the big, gray-haired man.

"Are you all right, sir?"

He got no answer.

As soon as Mr. Tony stepped into St. Patrick's, the Fifth Avenue din faded to a whispering hum. He blinked to accustom his eyes to the gloom. Then he crossed himself and turned toward St. Anthony's altar. It always amazed him how many people came to the cathedral in the middle of the business day. There were quite a few in the pews at the center. He chose a seat well behind them, lit a candle to St. Anthony, and put a dollar in the slot.

He knelt and closed his eyes. He began his usual "Hail, Mary," then stopped. This time he did not want indulgence for himself. This was for Philip. He told the saint how young Philip was, how he had sinned, and how he should be forgiven because he was a lost man who had meant no harm, ever.

He moved slowly out to the street, and headed back to work.

Philip tastes of cinnamon, and of salt. Little veins pulse just beneath his skin, and he is breathing hard, breathing with his whole body, all of him in her mouth and on her skin. Her hand grows numb from the weight of him.

318

The numbness in the hand becomes pain, and now only her hand is asleep. She has been lying on it. She turns over on her back and lets it flop onto the sheet, where it tingles as the blood returns.

Doe is awake, and Philip—dead. Buried yesterday.

*And what were you doing with him just now?*

Oh, God.

The interrogation room was almost square, and freshly painted in white. There were no windows or pictures, just two doors. One led to the cells. The other, leading to offices, had a one-way mirror. Sometimes the detectives left a suspect alone in the room and watched to see how he behaved. First offenders and the innocent were usually jumpy. Habitual criminals were calm.

Frank sat on a black foam-padded bench against the wall and looked at the two detectives. At first he had slouched as if he did not care, but now he was sitting upright with his hands on his knees, waiting for them to say something to him.

The one in the chrome swivel chair looked up from the typewritten report he had been reading.

"The Ross apartment," he said. "Saturday night."

"Some mess," said Frank. "I read about it in the papers."

"Why the hell didn't you contact us?"

Frank shrugged. "You know how it is, I didn't want to go asking for trouble." Smile. Make friends.

The detective in charge reached under his tie and scratched.

"Look," said Frank, "like I told your boys who picked me up, I had to push this fellow, he was making a grab. His getting killed is got nothing to do with me." Light a cigarette. Steady, now.

"The medical report says Ross died from a blow to the head."

"How could I know the queer would croak? I've hit guys twice as hard and shot craps with them an hour later."

The other detective shifted his weight in the chair. "You did time in the brig for fighting—"

"For chris*sakes!*" Frank threw his cigarette to the floor. "What was I supposed to do? Let him grab my cock? I know you gotta get somebody for this but it's not gonna be *me!*"

The detective raised his hand and then let it drop. "This isn't getting us anywhere. You better get a lawyer, you're gonna need one."

"What the hell for?"

"Ross is dead."

"Some town you got here—a fruit slips and conks his head and I get treated like I'm some kind of murderer." He was shouting now. "You let pansies run loose all over the goddamn streets and then you expect decent people to lay down for them?"

"That's enough," said the detective. "You want to say something before you get a lawyer, remember it can be used in court."

Suddenly quiet, Frank stared at the cigarette butt still burning on the floor. He stooped to pick it up, then straightened as a uniformed officer entered the room to take him out.

The two detectives looked at each other. Frank had been sweating the whole time; his smell hung in the air.

"Maybe it happened like he said."

"I dunno."

The first detective looked down at a pile of photographs taken by the police photographer. The one on top was of the nude corpse, face down on the bed.

He slipped the photograph and the report lying next to it into a manila envelope marked *Ross, Philip* and tucked in the flap.